Whack 'n' Roll

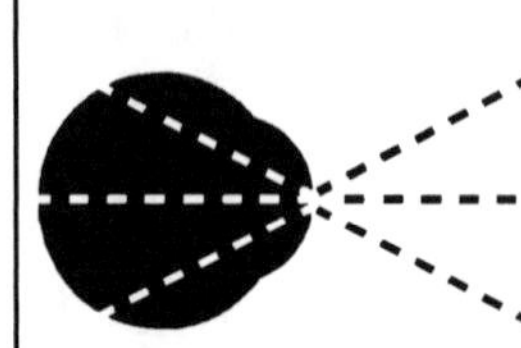

This Large Print Book carries the Seal of Approval of N.A.V.H.

A BUNCO BABES MYSTERY

WHACK 'N' ROLL

GAIL OUST

KENNEBEC LARGE PRINT
A part of Gale, Cengage Learning

GALE
CENGAGE Learning

De… London

GALE
CENGAGE Learning

This is a work of fiction. Names, characters, places, and incidents either are the product of the author's imagination or are used fictitiously, and any resemblance to actual persons, living or dead, business establishments, events, or locales is entirely coincidental.

The publisher does not have any control over and does not assume any responsibility for author or third-party websites or their content.

Kennebec Large Print® Superior Collection.
The text of this Large Print edition is unabridged.
Other aspects of the book may vary from the original edition.
Set in 16 pt. Plantin.
Printed on permanent paper.

LIBRARY OF CONGRESS CATALOGING-IN-PUBLICATION DATA

Oust, Gail, 1943–
Whack 'n' roll : a Bunco Babes mystery / by Gail Oust.
p. cm. — (Kennebec large print superior collection)
ISBN-13: 978-1-4104-1969-9 (alk. paper)
ISBN-10: 1-4104-1969-X (alk. paper)
1. Retirees—Fiction. 2. Murder—Investigation—Fiction.
3. Retirement communities—South Carolina—Fiction. 4. Large type books. I. Title.
PS3620.U7645W47 2009
813'.6—dc22 2009033480

Published in 2009 by arrangement with NAL Signet, a member of Penguin Group (USA) Inc.

Printed in the United States of America
1 2 3 4 5 6 7 13 12 11 10 09

To my husband, Bob

ACKNOWLEDGMENTS

Thanks first of all to Jessica Faust of BookEnds, LLC, my wonderful, fantastic, fabulous agent, for her enthusiasm and confidence in me. You helped birth the Bunco Babes, and I'll be forever grateful.

Thanks also to my very own bunco babes, Mary Ann, Janet, Chris, Barbara, Sondra, Mickey, Lise, Camille, Jean, Ellen, and Ann, who aspire to inspire, and succeed.

A special thank-you to the Purple Gang of SLV, true Red Hat sisters of the heart. Maureen, Fran, Carol, Jan, Claudell, Joan, Janet, Ann, and Rosemarie, I love you guys. Who would have guessed where playing golf together would lead?

Jim Montgomery, lieutenant, Detroit police department, retired, your advice on crime and punishment kept me on the straight and narrow when I tended to wander off into the land of make-believe. I take full responsibility for any errors or misinformation the reader might encounter. And Ben Jackson, you may be a retired policeman, but you still know how to think like an active one.

Mike McClain, I laughed out loud at seeing the first version of my Web page. I truly appreciate your dogged persistence in dragging technologically challenged me into the twenty-first century.

Last, but not least, my dear friend Patti Cornelius. You always seem to be there when I need you. A special big fat thanks for coming to my rescue with a title and cleverly naming my baby *Whack 'n' Roll.*

CHAPTER 1

"Kate McCall, stop daydreaming. It's your turn."

Monica's plaintive voice interrupted my mental inventory of things I still needed to do before bunco that evening. I shouldn't have let Pam talk me into playing golf when I should be home vacuuming. Reality check, reality check: golf versus vacuuming? No contest. Golf won hands down.

"I'm coming, I'm coming."

As usual I was going to be last to tee off. And I liked it that way. When it comes to procrastinating, I rule. I pulled my driver from my bag and dug a ball out of my pocket. Jim would be so proud — not to mention surprised — to know that I've taken up the game I used to complain about. I imagine him smiling down on me from the pearly gates. Granted, I'm not a very good golfer, but I do enjoy getting out on the course with some of the ladies from my bunco group. We call ourselves the Bunco Babes. Technically speaking, I'm not sure whether women of a certain age can still be considered "babes." But I believe with the proper attitude anything is possible. And the Babes have attitude up the wazoo.

"Connie Sue landed on the green." Monica pointed to the bright speck of pink 120 yards in the distance. She neglected to mention her shot landed in a sand trap. "Now let's see you make it across."

Monica tends to be competitive when it comes to golf. But Monica tends to be competitive — period. Even at bunco. And bunco, as aficionados know, is strictly a roll of the dice. No skill, no strategy. Simply a roll of the dice.

"You can do it, sugar," Connie Sue crooned. Once a cheerleader, always a cheerleader, I suppose.

Pam smiled encouragingly. "Make it across, and I'll let you wear the tiara tonight."

If that wasn't incentive, I didn't know what was. Pam was referring to the fact she was the reigning queen of the Bunco Babes. The tiara had been Connie Sue's idea. Figures, coming from a former Miss Peach Princess. At the end of each evening, a sparkly rhinestone tiara is awarded to the highest roller. This is the winner's to keep until next time we play. Then, after scores are tallied, the reigning queen relinquishes the crown to the new winner. Silly? Of course it is. Though some might loathe admitting it, I'd be willing to wager that everyone gets a kick out of wearing that tiara. It makes us feel special and appeals to our sense of fun. In other words, it makes us girls again.

"You've won it two times in a row," Monica reminded Pam. "Fair warning, pal. You're about to be dethroned tonight. I'm feeling lucky."

"Girls, girls, girls," Connie Sue drawled in her best Scarlett O'Hara imitation. "Don't make me have to give you a time-out." Connie Sue is the grandmother of twin toddlers. She likes to keep the rest of us up-to-date on parenting, lest we forget most of us once raised children of our own. Miracle that any of them survived, given today's theories.

I squinted across the narrow gully separating the elevated tee from the green, and sighed. I've always disliked the eighth hole. Nearly as much as I dislike the second, third, and fifth. There is no margin for error. Getting my ball on the green is a skill I have yet to acquire. If I'm lucky, it will land nearby. And let me tell you, that's a very big if. More often than not, my ball lands in the thick vegetation below.

I strode up to the tee box with more bravado than I felt, pushed my hot pink tee into the hard-packed ground, and prepared to say farewell to my pretty lavender ball, which in all likelihood I would never see again.

"Remember, sugar, left arm straight, knees flexed, feet shoulder-width apart." Connie Sue Cheerleader was at it again.

"Just keep your eye on the ball," Pam reminded, perhaps just a tad guilty for taking me away from my housework.

"What the heck?" I muttered. If Monica made it across that darn gully, maybe there was hope for a hacker like me. I took a deliberate backstroke just as Brad Murphy, the club's pro, had instructed. Then — for a split second — my attention strayed. Did I have enough crabmeat for the spread I planned to make for bunco? Or should I run by the Piggly Wiggly on my way home? Trust me, it's not a good thing when your attention strays in the middle of your golf stroke.

My driver *kachunk*ed as it connected with the ball. With a sick feeling in the pit of my stomach, I watched it arc against the blue

Carolina sky. Monica, Connie Sue, and Pam groaned when my ball hit the fringe of the fairway, struck a rock, then bounced backward — straight into the . . . crap. No other word for it.

"The sun was in my eyes," I said. A lie, a blatant lie.

None of us said a word as we climbed into our golf carts and navigated the steep, winding cart path to the bottom of the hill.

"Good luck finding your ball," Monica said as she dropped me off. I could tell from her smug expression that she was happy she wasn't the one who had to search through weeds, brambles, and whatever else.

I took an assortment of clubs out of my bag and headed for the spot where my ball had disappeared into the underbrush.

"I'll help you look," Pam offered. Her fluorescent yellow ball had managed to make it across the chasm, but just barely.

Ever leery of snakes, I used my eight iron to gingerly poke around. A warm breeze sent the reeds swaying and stirred up a sickeningly sweet odor. "Ee-yew!" I wrinkled my nose at the smell. "Something stinks in here."

Pam joined in the search. "Ee-yew," she echoed with a grimace when she, too, caught a whiff. "Maybe it's a dead body."

"Now who's been watching too much *CSI*?"

Pam and I are both crime and consequence junkies. *Criminal Minds,* all versions of *Law & Order, CSI* in Las Vegas, Miami, or New York — it didn't matter. Bring them on, the more the merrier.

"While we're on the subject, whose bright idea was it to play bunco the same night as *CSI*?"

"That's why we both bought TiVo," I said, poking at what looked like a plastic Wal-Mart bag.

Pam glanced my way and shook her head. "Look at the trash. Disgusting! Next thing you know the Road Warriors will have to patrol the golf course."

"Thank goodness for Road Warriors," I said. Pam was referring to the intrepid band of volunteers who, armed with grabbers and orange vests, ruthlessly defend the highways and byways against discarded soda cans and Burger King wrappers.

"I can't believe people throw stuff like this on the course." I took a final jab at the bag and let out a squeal as an arm — or what might once have been an arm — tumbled free.

No ladylike squeal from Pam. She let loose a shriek that could be heard clear to the clubhouse. A gray squirrel scurried for cover. My numb brain registered birds, too large to be crows, circling overhead. They looked more like turkey buzzards, true scavengers here in the South. They can pick a carcass clean in no time flat. The veggie burger I had for lunch threatened to return as my gaze returned to the . . . whatever.

Denial is a wonderful thing. One of the best defense mechanisms God ever invented. I stared and stared at the sickly gray pulp with a kind of morbid fascination. This couldn't be real, I tried to convince myself. Appendages just don't fall out of Wal-Mart bags. Or any other kinds of bags, for that matter. Serenity Cove has very strict policies against littering.

Could be an arm off a mannequin, I told myself. A fake arm. Could be someone's idea of a practical joke. A very twisted practical joke.

Pam clutched my sleeve. "Please, don't tell me —"

Before she could finish her sentence, Connie Sue and Monica hurried over to see what all the fuss was about.

"Dammit, Pam," Monica complained. "If you hadn't let out that scream, I could have parred that hole."

Connie Sue was the first of the pair to

spot the grisly find lying amid the weeds. She clamped a hand over her mouth, all traces of color leaching from her face.

About that time, Monica, too, spotted the object of interest. She pointed a shaky finger. "Is that . . . ?" she asked in a voice barely above a whisper.

"An arm." I nodded, no longer able to pretend the object was anything but an arm.

At my pronouncement, Monica promptly lost her tuna melt all over her brand-new FootJoys.

"Hey, ladies," a voice shouted from the tee box above us. "You're holding up play."

I recognized the man; I'd seen him at the fitness center during one of my sporadic workout sessions. After watching him hog the treadmill while others waited, I'd instantly cataloged him a first-class jerk. I wondered how he'd have reacted if he had been the one to find a dismembered body part in a Wal-Mart bag. Probably kept right on playing. It would, after all, be a shame to slow down play.

Ignoring him, I rummaged in my pocket for my cell phone. Tees and ball markers fell to the ground. Then I remembered I had left my cell in my bag on the cart. "Darn," I mumbled. My mind scrambled to come up with a plan, a protocol of sorts, but came up blank. Nothing so far in my life had prepared me for this kind of emergency.

"If you can't find your ball, lady, take a penalty and get on with it," the jerk's partner hollered.

"We found an arm," Pam hollered back.

The man took off his cap and scratched his head. "You found some yarn?"

"An arm!" My control snapped. Why did men refuse to wear hearing aids? "We found an arm!"

"Lady, I don't give a rat's ass what you found. Just move aside and let us play through."

Fortunately, just then, the ranger pulled up alongside our golf cart at the bottom of the hill. "Trouble, ladies?"

Before I could get two words out, the jerk yelled, "Bill, tell these women they need to brush up on golf etiquette."

"What's the problem, ladies?" Bill asked.

As one, all four of us pointed to the grisly discovery.

Bill climbed out of the golf cart and ambled over for a better look. After one quick glance, he became the second person that afternoon to baptize a pair of FootJoys.

Chapter 2

Management sure picked a fine time to install automatic hand dryers in the women's locker room, I thought as I helped Monica clean off her shoes. Toilet tissue just wasn't the same as paper towels. The crumpled Kleenex I found in the pocket of my shorts didn't work much better.

"This will have to do," I told her. What I didn't add was that her brand-new FootJoys would never again be the same. They were designed for mud and moisture, not regurgitated tuna melts.

"You're right."

I glanced up in surprise. Monica seldom agreed with anything I said. Not even when I was right. Beneath her tan, Monica's complexion was the shade of moldy olives. I made a mental note for any future decorating I might decide to do: Those shades of tan and green just didn't mix.

While I looked on, Monica toed off her

specially ordered AA narrows and pitched them in the wastebasket. "Think I'll go barefoot."

"Makes sense to me," I replied. Barefoot definitely seemed the way to go. These were extenuating circumstances. Just this once, the No Shirt, No Shoes, No Service rule would have to be ignored. No one wanted to smell barfed-on leather.

Monica bent over the sink and splashed cold water on her face. "I don't know how you can be so calm, Kate."

"I might look calm," I said, giving my hands a good wash with plenty of soap and water, "but I bet my blood pressure hit a record high."

Our eyes met in the mirror. "Who do you think *it* belongs to?" Monica voiced the question foremost in both our minds.

"It . . . ?" Strange way to think of a body part. Strange, but safe. Impersonal. Since I couldn't readily come up with a better euphemism for a severed arm, I just shrugged. "Guess we'll just have to keep our eyes peeled to see who's walking around lopsided."

"Kate!" Monica stared at me, aghast. "How can you be so . . . glib . . . at a time like this?"

"Times like this, one needs to be objective. I keep asking myself, what would Gil Grissom do?"

"Don't think I know him." Monica patted her face dry with the hem of her golf shirt. "Does he live here in Serenity?"

Monica doesn't watch much TV. She reads. Not just fiction, mind you, but literature, the esoteric type. She'd deny under oath that she ever picked up a book by James Patterson or Nora Roberts. Mention Danielle Steel, and she'd have palpitations.

I felt the absurd impulse to giggle. "No," I replied, trying to keep my lips from twitching. "Gil is from Vegas."

"Oh," she murmured, tucking her shirttail back into her microfiber shorts.

Someday I'll inform her that Gil Grissom used to be the main character in *CSI,* my very favorite TV show, but that could wait. I wasn't in the mood for explanations.

I peered at my reflection in the mirror. My reflection peered back. I noticed the roots of my short, Lady Clairol ash blond locks were in need of a touch-up. Behind rimless glasses, my sage green eyes, which I usually consider my best feature, had lost their sparkle. Guess finding an arm in a Wal-Mart bag can do that.

I jabbed the button of the automatic hand dryer. Hot air burst out with enough gusto to make the skin on my hands ripple. Another sign of aging, I thought glumly. Everything either ripples, sags, or wrinkles. I'm not usually this pessimistic. In fact, as a rule I don't mind getting older — as long as I don't look it or feel it. Go figure how that makes sense. However, finding an unattached body part was having an adverse effect on my sense of optimism.

"Guess we ought to get out there," I said, giving my hair a final fluff. "The authorities should be here by now. They'll want us to describe what we found."

Monica clutched her stomach, her face again that moldy olive green. "I think I'm going to be sick."

"Head between your knees." Placing my hand firmly on Monica's dark brown head, I gave it a nudge. Who would have guessed Monica of all people would suffer from a queasy stomach? Never hesitant to voice her opinion, confident in a way I often envied, Monica always seemed the strongest of our little tribe. "Take a deep breath," I ordered.

"OK, OK," she said at last, her voice shaky.

"Showtime," I said with false cheeriness, and shoved open the door of the restroom. One glance and I was tempted to turn tail and sequester myself in one of the stalls.

Maybe even spend the night there until things settled down.

Monica grabbed my arm. "Oh, my God," she whispered. "This place is a circus."

News travels fast here in Serenity. Never let it be said that the residents turned down an excuse to party. Serenity Cove Estates, you see, is a community of "active" adults — very active, indeed, when it comes to socializing. Of course, some whisper, the little blue pill does its share in keeping the activity alive and well — if you catch my drift. Folks here don't put off until tomorrow what they could do today. After all, one day you can be out on the course, the next, slip on a banana peel and end up awaiting a hip replacement.

The clubhouse grill, better known as the Watering Hole, strained at the seams to contain the multitude gathered to hear all the gory details. People lined the bar three-deep while the bartender along with one of the waitresses valiantly struggled to keep up with drink orders.

"Kate." Pam waved at us from across the room. "Over here."

Too late to turn back now. With Monica attached like a suction cup, I plowed through the crowd. I couldn't help but notice the jerk from the eighth hole along with his buddy holding court in the center of the room. Their names came back to me. Mort Thorndike and Bernie Mason. Like many my age, I occasionally suffer temporary memory lapses. But not to worry, I'm told. Senior moments, nothing serious. Everyone in Serenity has them. It's a downright epidemic.

"Yessir, we had our hands full dealing with a bunch of hysterical females back there," Mort, jerk number one, said to everyone within hearing distance.

"You got that right." Bernie, jerk number two, nodded his agreement. "Ladies looked like they would faint dead away any second, weren't for us."

Pompous fools! They remind me of that pair from *Sesame Street,* what's-his-name and what's-his-name. Mort, short and paunchy, and Bernie, his trusty sidekick, a string bean with a bad comb-over, were holding glasses of beer and obviously enjoying the limelight. Hysterical females, indeed! I wanted to set them straight right then and there, but bit my tongue. Time enough for that later.

Pam and Connie Sue were seated at a corner table. Someone had been thoughtful enough to provide each of them with a glass of wine. I could use one myself about now, but I didn't want to take a Breathalyzer before speaking with the authorities.

"Here, sit." Gloria Myers hastily vacated her seat at the table when she spied us. Janine Russell did the same. Nice ladies, Janine and Gloria. Both are fellow Bunco Babes as well as good friends. I first met them in a ceramics class, where I immediately became the poster child for uneven brushstrokes. Someday I'd return and finish the cookie jar I started months ago. No rush. Besides, everyone knows how fattening cookies are, and cookies are my weakness. Right up there next to chocolate. I blame them for the ten extra pounds I could stand to lose.

"You poor things," Janine clucked. "How awful." Janine, who could pass as actress Jamie Lee Curtis's stand-in with her short, chic silver hairstyle and slim figure, was a former nurse and the nurturer of our little tribe of bunco gamesters.

"Can we get you something?" Gloria asked. "Water, iced tea, maybe a nice glass of wine?" The bracelets on Gloria's wrist jangled as she motioned in the direction of the bar. Jewelry was Gloria's one — and only — concession to fashion. Shoulder-length salt-and-pepper hair, brown eyes, square jaw, minimal makeup. No muss, no fuss — that was Gloria. Her mother, Polly, was another matter entirely.

"Bourbon, straight up."

My eyebrows soared in surprise. This from Monica, a teetotaler?

"Good girl." Connie Sue patted Monica's hand. "Meemaw used to say nothing like a swig of bourbon for what ails you." I learned early on in our acquaintance that in Southern-speak *meemaw* translated means grandmother. Connie Sue is the only dyed-in-the-wool Southerner in the Bunco Babes. It never ceases to amaze me that after thirty-some years in Milwaukee, Connie Sue hasn't lost her accent.

I settled for my usual — iced tea, unsweetened, with lemon. Don't know how anyone can drink sweet tea, the beverage of choice here in the South. Ask me, it tastes like maple syrup straight off the shelf at the Piggly Wiggly. Iced tea is only one of many differences I've discovered between Ohio and South Carolina.

After Jim died, the kids thought I should return to Ohio, but for me, there's no going back. Don't get me wrong. Personally, I have nothing against Ohio. In fact, Toledo holds many fond memories, but Serenity Cove Estates is where I want to stay. It was love at first sight when Jim and I first saw the place with its pretty lake, loblolly pines, and magnolias the size of dinner plates. Next day we signed on the dotted line.

My reverie stopped when a hush fell over the crowd. All eyes turned toward the door. A man stood framed in the entrance, six feet, two inches, two hundred twenty pounds of pure muscle. His beige uniform was crisp and spotless, the creases in his pants sharp enough to slice cheese. He wore a shiny black holster on his hip and sported a shiny gold badge on his chest. His skin was the color of Starbucks Breakfast Blend.

"All right, folks, listen up." His deep voice, rich as molasses, bespoke a lifetime spent in the South. "I'm Sumter Wiggins, sheriff of this here county. Would the ladies who found the . . ." He paused. Clearing his throat, he started over. "Would the ladies who found . . . *it* . . . kindly step forward."

I guess "it" was the euphemism of choice. Monica gulped down her bourbon. Connie Sue and Pam did likewise with their wine. Was I the only one worried about a Breathalyzer? Heads turned our way, and everyone watched as we slowly rose to our feet.

Sheriff Sumter Wiggins herded us down a short hallway and into the manager's cramped office. After ordering one of the staff to bring in a couple more chairs, he closed the door on the gawkers lining the hall. No one wanted to be last to know what was going on. Can't say I blame them. I'm the curious sort myself.

A couple men brought in folding chairs along with a lot of clanging and scraping. Once they left, closing the door behind them, we, the four amigos, sat perched on the edge of our seats like sparrows on a clothesline.

Sheriff Wiggins lowered himself onto the edge of the desk, arms folded across an impressive chest. "From what I've heard, ladies, y'all have had yourselves an interestin' — lackin' a better word — round of golf."

None of us said a word. Not a single word. What was this world coming to?

The sheriff scowled down at us. "Ladies, no one is accusin' you of anythin'. I just need to ask y'all if anyone noticed anythin' out of the ordinary while you were on the course this afternoon?"

"You mean in addition to finding . . ." I caught myself just in time. If everyone was using euphemisms, I certainly wasn't going to swim against the tide. I rephrased my question. "You mean in addition to finding *it?*"

The sheriff's scowl deepened. In a good-cop, bad-cop scenario, my money would ride on him as bad cop. Sumter Wiggins didn't look the sort to tolerate fools or put up with nonsense. And he didn't seem the sort to call a dismembered arm by anything other than what it was — a dismembered arm.

"Let's try this again," he said. "One by one just tell me in your own words what happened this afternoon."

Our stories were all pretty much the same except for Monica's — she left out the part about my ruining her chances to par the eighth hole. Shows the state of shock she was in. In her usual frame of mind, she would have put that tidbit in the *Serenity Sentinel,* our weekly newsletter.

The sheriff listened, occasionally pausing to scribble something in his little black book. I was pleased to note that this was just how it was done on *Law & Order.* When we finished, he snapped the notebook shut and shoved it into his shirt pocket. "Don't suppose y'all might have a clue who . . . *it* . . . might belong to?"

Again, silence as thick as Jell-O.

"Anythin' else y'all want to tell me before I let you go?" Wiggins drawled, giving us a cold-eyed once-over.

Suddenly I was back in the second-grade

classroom of Sister "Hail Mary." My hand shot up of its own volition. "Sheriff . . . ?"

"Ma'am?"

Curiosity overcame temerity. "Can you really get fingerprints off a corpse?" Out of the corner of my eye I noticed Monica's face turning that odd shade of green.

"Kate," Pam protested feebly, but I knew she'd like to hear the answer, too. Both of us watched *CSI,* as well as the spin-offs, religiously every week.

"Really, Kate . . ." It was Connie Sue's turn to register an objection.

To his credit, Sheriff Wiggins didn't bat an eye. "Yes, ma'am, it's true that you can get fingerprints off a corpse," he said in that smooth-as-molasses voice of his, "but only when there are fingers attached to the limb. Seems like wild animals made the discovery before you ladies did."

Before I could shove her head down a second time, Monica passed out cold.

Chapter 3

In all the excitement, I had almost forgotten tonight was my turn to hostess our bimonthly bunco get-together. Adrenaline gushed through me like a burst from a fire hose. I raced around the house like a lunatic. I should never have let Pam talk me into a round of golf. In an hour, eleven ladies would descend, filling my house with chatter, laughter, and . . . questions. Lordy, they were sure to have questions galore about what the four of us had found on the golf course.

I stopped running around long enough to answer the phone. It was Monica.

"I've been thinking. Maybe you should find a sub for me. My stomach's still a little queasy."

I grasped the receiver tighter. "Monica, you can't do this to me. How am I supposed to find a sub at the last minute? We — I — need you."

"Well, I don't know. . . ."

"C'mon, Monica," I cajoled. "Just put on your big-girl panties and deal with it." I confess I'm not exactly sure what this means. I saw the slogan on a T-shirt once and for some reason it stuck in my head. All this time, I've been waiting for just the right moment to use it.

"OK," Monica agreed, albeit reluctantly. "See you in a bit."

"Great."

After hanging up the phone, I dragged the card table and folding chairs from the hall closet and set them up in the great room. The card table along with two other tables, one in the kitchen, one in the dining room, usually worked well for bunco. Twelve players, three tables of four. Next I placed three dice on each table along with score sheets and pencils. Since the kitchen table would be the designated head table, I put the bell Pam had once found at a garage sale in the center.

I stood back to take inventory. Something was missing. Something . . . From out of nowhere, panic attacked me. Snacks! I had completely forgotten about snacks. Bunco Babes can't survive without their munchies. I'd be kicked out of the group if I let that happen. I wondered whether I should hyperventilate, but decided there wasn't time.

Early on, the Babes and I — except for a couple who fancy themselves Martha Stewart — voted to keep it simple and just do snacks. I glanced at my wristwatch. It was too late for the crab spread that, before the hullabaloo, I had planned to whip up after golf. What to do? What to do?

Praying for inspiration, hoping for a miracle, I began rummaging through the kitchen cupboards. I found a can of chili sans beans nearly hidden on a shelf behind the soup. A survey of the refrigerator yielded a block of cream cheese perfectly intact without a hint of mold. An unopened bag of tortilla chips completed the bonanza. Voilà! Add a dash of hot sauce, and chili dip, my old standby, would be ready in a jiff.

Next I poured my stash of peanut M&M's and Hershey's Kisses into dice-shaped candy dishes and placed them on the individual tables. Now came the hard part. Usually I offer wine — both red and white, since I don't discriminate — as well as soft drinks to my guests. But tonight called for something special. Something a tad stronger. It had been a day to end all days. This in mind, I hauled out the blender and the margarita mix.

And not a minute too soon. The ladies arrived right on time. From the way they carried on, you'd think no one had seen one another in years. Let me tell you a little about ourselves. The Bunco Babes are a diverse group, ranging from blond and bubbly Megan, Pam's youngest, who at twenty is living with her parents while taking online college courses and figuring out what to do with the rest of her life, to Polly, our septuagenarian. Polly lives with her daughter, Gloria, whom I've already mentioned, in her own specially designed mother-in-law suite. Tara is our other "youngster." Tara is staying with her in-laws, Rita and Dave Larsen, until her husband, Mark, returns from Iraq. Rita suggested Tara as a replacement for one of our original members who decided to abandon Serenity Cove for a yacht in the Bahamas. Imagine! Like I said, we're a diverse bunch.

A frosty pitcher of margaritas and plenty of chocolate. Can't ask for a better combination, to my way of thinking. Judging by their response, the rest of the Bunco Babes seemed to think so, too. My spicy chili dip seemed to be a hit with the Martha Stewart crowd. After everyone had munched their fill and had drinks in hand, we took our seats around the tables.

Pam, tiara perched proudly atop her short reddish blond hair, rang the bell at the head table, signaling the game was about to begin.

Mind you, rules of bunco vary from group to group. Some rules might date back to your grandmother's time, others from the days you were changing diapers back in Toledo. One thing never changes, and that's no previous experience required. Just shake, rattle, and toss those dice.

For the uninitiated, there are six rounds in each set of bunco. The Babes and I play six complete sets before calling it a night. In each round, players try to roll the same number as the round. For instance, in round one, players attempt to roll ones; in round two, players attempt to roll twos, and so on and so forth, if you get my drift. One point is awarded for each "target" number rolled successfully. A player continues to roll as long as she scores one or more points. The round ends when someone at the head table, which controls play, reaches a total of twenty-one points and calls out, "Bunco!"

At first, all of us, by some unspoken agreement, tried to act as though nothing out of the ordinary had transpired that day. We were, after all, adults. Mature, sensible adults who strove to maintain a certain sense of decorum. We rolled a round of ones, then a round of twos, but by the time we started rolling threes, the margaritas kicked in.

"So, who do you think . . . *it* . . . belongs to?" It shouldn't have surprised me that Polly was the first to broach the heretofore unmentioned subject. Polly likes to remind anyone who will listen that at her age she has earned the right to say and do as she pleases. And she does.

"Mother, really," Gloria protested.

Polly proceeded to roll a series of threes. "Well . . . ?"

I had to hand it to her. Polly was persistent.

Next to me, Megan rolled three fives. "Baby bunco," she called out, and kept tossing the dice. Megan has an uncanny knack for winning the prize for the most baby buncos. Unfortunately she never seems to roll them when I'm her partner. "Baby buncos," by the way, occur whenever a player rolls three of a kind of any number except the target number, and count for five points. A bunco, on the other hand, occurs when someone rolls the three target numbers, and scores a whopping twenty-one points.

"Bunco!" Rita, a tall, full-figured brunette, called from the head table. We switched tables and changed partners.

Polly helped herself to a Hershey's Kiss. "I forget. What are we rolling?"

"Fours," Gloria said on a sigh. "Pay attention, Mother."

"Always do," Polly replied with customary cheerfulness.

"Regardless of who . . . *it* . . . belongs to, I'm sure it's no one we know." Rita, a commanding presence at nearly six feet tall with a matronly figure, picked up the subject along with the dice.

"Serenity Cove is far too civilized for something like that to happen here," Connie Sue volunteered from an adjacent table.

Janine clucked her tongue. "Poor soul. Probably a transient or hitchhiker." When she failed to roll a four, she slid the dice to Diane on her left.

Diane, an attractive woman with short chestnut brown hair and hazel eyes, is somewhat younger than most of us at forty-something. Diane works as the librarian in Brookdale, the small town down the road. She likes to brag about how she can multi-task. She proved it now by talking and throwing dice at the same time. "Transient or hitchhiker, the 'poor soul,' as you just said, didn't cut off his, or her, own extremity."

A temporary lull settled over us. The only sound was the click and tumble of dice.

"Maybe it wasn't cut off," Polly ventured at last. "I saw this show on TV once where —"

"Mother!" This time Gloria didn't try to hide her exasperation.

"Bunco!" Tara sang out as she rolled three fours, ending the round. I like Tara. Pretty and levelheaded, she's the sort of girl I'd pick for my son, Steven. For a moment, I let myself drift. How I wish Steven would settle down. I worry and wonder about him. Oh, he has friends, lots of them, but from what I can tell his friends are mostly male.

Again everyone rearranged themselves. Out of the corner of my eye, I saw Polly refill her margarita glass. Rita helped herself to more of the chili dip and tortilla chips. Connie Sue, who's perpetually on a diet, sneaked a handful of M&M's.

The discussion continued the minute the dice started to roll. "George and I wondered about the same thing, Polly." Nancy, the redhead from down the block who was subbing for our friend Claudia, jumped into the fray.

I craned my neck for a better look at Monica, seated at the head table alongside Pam. In my opinion, she looked a little pale, but maybe it was the overhead lighting. I hoped she was done vomiting and fainting. I just had the carpets cleaned last week. Carpet cleaning costs a small fortune these days. One has to watch pennies when one's on a fixed income.

"George," Nancy continued, giving a little flip of the wrist to add more pizzazz to her toss, "said *it* could have been chewed off by a wild animal. He said he saw a coyote the other day."

Suddenly my ears were filled with a loud clanging. At the head table, I saw Pam, her tiara now askew, ringing the bell with all the gusto of a town crier in days of old.

"Bunco!" she hollered.

Saved by the bell. Or was I? Rita and I won that run. I jotted down my score and started toward the head table. Uh-oh, I thought, glancing at Monica. I had seen that moldy-olive color on her face before. I raced for the ginger ale and soda crackers I had set aside for just such an emergency.

Alas, I was too late.

For the first time in the history of the Bunco Babes, the game ended after the first set. As my guests departed, we promised one another we'd meet again next week for a makeup game. Same time, same place. Different conversation.

Now, some people count sheep to fall asleep. Not me. Before Jim passed, I used to count his snores. The record for a sleepless night was 763. I'm considering buying one of those handy little devices guaranteed to lull a person to sleep listening to sounds of chirping birds, crashing waves, or the gentle patter of rain on the roof. Maybe if I search real hard, I can find one that emits snores — the deep, guttural, shake-the-bed kind of snores. Jim's kind.

Bright green numerals, large enough for me to see without trifocals, showed one a.m. on the clock I keep on the nightstand. Might as well give up. I had been tossing and turning since Jay Leno signed off. Normally the two margaritas I had at bunco would have left me sleepy. Not tonight. Kicking back the covers, I got out of bed and headed for the kitchen. Maybe a nice cup of herbal tea would settle me down.

I switched on the light, then reached into a cupboard for the still-unopened box of chamomile tea I had purchased at the Piggly Wiggly for just such an emergency. Wasn't that what Mrs. Rabbit always gave poor little Peter after he foraged in Mr. McGreg-

or's garden? Even Mrs. Rabbit would agree that finding an arm in a Wal-Mart bag had to be more upsetting than eating too many cabbages.

While I waited for water to boil, I stared out the kitchen window. Black as ink out there. Only light to be seen came from the window of a house catty-corner to mine. The Brubakers'. I live on Loblolly Court. Earl and Rosalie Brubaker live on the corner of Shady Lane and Loblolly. Nice to know someone else is awake at this hour. Probably Rosalie. She's the night owl, not her husband. Earl lives by the credo "Early to bed, early to rise." Wonder if Rosalie would be up for a friendly game of pinochle? Just kidding. Never been much for card games, though some day I might try my hand at bridge. Then again, maybe not. Bunco is more my speed. At the risk of repeating myself, no skill, no strategy, strictly social. Can't ask for more when it comes to a game.

The kettle's whistle startled me. If Monica could see me now, she wouldn't accuse me of being calm. I felt restless, jittery. A delayed reaction, I suppose, to the events of the day. My hand wasn't quite steady as I poured boiling water into a mug bearing the logo of a local bank. Water sloshed over the rim. Grabbing a dishcloth, I mopped up the spill.

Slumping down in a kitchen chair, I waited for my tea to cool. My mind kept replaying what had happened that afternoon. If I hadn't topped my drive, we might never have found the . . . *it.* And, let me tell you, *it* was not a pretty sight.

As I already mentioned, along with cookies, chocolate, and *CSI, Law & Order* is another weakness of mine. The character Lennie Briscoe, played by the late Jerry Orbach, is a personal favorite. Lennie has a God-given talent for wisecracks no matter how gruesome the scene. How does Lennie do it? How can he and his cohorts be so nonchalant week after week?

"Duh!" I muttered out loud, and resisted the urge to slap myself on the forehead. Could it be because Lennie and his cohorts are played by actors? Could it be because their crime scenes are make-believe? Could it be because the blood is really ketchup? Duh! If there was any lesson to be learned from yesterday afternoon, it was that mangled arms are one thing on TV, another entirely up close and personal.

I took a sip of chamomile tea. Not bad, but definitely an acquired taste. Getting back to . . . *it.* If my ball hadn't landed in the crud back on the eighth hole, *it* might never have been discovered. Those turkey buzzards would have picked it cleaner than a tray of free hors d'oeuvres at happy hour. And that would have been a real tragedy. The rightful owner of . . . *it* . . . deserved better. Deserved some dignity, some respect. Body parts, even those in Wal-Mart bags, shouldn't be discarded like yesterday's newspaper.

If I live to be a hundred like Aunt Catherine, my mother's oldest sister, I don't think I'll ever forget how that arm had looked. The mention of *that* word had me sitting up straighter and squaring my shoulders. There, I had gone and done it. I had said the forbidden. If I may paraphrase Shakespeare, an arm by any other name is still an arm. Not an *it.*

Small wonder Pam had screeched like a banshee when that arm tumbled out. The best I could muster at the time was one pathetic little squeak. My vocal cords seemed paralyzed. Something that doesn't happen often. If you don't believe me, ask any of the Babes. Instead of hollering my head off, I had stared and stared and stared. The flesh — at least what was left — had been a swollen, mottled grayish black, the edges ragged. I shuddered. What kind of person could do that to another human being? Surely, as Connie Sue had pointed out at bunco, no one here would do such a thing. Serenity Cove Estates is much, much too civilized.

I laced my fingers together and frowned into my teacup. Something nagged at me, but I couldn't quite pin it down. Then it came to me. *It* . . . er, the arm . . . had been wearing a ring. Either a silver or white gold band had been nearly hidden by the engorged flesh at the base of one knuckle. If I closed my eyes, I could still picture it. Instead, I kept them open. Wide open. If I tried to picture that ghastly sight, I'd never get any sleep.

I shoved my tea aside. Maybe a game of pinochle wasn't such a bad idea after all. A glance across the way showed the Brubakers' light still on. Earl and Rosalie had moved into Serenity Cove Estates about the same time as Jim and I. For a while, Rosalie and I were pretty good friends. That was until she discovered golf. Golf with a capital *G.* Where that game is concerned, we're not in the same league. And I mean that both literally and figuratively. We're still on good terms, and she occasionally subs for bunco, but our paths seldom cross anymore. Maybe now was the time to renew acquaintances.

Before common sense had a chance to kick in, I hightailed it out the door.

Chapter 4

To my chagrin, Earl Brubaker, not Rosalie, answered my knock. It was clear from his rumpled khakis and a once-upon-a-time-navy golf shirt that he hadn't been to bed yet.

"Kate!" Earl gaped at me in surprise. "What the hell are you doing here this time of night?"

I gaped back. The seconds ticked past. Earl had posed a good question. Too bad I didn't have a good answer. Or, for that matter, any answer at all. I shifted from one foot to the other. "I couldn't sleep and happened to notice your light was on. What's that old saying, 'Misery loves company'?"

"And your point is . . . ?"

"I'm the company." I beamed him my brightest smile.

Judging from the man's dour expression, my feeble attempt at humor went right over his head. He stood planted in the doorway like a mighty oak, unsmiling, silent. The man always put me in mind of a basset hound with his sad, brown eyes and droopy face. Tonight was no exception.

I frantically scanned my limited repertoire for a plausible excuse for my late-night/early-morning visit. "Could I borrow a cup of sugar?" I winced at hearing those words pop out of my mouth. How lame can you get?

"Sugar?"

Sugar seemed a foreign word to Earl. Maybe I should have tried a simpler request. Maybe flour or, simpler yet, salt. But I was on a roll now. I had regained my footing. "Yes, sugar," I ad-libbed. "I thought I'd bake a nice batch of chocolate-chip cookies for Sheriff Wiggins and his men. They couldn't have been nicer this afternoon."

He dragged a hand the size of a catcher's mitt over his stubbled jaw. "Sure, I guess," he mumbled. "Come on in."

"Thanks." As I followed him to the back of the house, I glanced around, nonchalantly I hoped, but saw no sign of Rosalie. At least I hadn't disturbed her with my sudden need for nocturnal companionship. She wasn't as gullible as her husband. She would have seen through me in a flash.

Earl switched on the kitchen light. Dirty

dishes were piled high in the stainless steel sink. The granite countertops were cluttered with newspapers and stacks of mail. Strange, I thought. This wasn't like Rosalie. She might not have been much of a cook, but the woman kept her kitchen spotless. My sense of uneasiness crept up a notch. What the heck was I doing in Rosalie's kitchen with her husband in the middle of the night?

Earl shuffled across the room. "Who did you say you were baking cookies for?"

"Sheriff Wiggins and his deputies. They were awfully patient with us this afternoon." I clutched my robe tighter around my neck. What had I been thinking to head over here in my pajamas at this ungodly hour? Heaven knew, if Jim were still alive, he'd have had a conniption fit at my calling on a neighbor in my nightclothes.

"What happened this afternoon?" Without waiting for an answer, Earl poked his head inside the pantry and began rummaging around.

"You didn't hear?"

"Hear what?"

I let out a sigh. Surely he must be the only person within a fifty-mile radius that hadn't heard the news. "My friends and I found an . . ." I fumbled for a suitable word. While I could call a spade, a spade, and an arm, an arm, not everyone had my fortitude. "We found an odd . . . part . . . on the golf course this afternoon."

"Found some art?"

Please, Lord, not again, I prayed. Not another man in need of a hearing aid. Maybe I should go into the business. Probably make a fortune. I sighed and took the easy way out. "That's right, Earl. We found some art."

He emerged from the pantry triumphantly clutching a half-empty bag of sugar and handed it to me. "No need to get all worked up."

Now that I had the sugar I really didn't need, it was time to go. "Well, thanks for the loan. I'll replace it next time I'm at the Piggly Wiggly." As eager as I'd been earlier to trot over to the Brubakers', I was now even more eager to trot back home.

I turned and headed for the door with Earl trailing behind. "Sure glad I didn't wake Rosalie," I said over my shoulder. "Tell her I said hello."

"I would, but Rosalie isn't here."

I stumbled to a halt, nearly tripping over the sill. "Isn't here?" The possibility hadn't occurred to me.

Earl's hand was on the door, poised to close it. "She's in upstate New York visiting the grandkids. Should be back next week or so."

"I'm surprised you didn't go with her."

"I'm not big on little kids," Earl admitted grumpily. "Last time our daughter visited, her youngest picked all my prize orchids for a bouquet. Sure hope by their next visit he'll be old enough to tell the difference between a dandelion and a phalaenopsis."

I resisted the urge to roll my eyes. Phalaenopsis? Give me a break. Most adults, much less children, probably had never even heard the word. Poor child. No wonder Rosalie left a curmudgeon like Earl behind when she took off to visit the grandkids.

Home again, I dumped my chamomile tea, which had grown stone-cold in my absence, down the drain. So much for it being as soothing as a field of wildflowers.

Feeling as restless as ever, I wandered into the library. Calling the small room a "library" always seemed ostentatious. When I think of a library, I think large. Large and filled floor to ceiling with books. That hardly describes a room the size of a guest bedroom with a solitary magazine rack. Our builder kept correcting me whenever I referred to this space as a den. Dens, he insisted, were passé. Family rooms, he informed me, were now called great rooms.

And every new home, he had said, absolutely must have a master bedroom suite.

"Well, la-di-da," I had said.

Besides the aforementioned magazine rack and Jim's recliner, the library/den is also where we keep the computer. Now that Jim isn't always sitting in front of it playing solitaire, I've learned how to surf the Net. Who knows? Someday I might even have my own MySpace page. Wouldn't my granddaughters, Jillian and Juliette, be impressed? They'd think their grandmother was "hip."

Do youngsters still use that expression? Here in Serenity mention *hip* and people instantly associate it with *replacement.*

I powered up the computer and surfed until I found just what I was looking for. A honey of an electronic marvel called the Sandman. Clinically tested, the Sandman is a device guaranteed to help people achieve deeper states of sleep and relaxation. It emits sounds. Waves on a beach, rain on the roof, wind in the willows. It can even be programmed to sound like a thunderstorm. Not exactly Jim snoring, but I'd wager it's a close second.

Satisfied with my purchase, I stifled a yawn and turned off the computer. As I made my way through the darkened house, I noticed a light still burned at the Brubakers'. And once again, I thought this odd for a man who liked to retire early.

Chapter 5

I zigged right when I should have zagged left. I zagged left when everyone else in class zigged right. Flowing Chi definitely wasn't flowing this morning. My *dantien* was nowhere to be found. I sneaked a peek at Pam. Her Tai Chi moves seemed as smooth and graceful as ever. But Pam can dance the Electric Slide with the best of them, while I watch from the sidelines. I envy her sense of rhythm. I'm a klutz when it comes to coordination. That's the reason you'll never find me on a tennis court. I took tennis lessons — once. Never made it past the serve. A pity because I loved those cute little outfits all my friends wore. No, Tai Chi is more my speed. Concentration, flexibility, balance. To my way of thinking, these are more useful to a senior citizen than a killer backhand.

"Next we'll do Fighting Tiger," Marian, our instructor, crooned in that soft singsong she uses to lead us through our paces. "Step out to the left."

Normally Fighting Tiger is one of my favorites. It makes me feel like Chuck Norris about to kung fu one of the bad guys on a rerun of *Walker, Texas Ranger.* I brought up my shoulder, made a fist, shifted my weight, and, once again, zigged when I was supposed to zag. I felt the heat of Marian's glare. Her look reduced me to the only six-year-old in a ballet recital who was out of step. I could almost hear the audience snicker.

Finally class was over. We performed the closing ritual, stepping back out of Tai Chi with the left foot. I started to use the right but, thank goodness, caught myself in the nick of time. Don't want Marian to have a hissy fit. Or irritate the Tai Chi gods. That reminds me of another reason I love bunco: You don't have to be coordinated.

Pam gathered up her belongings. "I told Connie Sue and Monica we'd meet them for breakfast. Hope that's OK. Don't take this the wrong way," she said, turning and giving me the once-over, "but you look awful."

"Thanks," I muttered. "What are friends for if they can't be honest?" I tried to shrug off Pam's comment. But deep down I wondered if sometimes honesty wasn't a bit overrated. Who needs to be told they look like a hag?

"The girls said they'd meet us at the café."

"Lead the way." I picked up my purse, which weighs a ton, and slung it over my shoulder. Actually the fact that it weighs so much eliminates my need to visit the workout room. At least that's how I rationalize it. Someday I plan to schedule an appointment with the personal trainer, but what's the rush? The fitness room isn't going anywhere.

I followed Pam outside and climbed into her cherry red golf cart. Pam always travels by golf cart whenever possible. Since it's electric, it saves on the cost of gasoline. Personally I think Pam enjoys tooling around in a vehicle she can park without scraping fenders. Not that she's a bad driver, just a bad parker.

The Cove Café is located right around the corner from the Recreation and Fitness Center. All one has to do is follow one of the many asphalt pathways that wind throughout Serenity Cove like a spool of ribbon.

Monica and Connie Sue were seated at our favorite table when we arrived.

"Good heavens, Kate, you look terrible," Monica said the moment she spotted us.

I tried not to wince. When Jim and I first started dating, I could stay up half the night and still look fresh as a daisy the next morning. Now one sleepless night, and friends line up to tell me I look like something the cat dragged in.

"Not to worry, sugar," Connie Sue drawled, "I've got just the thing." She dug through her bag and produced a small, expensive-looking gold vial. "It's the latest rage. Dab a little of this under your eyes. It'll work wonders on those dark circles."

"Fine," I said, knowing I sounded more grumpy than grateful. When it comes to health and beauty tips, there's no one better than Connie Sue. Lest we suffer a senior moment, Connie Sue is quick to remind us she was once a reigning beauty queen. To this day, she wages a valiant battle against the ravages of time. From all appearances, she is holding ground. Thanks to the help of a skilled colorist, her hair is still the same honey blond it was the day the rhinestone tiara that we now use for bunco was placed on her head. Countless hours in land aerobics and tennis keep her figure a trim size eight. If I didn't love her so much, she'd be easy to hate.

"Trouble sleeping last night?" Monica asked.

I nodded. Unless tortured, I wasn't going to volunteer any information about my middle-of-the-night sojourn to the Brubakers'. I offered a silent prayer of gratitude that Rosalie hadn't been present to witness my foolishness.

"Me, too," Monica sighed. "I took one of the sleeping pills the doctor prescribed for Fred after his prostate surgery. Wasn't for that, I couldn't have slept a wink either."

"I know exactly what y'all mean," Connie Sue confided. She leaned forward as though imparting a state secret. "This whole place is simply buzzing about . . . *it.*"

"*It* can't possibly belong to anyone here in Serenity," Monica said in her usual matter-of-fact manner, rehashing what the Bunco Babes had talked about the night before.

Pam and I exchanged glances. We had watched too many episodes of *Law & Order* not to know that crimes were full of quirky little twists and turns.

"Thacker thinks *it* probably belongs to a person from somewhere miles from here. Myrtle Beach, or maybe Charleston." Connie Sue has a habit of quoting her husband's opinions on a variety of subjects. To her way of thinking, Thacker Brody might as well have been a Supreme Court justice handing down life-altering decisions. To my way of thinking, Thacker Brody is a pompous fool. But Connie Sue adores him, so we all tolerate him the best we can.

A waitress I had never seen before appeared with menus tucked under one arm and holding a coffeepot in the other. *Marcy* was written on a piece of masking tape fastened to a borrowed name tag. Her frizzy brown hair looked overpermed, and her disposition, judging from her scowl, underdeveloped. "Y'all want coffee?"

We exchanged glances. *Where was Vera?* I sensed the four of us were all asking ourselves the same question. Without a doubt Vera was our favorite waitress at the Cove Café. Not that I'm boasting, but I'm equally certain we were her favorite customers. Vera wouldn't have had to ask what we wanted to drink. She'd know.

"No coffee for me," Monica said with a vigorous shake of her head. "I'll have Earl Grey."

The waitress stifled a yawn. "Who's he?"

"It's not a *he,*" Monica huffed. "It's tea."

"Well, why didn't you just say so?" Marcy shrugged diffidently. "Can't expect me to know everything."

"Just water." Connie Sue's smile seemed a bit forced. "Lemon, no ice."

I eyed the pot Marcy was holding with

anticipation. "Coffee, and lots of it."

"Me, too," Pam echoed.

"No wonder y'all can't sleep at night," Connie Sue scolded after Marcy left to fetch Earl Grey and ice-water-lemon-no-ice. "Too much caffeine isn't good for a body."

"She's right, you know. I just read the results of a recent study —"

"Enough about coffee, y'all," Connie Sue interrupted Monica before she went off on one of her tangents. "There are serious matters here that need discussing."

Pam picked up the thread of our previous conversation. "In all likelihood, *it* might even belong to someone from out of state. Maybe Georgia, or possibly Florida."

"I agree," Monica said, nodding in agreement. "Serenity Cove Estates simply isn't the type of place where that type of thing could possibly happen. People here are much too friendly — too civilized."

"Thacker said," Connie Sue continued, "no one in their right mind would commit such a crime, then leave the evidence right in their own backyard, so to speak. He said whomever did such a horrible act would want to get anything incriminating as far away as possible."

I fought the urge to roll my eyes at hearing Saint Thacker's name mentioned repeatedly. We were quiet until Marcy returned with beverages for Connie Sue and Monica. However, the tea she set in front of Monica bore the name Lipton on its tag, not the earl's. Connie Sue's glass held more ice than water with no lemon wedge in sight. But Pam and I lucked out as Marcy topped off our cups.

"This is Lipton's." Monica pointed an accusatory finger at the tea bag.

Marcy deflected Monica's stare with one of her own. "This is all we got."

The dueling stares ended in a draw. Connie Sue took up the challenge as she picked up her glass and handed it back to Marcy. "I asked for water, lemon, and no ice."

"Whatever . . ." With a put-upon sigh, Marcy trudged off in the general direction of the kitchen.

"If I were you, I'd make sure she doesn't spit in your glass," I advised Connie Sue. "I saw a movie once when a waiter did that after a customer ticked him off. The guy got some terrible disease and nearly died."

"Really, Kate," Connie Sue scolded. "The things that come out of your mouth."

"Like yesterday," Monica quickly chimed in as if we actually needed her opinion, "when you asked Sheriff Wiggins about taking fingerprints from a corpse. It's all your fault I passed out. Thank goodness I came to before someone dialed nine-one-one."

"Kate has an inquiring mind."

Pam, bless her heart, rose to my defense. I reminded myself to thank her later. Maybe give her some of those chocolate-chip cookies I intended to bake for the sheriff. I've even seen Connie Sue sneak one or two of my cookies when she thought no one was watching. No fooling me, no sirree. I can spot a fellow chocoholic a mile away.

The waitress returned, plunked down a water glass only two-thirds full. A shriveled slice of lemon clung to the side like lichen to a rock. She pulled out a pad. "You ladies ready to order?"

We perused the menus while Marcy waited, pencil poised. I don't know why we waste time with these little rituals when we always order the exact same thing. I suppose there's a certain comfort in going through the motions.

Snapping her menu shut, Monica was the first to order. "I'll have an egg white omelet with extra veggies."

Connie Sue's forehead scrunched the way it always did when she was deep in thought. Once, after a second glass of wine, she whispered to me that she was considering

Botox. When she realized what she had said, she swore me to secrecy.

"I'll have my usual, wheat toast unbuttered and the fruit cup," she said at last.

That should have been my choice. Nice, sensible, low-cal, low fat. But instead I heard myself say, "Two eggs scrambled, bacon crisp, toast, and hash browns. No grits."

"I'll have the same," Pam said, shooting Connie Sue and Monica a defiant look.

As Marcy strolled off in the direction of the kitchen, Monica turned to Pam. "You've been awfully quiet on the subject. Who do you think *it* might belong to?"

I'd had enough. "For crying out loud, ladies, can we please stop calling it an *it?* It's not an *it.* It's an arm!"

Monica glanced over her shoulder to see if any of the other diners might have overheard my mini-explosion. If anyone had, they pretended not to notice.

Connie Sue picked up her glass, stared into it, then set it down again without drinking. Maybe she had taken my warning to heart after all. No telling what an irate waitress might do when she thought no one was looking.

Pam reached over and patted my hand. "You're absolutely right, Kate. It's time we stop treating *arm* as though it's a dirty word."

"Thank you," I mumbled, feeling mollified and foolish all mixed together.

Monica and Connie Sue, looking properly chastened, murmured their agreement. After clearing her throat, Monica returned to the subject at hand. "All right, Pam, you've been awfully quiet. Give us your take on the subject."

Pam toyed with the handle of her coffee cup. "I can't believe something that awful might have happened to someone we know — someone from Serenity. Guess I have to go along with the notion that *it* was brought here by a person from somewhere else in an attempt to hide their crime."

I suppressed a shudder. The image of a wild-haired maniac flinging various and sundry body parts about as he, or she, traveled through the countryside made me cringe. It conjured the notion of guests happily tossing rice at a wedding. Did wedding guests still toss rice? Or was that now politically incorrect? Later, I'd consult an etiquette book. Or, better yet, ask my daughter. Whether Martha Stewart or Julia Child, Jen always does everything by the book. She takes after Jim's side of the family in that respect.

"This kind of talk surely can't be good for the digestion. Let's change the subject, shall we, girls?" Connie Sue said, smoothing her always-perfect honey blond locks. "Has anyone heard from Claudia?"

We cast expectant glances around the table. Claudia Connors is another member of the Bunco Babes and the most outrageous by far. Claudia, a divorcée, has recently taken up online dating. That was how she met Lance — whom, by the way, none of us has yet so much as caught a glimpse of. And this Lance person persuaded Claudia to join him on an RV trip out west. Names like Yellowstone, Yosemite, and the Grand Canyon had flowed from Claudia's lips as easily as the lyrics of her favorite Beatles tune. All the Babes tried to talk her out of taking off with a man she scarcely knew, but there was no reasoning with her.

"Any of you ladies receive a phone call from her?" I asked hopefully. "Or maybe a postcard or e-mail?"

"I haven't heard a word from her — not a single, solitary word," Connie Sue said after a lengthy pause.

"Neither have I," Pam admitted.

"Well, as we all know, Claudia always forgets to turn on her cell phone." Monica's tone implied a mental defect of some sort. Truth be told, I often suffer from the same malady as Claudia. But, coward that I am, I took the path of least resistance and held my tongue.

The fact of Claudia's prolonged radio silence struck home. Uneasy glances flitted from one to the other. None of us wanted to voice our mutual worry out loud. But all of us, I'm sure, shared the same concern. Claudia was unaccounted for. No phone calls, no postcards, no e-mails. Where was she?

And was she all right?

Marcy appeared just then bearing a tray with our breakfast orders. Her mouth thinned in an uncompromising line, she set Monica's omelet down in front of Pam and my scrambled eggs, bacon, and hash browns in front of Connie Sue.

"You're new here, aren't you, dear?" Connie Sue deftly switched plates.

Monica was more to the point. "Where's Vera?" she asked.

"Gone." Marcy shrugged, nonplussed. "She just up and left."

What was this, I wondered, an epidemic of missing women? Claudia, and now Vera. Not to mention Rosalie Brubaker's prolonged absence. I toyed with my eggs, no longer hungry.

CHAPTER 6

I was still miffed an hour later. Leave it to Monica to push my buttons. I didn't think my question to the sheriff about taking fingerprints off a corpse was so out of line. For the life of me, I couldn't figure out why Monica was in such a snit.

I filled an entire cookie sheet with neat little balls of dough before I realized my mistake. I wanted to both laugh and cry when I realized my blunder. In my current state of discombobulation, I had neglected to add the key ingredient — the chunks of mouthwatering dark chocolate that make my cookies special. Stupid, stupid, stupid! I felt like banging my head on the counter. A mind is a terrible thing to lose.

Disgusted at my oversight, I dumped the entire pan load of cookie dough back into the mixing bowl. No wonder I couldn't concentrate. I was worried sick about Claudia.

Claudia has an adventurous streak I've always admired. She'd single-handedly raised two sons after her auto-exec husband left her for his busty, twentysomething secretary. A cliché, I know, but it happens. By dint of hard work and determination, she became a top-selling Realtor in Oakland County, Michigan, while seeing her boys through college. One of her sons is a successful surgeon somewhere in Chicago, the other an aeronautical engineer in Seattle. After years of putting her boys first, Claudia decided it was time to kick up her heels. She sold her home in Farmington Hills, bought a house here in Serenity Cove Estates, and settled down to enjoy the good life.

I dumped enough chocolate into the mixing bowl to induce a diabetic coma. No need for an electric mixer, I thought as I whipped the spatula through the cookie dough at high speed. Still, I couldn't get Claudia out of my mind. Wild and wacky, Claudia is the Bunco Babe version of Auntie Mame. Drama Club, Novel Nuts, and the Serenity Singers — Claudia dived into these activities with abandon. Recently, however, she had discovered a new interest. Internet dating. Claudia, being Claudia, embraced this new hobby with her usual zest. Now, on a whim, she had gone off with a man she barely knew — a virtual stranger. She had pooh-poohed warnings from the Bunco Babes, insisting she knew what she was doing.

But did she?

I remember reminding Claudia that Ted Bundy seemed like a perfect gentleman, too, until women started showing up dead. Claudia had been gone over a week without a single word to any of us. I needed to make sure Sheriff Wiggins put Claudia's name at the top of his missing-persons list.

For the second time that morning, I rolled perfect little balls of dough and lined them on the baking sheet like good little soldiers. And if Claudia weren't worry enough, there was also the matter of Vera's unexplained absence.

Vera always struck me as the sensible and down-to-earth sort. Definitely not the type to just up and leave a perfectly good job as waitress at the Cove. Granted, I didn't know much about the woman's personal life, but I promised myself to find out more next chance I got.

I glanced out the window and watched Earl Brubaker back down his drive. I tried to remember the last time I'd seen Rosalie, but couldn't seem to recall how long it'd been. I wondered if I should add her to my missing-persons list.

With concerned citizens such as myself, there'd be no need for a hotline. Why, the sheriff would probably be downright grateful for my assistance. And even more grateful once he got a taste of the treats I was bringing him. I smiled at the thought.

Just as I was about to pop the pan of cookies into the oven, the kitchen filled with smoke.

"Damn, damn, damn," I swore aloud, glad no one was around to hear me.

I cracked open the oven door and immediately spotted the problem. With all the goings-on, I had forgotten to clean the spills from an apple pie that had baked over. Apparently a self-cleaning oven doesn't just clean itself.

My eyes watered from the smoke. I cranked the kitchen window wide, then flipped the switch for the overhead fan. I waited for the blades to whirl and clear the air, but nothing happened. Absolutely nothing. I flicked the switch a couple times for good measure. Still nothing.

"Damn, damn, damn," I swore again, louder this time. I always feel so helpless when things around the house need attention. In all our years together, I had depended on Jim to fix things. He could unclog a drain, repair a dishwasher, or install a ceiling fan. You name it, Jim could do it. Of course, in the process, he made my limited use of swearwords seem amateurish.

Thank goodness for double ovens, I thought. While waiting for the convection oven to preheat, I reached for the phone. Why let your fingers do the walking when you have friends like Pam? Pam has been in Serenity Cove the longest of any of my friends. She's the go-to person when I want information. Looking for carpet cleaners, a window washer, or a landscaper — Pam is the person to ask.

Pam picked up on the third ring.

"I have a problem," I explained, getting straight to the point. "The fan in my kitchen just committed suicide. Do you happen to know a good handyman?"

"Give me a sec." I could hear the rustle of pages at the other end of the line. Pam rattled off a number. I scribbled it down. "You'll like him. He's a real gem."

"Does this 'real gem' have a name?"

"Yeah, of course," Pam said with a laugh. "It's Bill — Bill Lewis. As a matter of fact, you met him yesterday."

"I did?" If I had, he certainly failed to

make much of an impression. Then again, other matters had made too much of one, but I didn't want to go there.

"Bill also works as a ranger on the golf course."

"Bill . . . ? The guy who barfed?"

"The one and only. Give him a chance, Kate," Pam urged. "Don't condemn the guy because he has a sensitive stomach."

I glanced up at my dead ceiling fan and heaved a sigh. "OK, OK, I'll call him, but he better not lose his lunch all over my nice clean kitchen floor."

"Just don't have any nasty surprises in store for the poor man."

I doodled a chain of daisies on the pad where I had written Bill's number. "I know it's only been an hour since the last time we talked, but I don't suppose you've heard from Claudia?" I asked, trying to keep my tone casual.

"No, not a word. I have to admit, Kate, I'm concerned. Do you think we should try to contact her sons? Ask them if they've heard from their mother?"

I thought about this for a moment. "I hate to worry them. Besides, we still don't know whether the arm belongs to a man or a woman. Let's wait until we find out more before sounding the alarm. For all we know,

Claudia is busily snapping pictures of the Grand Canyon."

"I still don't like the fact she was so secretive about this new man in her life."

"Maybe he's a lot older than she is."

"Knowing Claudia, he's probably a lot younger."

"Maybe he has two heads."

"Or weighs six hundred pounds."

"Seriously, Pam, if Claudia isn't enough to worry about, what do you make of Vera taking off like that?" I could picture Pam's brows drawing together in a frown.

"It's possible Vera decided to take a vacation on the spur of the moment."

Pam has a tendency to look at the bright side of a situation. A trait I find downright irritating at times. "Yeah," I sneered, "maybe she won the lottery and took a cruise to the Greek Isles."

"No need to be sarcastic," she chided. "There's probably a simple explanation. For example, there could be an illness in the family, and Vera was called away to care for them. Hate to cut this short, Kate, but I've got to run, or I'm going to be late for the dentist."

"Better you than me," I said. Personally I'd rather have gallbladder surgery than see the dentist. Surgeons give you general anesthesia. Dentists don't.

After we disconnected, I gave Bill Lewis a call, and he agreed to drop by Sunday afternoon to check out the fan. Satisfied that my problem was under control, I packed a couple dozen cookies in a plastic take-and-go container and headed out the door.

Chapter 7

The Brookdale County Sheriff's Department was housed in a single-story brick building just off the town square. I pulled into a parking spot down the block. I'd never had cause to turn down this particular side street before. Certainly never had cause to visit the sheriff. But then I never had two friends AWOL with a madman on the loose.

I took a minute to study the building in more detail. It looked so . . . ordinary. I had envisioned something far grander. Something more Southern with pillars or at least a veranda. Something . . . stately. Whatever I'd expected, this certainly wasn't it. Its neat brick exterior reminded me of the thousands upon thousands of ranch-style homes popular in the Midwest. The trim around the windows and doors looked as though it had recently received a fresh coat of white paint. Pots planted with cheery purple and yellow pansies flanked each side of the entrance. A large gold emblem emblazoned on the door proclaimed it the official domain of Brookdale County sheriff Sumter Wiggins. Stifling my disappointment, I pushed open the door.

A girl with lank, shoulder-length hair and wire-rimmed glasses too large for her small face sat before a computer screen at the front desk. The nameplate read TAMMY LYNN SNOW. She glanced up from the screen and gave me a tentative smile. "May I help you, ma'am?"

The inbred politeness of Southerners never fails to impress me. When they address you, it's always "Yes, ma'am" or "No, ma'am." So different from their Northern counterparts. Folks there could take a page from their book.

I explained to Tammy Lynn that I was here to see Sheriff Wiggins. The whole time I kept thinking Connie Sue would give her eyeteeth to get her hands on the girl. Tammy Lynn had great bone structure. Even I could see that. The girl was in dire need of a makeover. With the right hairstyle and a little makeup, the girl could be a knockout. But all that potential was hidden beneath a well-scrubbed face and clothes more befitting her granny. On second thought, make that her great-granny. After all, I'm a grandmother myself and like to think I still possess some fashion know-how.

"Do you have an appointment, ma'am?"

"Ah, no. Sorry," I admitted rather sheepishly. In the commotion of my kitchen filling with smoke, a suicidal ceiling fan, and finding a repairman, calling for an appointment never entered my head. And if it had, I would have ignored it. I'm a true believer in the element of surprise. Especially when the "surprise" comes bearing gifts. "I'm positive the sheriff will want to hear what I have to say. I promise I won't take up much of his time," I tacked on for good measure.

Tammy Lynn picked up a phone and relayed to the sheriff the message that he had a visitor. She nodded several times, then hung up. "Ma'am, he'll be with you shortly. Please have a seat."

I plunked myself down in one of the molded plastic chairs and prepared to wait. The girl resumed pecking away at the keyboard. Dog-eared copies of *Field & Stream* and *Popular Mechanics* stacked on a corner table didn't interest me. I used the time instead to examine my surroundings. The walls were covered in a faux-walnut paneling, the floors a nondescript brown linoleum. Various official-looking certificates hung in cheap plastic frames. If anything, the interior was a bigger disappointment than the exterior. It was downright . . . boring. I might as well have been at the tax assessor's office.

The sheriff's department was nothing like the energy-charged headquarters on *Law & Order.* Thanks to my local cable station, I watch reruns faithfully each evening. Only the perfunctory "Most Wanted" posters tacked on a bulletin board near the door hinted this might be a law-enforcement establishment. But even that was ho-hum. I see these same bearded, unsmiling faces every time I mail a package at the post office. Nevertheless I committed each face to memory — just in case. A woman living alone can't be too careful.

The intercom buzzed just then. Tammy Lynn looked up from her keyboard and gave me a timid smile. "Sheriff Wiggins will see you now."

I smiled back, collected the cookies and my handbag from an adjacent chair, and walked down a short hallway to a door marked COUNTY SHERIFF.

Sumter Wiggins was just as impressive on second viewing. All hard muscle and bad attitude. Some might even call him intimidating. But not me. I'm too old to be easily intimidated. In spite of the little pep talk I gave myself, however, I felt a faint flutter of apprehension as I took the seat he indicated.

"Miz McCall," he drawled in that velvety baritone. "What brings you here instead of out on the golf course this fine afternoon?"

I wonder if anyone had ever told him that voice of his could earn more money in a week dubbing commercials than he could in a year as county sheriff. Not that I had any direct knowledge of this, mind you, but I always make a point of reading the entertainment section of the paper. One picks up interesting tidbits from time to time.

I plunked the take-and-go container of chocolate-chip cookies on the desk in front of him. "I thought you and your men could use a little treat while trying to break the case."

"The *case . . . ?*" The word fairly hummed with skepticism and disapproval.

"The case of the missing appendage," I hastily supplied, lest he'd forgotten our find of the day before. "Sounds like the title of a Nancy Drew mystery."

Not a glimmer of recognition crossed his face at the mention of my girlhood heroine.

"Surely you've heard of Nancy Drew?" I asked. Hoping to enlighten him, I rattled off several titles that came to mind. *"The Secret of the Old Clock*? *The Hidden Stair-*

case? The Clue in the Diary?"

His expression remained impassive.

I forged ahead. "My all-time favorite is *The Password to Larkspur Lane.* I must have read it a dozen times." I was momentarily transported back to my youth where I devoured every book written by my idol, Carolyn Keene. Heard she died at her typewriter at the ripe old age of ninety-six. Not a bad way to go, for a writer, that is.

"No offense, Miz McCall," he drawled, "but if I want to discuss books, I'll join Friends of the Library."

Well, that certainly put me in my place. "Sorry, Sheriff. I do tend to ramble on and for that I apologize. I just assumed a man in your profession would be a mystery buff."

The sheriff sighed. "Don't mean to be rude, ma'am, but I've got a full schedule."

"Of course you do," I replied primly. "Far be from me to take valuable time away from your investigation."

He looked hopeful as he reached for his little black notebook. "Have you, by chance, remembered a detail you might have forgotten in all the excitement yesterday?"

"Well . . ." I could feel myself puff with pride. I had become part of an official police investigation. Wouldn't my children be impressed to learn I was working closely with the sheriff's department? "Actually, Sheriff, I do have a couple leads that might help solve our case."

"*Our* case?"

I swear I saw him wince, but he recovered admirably and reached for a pen.

"Now we're making progress."

"My friend Claudia took off on a trip out west with a man she met on the Internet." I leaned back and waited for the impact of this to fully sink in.

"That's it?" he asked after a prolonged pause.

"In an RV," I added. "No one's heard a word since she left. Some of the Bunco Babes, as well as myself, have tried calling her, but no luck. Granted, Claudia's notorious for forgetting to turn on her cell phone. Said she had enough of phones ringing day and night when she was in real estate."

"Does this Claudia have a last name?"

"Of course, she does," I said with a little laugh. "It's Connors. Claudia Connors." How absentminded of me. This just goes to show how upset I was about her disappearance. Sheriff Wiggins must surely have thought I was nothing more than a ditzy, harebrained woman with too much time on her hands.

"If that's all . . ."

His lack of enthusiasm was evident — even to a ditz — as he jotted Claudia's name in his book.

It would have been easy at this point to beat a hasty but dignified retreat, but I refused to let his attitude deter me from accomplishing what I had set out to do. I drew myself up straighter in the chair. "There is one more thing you may want to know since you're looking into missing persons."

He regarded me silently. His dark eyes could bore straight through a person. But like I said before, I'm not easily intimidated. After all, it's not like I'm a felon with something to hide. Nevertheless . . .

I leaned forward and lowered my voice. "Vera up and left without a word." I debated whether to mention Rosalie, but decided against it . . . at least for the time being.

Sheriff Wiggins sighed heavily. "Is this Vera another of your bunco ladies?"

"No, no. Vera is our favorite waitress at the Cove Café."

"I see. Suppose you tell me what you know about Vera. I'll take it from there."

"Vera wasn't at work this morning, and this new waitress, Marcy, couldn't keep our orders straight. Naturally we asked about Vera."

"Naturally."

I ignored the thinly veiled sarcasm. "All Marcy could say was that Vera 'up and left.' It isn't like a woman of a certain age to just walk away from a perfectly good job when tips alone would make her want to stay."

"Does this Vera have a last name?"

Sheriff Wiggins waited, pen poised, while I pondered his question. I was reminded how very little I knew about the woman who served me breakfast two or three times a week. "I'm sure Vera does have a last name, but I don't think I've ever heard it," I admitted slowly, then brightened. "Surely the folks who hired her can tell you."

"And you think I need to check into the matter because . . . ?" He paused, leaving me to fill in the blank.

"Because . . ." The man was trying my patience. He could, at the very least, pretend to be a teensy bit grateful for the information. I read the news. I watch TV. The police are always asking concerned citizens to step forward.

"Because," I began anew, "the arm we found yesterday belongs to someone. I believe it's proper police procedure to account for anyone who might be missing. Especially those missing under rather mysterious circumstances."

"Don't mean to be disrespectful, ma'am,

but what makes you an expert on police procedure?"

"Because I've watched *every* single episode of *Law & Order,* that's why," I fired back.

My retort left him at a momentary loss. Sheriff Sumter Wiggins certainly failed to measure up to *Law & Order*'s Detective Lennie Briscoe when it came to witty repartee. First Nancy Drew, now *Law & Order.* I could see by the expression on the sheriff's face that he wasn't taking me seriously. How hard could it be to track down a couple of missing women who had gone AWOL? I bet I could do it myself if I set my mind to it. I had half a notion to do just that.

"If that's all . . ."

It didn't take a ton of bricks to hit me over the head. I can tell when I'm not wanted. I got to my feet and slung my purse over my shoulder. The sheriff rose as well. Apparently his mama drilled good manners into her boy — if not a sunny disposition.

"Enjoy the cookies, Sheriff. Chocolate chip are my specialty."

"Kind of you, ma'am, but I don't eat cookies."

Doesn't eat cookies? That stopped me dead in my tracks. What kind of person doesn't eat cookies? Not even Connie Sue, who watches her weight like a hawk, has that much willpower. Clearly the man wasn't human.

I could feel my cheeks burn as I marched past Tammy Lynn and out the front door. Sheriff Sumter Wiggins was insufferable. My meeting with him had definitely gotten off on the wrong foot.

Or in this case — pardon the pun — on the wrong arm.

Chapter 8

The whole town was still buzzing the next day when I ducked into the Piggly Wiggly. And I don't mean just Serenity Cove Estates, but Brookdale as well. Brookdale happens to be the county seat and, as the crow flies, is the town closest to Serenity. It's not very big as towns go, but one can find the essentials of life situated around the town square. In addition to the ubiquitous Chinese and Mexican restaurants, there's a quaint little tearoom, a video store that doubles as a nail/tanning salon, a used-book store, and a couple of antiques shops. Flanking the square like nineteenth-century bookends are the county courthouse at one end and the opera house at the other. Cute and quaint. Brookdale could double as a set for a Disney movie.

If I get a hankering to visit a mall, I hop in the Buick and drive another twenty-five miles or so down the road. I have to admit I don't hanker as much as I did when I was younger. Malls, it seems, have lost their luster. If that's a sign of aging, then so be it.

In an area where a hole in one makes headlines, finding a body part is *huge.* Everywhere I went, it's all people were talking about. Having been one of the discoverers made me somewhat of a celebrity. Given my druthers, I certainly wouldn't have picked a dismembered appendage as a means for my fifteen minutes of fame. I would have chosen something more in line with winning the South Carolina Lottery. Or a dream vacation to Fiji on *Regis and Kelly.*

"Kate!" A woman's voice exclaimed from behind me.

Seemed like I couldn't wheel my shopping cart, or buggy as they're called here in the South, halfway down the produce aisle before being waylaid by someone eager to get the lowdown. I stopped sniffing a cantaloupe and glanced over my shoulder.

"Hello, Shirley," I said, recognizing the woman. Shirley Buckner and her husband, Jerry, attend the same church as I do. Jerry sings in the choir. Shirley organizes bake sales. A nice couple. A little on the dull side, but nice.

"I heard what happened the other day."

"You and half the county, it seems." I set the melon back in the bin and picked up another. Don't know why I bother with the sniff test. It never seems to help. Truthfully, I sniff only when others are around so it looks like I know what I'm doing. If no one's watching, I just grab the nearest melon and move on.

"It must have been horrible."

"You might say that," I replied, giving up on smell-the-cantaloupe.

"Jerry and I were talking over breakfast. Do you suppose the rest of that poor soul will ever be found?"

"I have no idea, Shirley." I placed the melon in my cart . . . er . . . buggy. "I only hope someone else does the honors next time."

Shirley searched through the mound of melons as if she actually knew what she was doing. "I heard people say" — she dropped her voice to a whisper — "*parts* are probably scattered all across the state from one end to the other."

"Couldn't help but overhear what you were talking about." A second woman joined us. Apparently Shirley's whisper needed more practice. "It's awful, just awful. Isn't it?"

Sheesh! Did she expect me to disagree?

"It certainly is," I murmured, edging away from the cantaloupes and heading toward the tomatoes. I'm much more confident around tomatoes. It's much easier to spot a ripe one. Just zero in on red.

The woman, who I seemed to remember went by the name Bootsy, followed. "We never even used to lock our doors. Now my husband is talking about putting in a security system."

Shirley, not about to be left out of the conversation, abandoned melons for Roma versus vine-ripened. "We're considering getting a dog. A rottweiler, or maybe a pit bull. One that will be a good watchdog and protect us."

"What about you, Kate? You live alone. Aren't you frightened?"

"To be totally honest, ladies, I haven't given the matter much thought." I could tell by their looks of disapproval they weren't happy with my answer.

"You really ought to take this more seriously," Bootsy advised. "A woman living alone can't be too careful with a madman on the loose."

"Bootsy's right, you know." Shirley squeezed a beefsteak, nodded once, then bagged it. "Maybe *you* should consider having a security system installed."

"Or get a dog," Bootsy chimed.

"I heard the Humane Society is a great place to adopt a pet."

"A friend of mine . . ."

I abandoned the produce section in favor of frozen foods and a quick escape. Last seen, Shirley and Bootsy were still arguing the merits of security systems versus guard dogs. I had no immediate plans for either.

I kept my shopping to a bare minimum to avoid a repeat of the conversation I'd just had with the two women. It's rare I enter the Piggly Wiggly with only five items on my list and leave with only five. Usually my cart . . . er . . . buggy is full. It seemed a shame to pass the "buy one, get one free" items. But today I made an exception. I didn't want to talk about "arms" or, worse yet, whom they might belong to.

I was loading my groceries into the car when I heard sirens. Mind you, sirens aren't something we often hear around here. In Toledo, no one batted an eye at the sound. Police, fire, ambulance. Emergency vehicles were an everyday occurrence. But here it's different. More personal. Here people know one another by face if not by name. No one wants a catastrophe to befall a neighbor.

I glanced over my shoulder in time to see the sheriff's cruiser whiz by. This was followed by, not one, but two more. Lights flashed, sirens wailed. Something was up. Something was definitely up.

I did what any other red-blooded citizen would do. I jumped in my car and followed in hot pursuit.

At first I had a hard time keeping up. Couple times I worried I'd lose sight of them altogether. Couldn't let that happen. I put the pedal to the metal and floored it. I had no idea the Buick could even go that fast. It certainly never had with Jim behind the wheel. I deliberately avoided glancing at the speedometer. It would probably scare me. In this situation, the adage "Ignorance is bliss" suited me just dandy. I only hoped that drivers who pulled to the side of the highway at the sight of flashing lights would assume I was part of the procession and stay clear.

Brake lights flashed ahead of me. I whipped the wheel and made a hard left. The Buick shuddered. Tires squealed. I burned rubber and was proud of it. Another first.

The posse had left the highway and headed down a road that led to the state park. Signs flew past. Brown signs with arrows. RANGER'S STATION. PICNIC SITE. BOAT RAMP. CAMPGROUND.

I rounded a bend in the road, then slammed on the brakes. I narrowly avoided plowing into a sheriff's vehicle parked half in, half out of the road. I hopped out of my car and looked around to get my bearings.

A dozen or so RVs and motor homes, some the size of a Greyhound bus, were parked in a section that afforded campers hookups for water and electricity. Where were the tents? I wondered. What happened to sleeping bags on the ground? Did campers still cook on Coleman stoves? Did people still gather around campfires and toast marshmallows? These pithy questions would have to wait. Right now I had a mystery to solve.

A small group of people clustered near a humongous motor home. The sort you hate to get behind on the interstate. The kind that sports a custom-made license plate holder proclaiming for all the world to see that June and Ward are TWO FOR THE ROAD. A jean-clad woman in her forties, her dark hair pulled back into a ponytail, had watched me come to a screeching halt behind the sheriff's cars. She cupped her hand around her mouth and bellowed, "Follow the trail."

I did just that, pleased beyond measure that I'd been mistaken for official law enforcement. The trail was clearly marked and easy to follow. It meandered through woods thick with pine and hardwood. My sneakers made little sound on the pathway paved with fallen leaves, pine needles, and a few scattered acorns.

One hundred yards or so down the trail, I heard male voices just off to my right. I veered off the beaten path and headed in that direction. I hadn't gone far when I stopped. I spotted half a dozen men forming a loose semicircle near a giant oak. I instantly recognized Sheriff Wiggins. I assumed — shrewdly on my part — that the other two uniformed men were his deputies. Judging from the jeans and T-shirts, I guessed the remaining men were either campers or fishermen or both. A dog lolled nearby. I slipped behind a tree — one within hearing range — and waited. Having come this far, I didn't want to be shooed away before finding out something of interest.

Everyone seemed to be pointing and talking all at once. All, that is, except Sheriff Wiggins. The sheriff simply stood there, arms folded across his massive chest, and gave each of the campers/fishermen the once-over with eyes sharp as drill bits.

It was then I caught my first whiff. That same sickeningly sweet odor I had first smelled on the golf course the other day. I forced myself to breathe through my mouth lest I suffer a similar consequence to what Monica had. My sneakers weren't brand-new, but they didn't deserve the same fate as Monica's FootJoys.

I read once, or maybe saw on TV, that police officers and other crime-scene investigators rub Vicks VapoRub under their nostrils to help deal with such smells. Sure wished I had some right now.

"Cordon off the area," Sheriff Wiggins ordered.

I watched in fascination as one of the deputies unrolled a spool of yellow crime-scene tape and began winding it around an area roughly the size of my laundry room.

The sheriff turned to the second deputy. "Call the coroner. Tell him to get here ASAP."

"Yessir." The deputy turned away, pulled out a cell phone, and began punching in numbers.

What had they stumbled across? I wondered. But deep down I already knew. I peered out from my hiding place, trying to get a better look.

"Better call SLED as well." Not once did the sheriff raise that deep Southern baritone — he didn't have to. His well-trained deputies jumped to obey each command.

SLED? I frowned. What did that mean? Was *sled* another name for a stretcher or gurney? A device used to transport a body? I made a mental note to check this out later.

Sheriff Wiggins pulled out his little black book and turned his attention to the campers/fishermen. "Did you, or anyone else, do anything that might have disturbed the site?"

"No, sir," the oldest of the trio replied. He was about retirement age with thinning hair and a ruddy complexion. "No, sir," he repeated more emphatically. "We kept our distance, except for Sherlock here."

I studied the dog lying near a fallen log. It was black with a pink tongue and bright eyes. Drawing on my rather limited knowledge of the species, I'd say Sherlock was a mutt. Maybe part Lab, part springer spaniel? Or maybe not. He, or she, could be almost any large-dog combo. Like I said, when it comes to dogs, my knowledge is limited. Don't get me wrong. I love animals, dogs especially, but Jim claimed to be allergic, so we never had pets. Not even when the kids were little.

The youngest camper spoke for the first time. "Wasn't for Sherlock nosin' around, we woulda kept right on walkin'."

"Thought at first a deer might've died and been left to rot," the third man ventured. Someone should tell the guy his shirt was one size too small. It bore the image of an outdoor grill and the message BORN TO BARBECUE. By the looks of him, he had eaten a few barbecues too many.

"Couldn't have been buried more than two feet deep." This from the first man to speak.

The sheriff, I noted, scribbled all this down in his little spiral notebook. Next time I visited an office-supply store, I'd have to get me one of those. Use it as kind of a journal to record the facts of the case.

"Only a corner of a trash bag was sticking out of the ground until ol' Sherlock started digging."

The youngest one pulled off a ball cap bearing an Atlanta Braves logo and wiped his brow. "Even then we couldn't tell what was inside."

Trash bags certainly seemed used for a lot more jobs these days than hauling out trash. I craned my neck for a better view. Thank goodness the men were too focused on one another to notice little old me peeking out from around an oak.

"Almost screamed like a girl when I got an eyeful of what's in it," said man number two.

I wanted to scream like a girl myself. And I would any minute now if someone didn't just come out and say what was inside the bag.

The sound of leaves crunching on the trail behind me accompanied by the murmur of voices alerted me to the fact that I had company. A backward glance confirmed that I had company indeed. Lots and lots. Too much, in fact. To my dismay, the group I had seen earlier at the campground had apparently decided to join me.

The sheriff looked over at the interruption. His dark gaze swept over the assembled crowd, spotted me, and pinned me with a scowl. I waved.

He didn't wave back.

Instead Sheriff Wiggins lowered his head and spoke to his deputy. The scowl on the deputy's dark face was a pretty fair imitation of the sheriff's as he strode our way.

"Sorry, folks," the deputy said, his tone polite but firm. Very firm. "I'll have to ask you to step back."

"What's going on?" the woman with the ponytail asked. I assumed her to be the group's designated spokesperson. I was happy to learn I wasn't the only curious soul.

The short, chubby woman next to her held a hand over her mouth. "Ee-yew! What's that smell?"

The deputy's frown deepened. I had the feeling he wasn't about to leak a smidgen of information — at least not with his boss within earshot. Regardless, I decided to give it my best shot. "I think I saw you at the sheriff's office yesterday just as I was leaving." I gave him a friendly smile, trying to disarm him with my charm. I read the name off the brass plate pinned above his breast pocket. "Pleasure to meet you, Deputy Preston. I'm Kate McCall."

I could tell from his expression my name registered.

I smiled wider. What harm could it do? "I'm the lady who brought the chocolate-chip cookies," I added, hoping he had a sweet tooth.

"Sorry, Miz McCall. The sheriff said not to say a word — to you or anybody." He cleared his throat, then, looking past me, addressed the woman with the ponytail. "Sorry, ma'am, but I'm going to have to ask y'all to leave."

"You can't do that," she protested. "I have an annual park pass." I didn't know the woman, but I liked her already. We might have been twins separated at birth — if it hadn't been for the difference in our ages.

"Preston . . . ?" Sheriff Wiggins called over. "Is there a problem?"

"No problem, sir. None I can't handle."

Ponytail wasn't about to give up without an argument. "It's not against the law to gather in a public place. It's even in the Constitution, guaranteed by the Bill of Rights."

Now, I didn't know if this was correct or not, but it sounded good to me. You go, sister, I told her silently. No need for me to add my two cents' worth with her doing such an outstanding job.

Sheriff Wiggins must have sensed a mutiny in the making. Thumbs hooked in his belt, a no-nonsense expression on his face, he turned and approached our little group. "Bill of Rights or no Bill of Rights, folks, if you don't leave this minute, I can and will arrest the lot of you for obstruction of justice. This here is a crime scene."

We left.

CHAPTER 9

Crime scene?

That told me everything I needed to know. I trudged back to the campground, accompanied by the merry band of bystanders. My mind raced. Just what had Sherlock managed to find, or, more aptly, managed to dig up? Was the puzzle finally solved?

"Want to hang out?" the woman with the ponytail asked. "Have a cup of coffee?"

"Sure." I snapped up the opportunity to stick around. The sheriff and his men had to leave the woods sometime. Besides, I wanted to be there when the coroner arrived with his sled — whatever the heck that was. Couldn't wait to tell the Bunco Babes about my latest adventure.

"Name's Donna," said the woman formerly known as the-woman-with-a-ponytail. She indicated her chubby companion. "This here's Betty Lou, my sister-in-law."

"How do you happen to know the sheriff?"

Betty Lou asked.

"It's a long story," I replied, accepting the mug of coffee Donna poured from an industrial-size thermos. Except for the two women, the campers had drifted away. But that was A-OK with me. I'd had enough being at the center of attention.

Betty Lou plunked herself down in a canvas chair and motioned for me to join her. "Take your time, sweetie. Looks like it's going to be a long afternoon."

The women were a good audience — almost, but not quite, as good as the Babes. Both of them listened with rapt attention while I recounted what had happened the other day on the golf course.

"What do you think the guys found back there?"

Donna's question hung in the air. Neither Betty Lou nor I voiced an opinion. Don't know about Betty Lou, but I had plenty of opinions, but kept them to myself.

At last, Betty Lou heaved herself out of the chair and marched off in the direction of a spiffy red and silver Winnebago that probably cost more than my house.

"Hey, Betty Lou," Donna yelled. "Where you goin'?"

"I'm packing up," she yelled back, not breaking stride. "I'm not gonna spend another night in this place. It ain't safe."

"S'cuse me, Kate," Donna said, dumping out the dregs in her cup. "Wait up, Betty Lou. Eddie and me'll be right behind you. He caught enough bass for one fishing trip."

I watched in admiration as the pair disassembled their campsites. Their movements were economical and well rehearsed, but then again they had no tent stakes to pry out of the ground, no air mattresses to deflate. Not like the times Jim and I had taken the kids camping. In no time at all, Betty Lou and Donna had whisked the checkered cloth from the picnic table and folded canvas chairs into matching pouches. Bit by bit the motor homes were ready to roll.

I stood off to the side and tried to stay out of the way. Other campers saw what the sisters-in-law were doing, and one by one began to follow suit. I wasn't as easily deterred. I sat on a tree stump, prepared to stay as long as necessary.

I didn't have much longer to wait before a white van drove up and parked behind my Buick. I felt a certain sense of satisfaction at the sight. I was blocked in. No way the sheriff could expect me to leave a "crime scene" with the coroner's van practically on my rear bumper.

My stump provided a ringside seat for all the action. How the Bunco Babes would love this, Pam especially. Local police, state police, and men from the sheriff's department filed back and forth talking into cell phones and barking into walkie-talkies. I caught a word here, a phrase there. One word in particular stuck in my head.

Remains.

My earlier suspicion was confirmed. The arm we had found on the golf course was about to be reunited with more of its body.

I stayed at the campground until men from the coroner's office loaded a gurney carrying a black vinyl mound — a mound too small to be an entire body — into the back of their van and pulled away. Soon various law-enforcement officials began to drift back to their vehicles and leave. It was time to make my getaway before Sheriff Wiggins showed up and gave me the evil eye.

By now the campground was nearly empty. Donna waved as she and Eddie followed by Betty Lou and her husband pulled out of the park. Betty Lou, her nose buried in a map, didn't look up. No doubt she was searching for somewhere *safe.*

My brain buzzed with questions as I got behind the wheel of the Buick. Would the coroner now be able to identify the victim? I said a little prayer that Claudia and Vera were off somewhere having fun. That Rosalie was having a great visit with her grandkids. I crossed my fingers that the small mound zipped inside the vinyl bag belonged to some unfortunate stranger and not a friend.

Who would commit such a heinous crime? I wondered. The consensus was that the perpetrator couldn't possibly be from Serenity Cove Estates or Brookdale. In this instance, I hoped consensus was right on target. But what if it wasn't? It worried me no end that Claudia and Vera were unaccounted for. And I'd rest a lot easier when Rosalie returned from Poughkeepsie. I wanted to do something, but what . . . ? It wasn't my nature to sit back and wait.

I kept to the speed limit on the drive back to Serenity Cove Estates. No need to rush. My stomach rumbled, reminding me I hadn't eaten since breakfast. A glance at my watch showed me it was later than I had thought. Somehow I wasn't in the mood to cook. A common occurrence since Jim passed away. My freezer is filled with frozen dinners and, my favorite standby, gourmet pizzas. Neither held any appeal tonight. On the spur of the moment, I decided to get a bite at the Cove Café.

By the time I got there, except for two couples at a table near the window, the café was deserted. Most folks on fixed incomes like to take advantage of the early-bird specials. That time was long past. I parked myself at a corner table and looked around.

No sign of Marcy — good. No sign of Vera either — bad.

Beverly, a waitress I knew slightly, greeted me with a tired smile and handed me a menu.

"A slow night, Beverly?" I like to address people by their given names whenever possible. Gets a bit tricky at times with those darn senior moments popping up when you least expect them. Those memory cells in the brain just don't cough up information like they used to. It takes a while, but eventually stuff does float back. I heard as long as that happens, not to worry. It's when those names and places don't come back — ever — that you're in deep doo-doo.

"It was busier than usual early on. Seems all folks want to do is talk about that thing some ladies found out on the golf course."

"Ah, yes, the *thing.*" Had *thing* become the new catchphrase for *it?*

"What can I get you to drink?"

"Coffee," I said, then reconsidered. "Better make that decaf." I didn't need another sleepless night while waiting for the Sandman to arrive.

Beverly left and returned minutes later with my decaf. "Have you decided what to order?"

"What do you recommend?"

"There's still some meat loaf special left."

"Sounds good." Comfort food. Just the ticket.

The occupants of the window table got ready to leave. The men signed their tabs and pocketed their credit cards, and the couples left together amid promises to get together soon.

After placing my order, Beverly returned and began clearing the table. She looked my way. "Your dinner should be out in a jiff."

"No hurry. I've got all night."

The instant the words were out, I wished them back. The poor woman looked dead on her feet. "Sorry. How insensitive of me. You probably can't wait to lock up for the night."

"Take your time. Customers or not, management insists we stay open till nine." She slowly made her way back toward the kitchen with a tray of dirty dishes.

I took a sip of coffee and decided to take

advantage of the situation. This would be the perfect opportunity for an impromptu investigation. I'd rest easier tonight knowing Vera was somewhere enjoying herself.

"Looks like it's been a long day," I said when Beverly returned with my meat loaf.

"You can say that again. I pulled a double."

I looked at Beverly more closely. She appeared to be in her mid-fifties with a liberal amount of gray mixed in with the brown strands. The smudges under her eyes were too dark to be hidden by concealer. I'd bet she'd like nothing better than to kick off her shoes and put up her feet. "I assume working a double means you pulled an extra shift?"

"One of the girls who works breakfast and lunch needed time off. Left us shorthanded."

I dipped my fork into the mashed potatoes. "You mean Vera?" I asked with studied innocence.

"Yeah." Beverly started collecting salt and pepper shakers from the various tables. "Vera didn't give much notice, but since she's been here the longest, management decided not to make a stink."

"My friends and I wondered what happened to her. The new girl, Marcy, kept mixing up our orders."

Beverly grunted. "Don't surprise me none. Marcy isn't cut out to be a waitress."

I heartily agreed, but didn't voice my opinion out loud. With the kind of service Marcy provided, she'd starve to death if she had to depend on tips. I sampled a small piece of meat loaf and was pleasantly surprised. Not bad. Not as good as mine, but not bad. Or maybe I was hungrier than I thought.

Beverly took a seat at an adjoining table and proceeded to refill the shakers. "Marcy said she's looking for another job. Complains folks here are too fussy."

And I had a pretty good idea whom she was calling fussy. "Maybe she'll be happier in a job where she doesn't have to deal with people on a regular basis."

"Now, take Vera, on the other hand," Beverly went on. "She's always saying how much she likes everyone. We sure miss her around here."

I phrased my next question with care. "Did Vera happen to say how long she'd be gone?"

Beverly shrugged. "No one seems to know. Not long, I hope. Can't take too many of these doubles. My dogs are barking."

I went back to cutting my meat loaf into

small, bite-size pieces. "Well, my friends and I hope Vera'll be back soon. Where did she go, by the way?"

"Didn't say."

My interrogation skills needed honing. But determination has to count for something, doesn't it? "Did Vera take her family with her?" I had no idea if Vera even had a family, but what the heck. Throw out the question and see what happens, right? Cops do it all the time on TV.

"Family?" Beverly screwed tops back on the saltshakers. "Nah. All Vera's got is a daughter. Lisa's pregnant and expecting her third kid next month."

A red flag went up. Why would a woman whose only daughter was eight months pregnant just up and leave with no explanation? I didn't like where this conversation was leading. "I don't recall Vera ever mentioning a husband. What's he like?"

"Him?" Beverly practically spit the word. "That no-good so-and-so?"

"I take it you don't think much of him."

"If you ask me, he's nothing but a lying, cheating scumbag."

Tell me how you really feel, I wanted to say, but didn't. "Why is that?"

Beverly glanced around to make sure no one could overhear. "Don't know why Vera stayed with the rat as long as she did. I'da left him the first time he took a swing at me."

"He hit her?" I asked, genuinely shocked.

Beverly nodded. "Over the years, she came in many a time with bruises she tried to cover up and make excuses for. She finally kicked the bum out. Smartest thing she ever did."

"They're divorced, then?"

"Yep. I heard ol' Mel wasn't none too happy Vera got to keep the house. Got a small settlement, too. That really got Mel's goat. Judge told him to pay up or else."

I sat back to digest this bit of gossip. Seeing as how I had pushed my plate aside, Beverly wandered off to get my check. It was nearing the witching hour of closing time, and she was eager to quiet her barking dogs.

Well, I thought to myself as I drained my second cup of decaf, the meat loaf special was worth every penny. I silently congratulated myself. My interrogation techniques weren't so bad after all. I had learned Vera had not only an abusive husband but an angry one as well.

Chapter 10

Bill Lewis was a rare find. Especially here in the South. It's not easy to come across a repairman who actually shows up, not only on the day he says he will, but at the appointed time as well. I've often thought there ought to be a separate zone called Southern time. I remember once being assured by the cable guy that he'd come first thing in the morning only to have him ring the bell just as Jim and I were sitting down to dinner. I did what any Yankee would do. I invited him to join us. And he did. When it comes to Southern hospitality, I'm a fast learner.

"I'm not too early, am I?" Bill asked, almost apologetically.

I glanced at my watch. Actually he was ten minutes early. What a strange concept. If I wasn't careful, Bill Lewis would spoil me for the whole lot of handymen and subcontractors all rolled into one. I'd have to remember to call Pam later and thank her for passing along Bill's number.

"You must be from up North," I said by way of a greeting.

"Battle Creek, Michigan," he returned with an easy smile. "That's right about here." He held his hand up, palm out, and pointed to a spot somewhere near the middle. I'd seen other Michiganders perform this little trick to explain exactly where they hailed from. It must be handy to have a state shaped like a mitten. Try that with any other state and see what happens.

"Thanks for coming, especially on a Sunday," I said as I led him down the short hallway, past the laundry room, and into the kitchen.

"Sorry I couldn't get here sooner. Nice place you have here," he said, looking around.

"Thank you. Jim and I like it." There I slipped and did it again. Went and used the wrong tense when it came to speaking about my late husband. Old habits die hard when you're married as long as we were.

Bill started speaking before I had a chance to correct my error. He pointed to the defunct object in question. "If I remember correctly, this fan here's the culprit."

"I have no idea what's wrong with it. It

worked just fine last time I used it." I hated hearing the damsel-in-distress undertone in my voice. Maybe I should have noticed something. A warning of sorts. Sparks flying? A funny odor, or a grinding noise. Something . . . ?

He shrugged. "Most times these things just happen. Work fine one minute, break the next."

Bill was definitely my kind of guy. No blame pointing. Just it works, or it doesn't work. Simple as that. And if that wasn't enough to recommend him, he came with a full head of silver gray hair. No mean accomplishment for a man over sixty. I hadn't noticed this in all the hubbub at the golf course. Either Bill had worn a ball cap or my powers of observation were as kaput as my ceiling fan.

"Don't suppose you have a ladder handy?" he asked.

"There's a stepladder in the garage. Will that do?"

"Perfect, just the thing. I'll get it and be right back."

Yes, indeed, Bill Lewis was a fine-looking man. The combination of silver gray hair and Paul Newman baby blues were enough to make my heart flutter. Most of all, I liked his smile, kind of sweet, a little shy. I could feel a hot flash coming on. Or a power surge, as the Babes call them. Shame on me for noticing such things at my age. And Jim gone less than two years.

When Bill returned minutes later carrying the stepladder, I noticed he had strapped on a tool belt. There's something about men and tool belts. Whatever it was, it was nudging my dormant hormones back into life.

"Is the switch off?"

My switch was definitely on — and humming. But I gathered that wasn't the one he meant. "Ah . . . yes," I stammered after double-checking the wall plate to make sure.

Bill climbed the ladder and began tinkering. A screwdriver here, and a wrench — or maybe it was a pliers — there. Always had trouble keeping the two straight. I wasn't sure what I should do next. Make myself scarce or stick around and watch? I elected to stay — in case he needed help of course.

"Hate to give you bad news, but looks like the motor shorted out." Bill had climbed down to give me the bad news face-to-face. "Only thing you can do is replace it with a new one."

Now, normally I love shopping as much as the next woman, but that doesn't include home-improvement stores. Looking through aisle after aisle of electrical and plumbing gadgets bores me to tears. Given a choice between Macy's and Lowe's, I'll take Macy's in a heartbeat. Maybe I'd feel differently if Lowe's and Home Depot had preferred-customer sales. I'd whip out my Visa so fast it would make heads spin.

"What exactly am I supposed to do with the fan once I bring it home?" I asked, hearing the damsel-in-distress note back in my voice.

"That part's easy." He gave me that shy smile that I found so endearing. "All you need to do is give me a call. I'll come right over and hook it up for you."

"I can't tell you how much I appreciate this." I smiled back. "Don't know what's come over me, I completely forgot to ask how much you charge. What do I owe you?"

"Don't worry. You'll find my prices reasonable." He tucked the screwdriver and wrench/pliers back into slots on his tool belt. "I don't do this for the money so much as it gives me something to do with my time."

"Hope I haven't kept you too long." The words came out in a rush. I needed to keep my mind on business or else I'd have another of those hot flashes.

"No problem. Happy I could help."

"I don't want to keep you," I said, even

though I did — want to keep him, that is. "Your wife probably has dinner waiting and doesn't want it getting cold." Could I be any more obvious? I employed a trick all women learn in infancy. I looked at his left hand — discreetly, of course — to see whether he wore a wedding band. He didn't.

Bill's expression clouded. "There is no wife. Not anymore, that is. Margaret died before I moved here."

"Oh, I'm sorry. I didn't know."

"No way you could," he said. "She got cancer just before I was set to take an early retirement. After she passed away, I decided a change of scenery would do me good."

The moment seemed right to set matters straight. "Jim, my husband, died almost two years ago. Had a massive coronary right in the middle of the Super Bowl." I toyed with the end of a dish towel that was sitting on the counter. "Poor Jim. He never lived long enough to find out he had won fifty dollars in the football pool. I'm still getting used to his being gone. It's lonely at times."

Bill nodded sympathetically. "Know what you mean. I try to keep myself busy. I ranger part-time at the golf course, do odd jobs, have some hobbies."

"What sort of hobbies?" Did that sound pathetic or what? I definitely needed a refresher course in Flirtation 101.

Fortunately Bill didn't seem to notice. "Woodworking mostly. I just got reelected president of the Woodchucks."

Were woodchucks the same as groundhogs? Cute furry little things? "Woodchucks?"

Bill chuckled at my obvious puzzlement. "That's what the woodworking club here in Serenity Cove Estates calls itself, the Woodchucks. I'm nearly done making a cradle for my son and his wife. They're expecting their first baby in the spring."

"A cradle, how lovely! I'd love to see it when it's finished." The words were no sooner out of my mouth than I felt a blush warm my cheeks. He must think me a brazen man-chasing hussy. Here I scarcely knew the man, and I was inviting myself over to his place. Funny what a pair of pretty blue eyes and a full head of hair can do to a woman's common sense. Not to mention the tool belt.

I stole a glance his way and could swear he was blushing, too. Here we were, two mature adults who should know better, acting like a couple of teenagers.

"I'd appreciate you giving it a once-over. I could use a woman's opinion. Soon as I give it a final coat of varnish, I'll give you a call."

With that, he picked up the stepladder and returned it to the garage. A minute later he was back. "Ah, Mrs. McCall . . . ?"

"Kate," I interrupted before he got any further. "Friends call me Kate."

His Paul Newman blue eyes swept over my kitchen before pinning me like a butterfly to a mat. "What I'd like to do, Kate, is apologize for the other day at the golf course."

I could've pretended I didn't know what he was talking about, but why play coy? "There's nothing to apologize for, Bill." I liked the fact that we were now on a friendlier, first-name basis. "Don't think I've ever been so happy to see a ranger on the course as I was then. You couldn't have arrived at a more opportune time."

"Well, I'm embarrassed about what happened next. I've been a hunter all my life, and no one's ever accused me of being squeamish."

"You weren't the only one who lost their lunch that day," I said, recalling Monica's reaction. "My friend threw up all over the brand-new FootJoys she had to special order. She ended up tossing them in the trash."

Bill's expression remained glum. "Sure was a sight. For a minute there, I wasn't sure what I was looking at. Couldn't believe my eyes."

I shuddered at the memory, then banished it from my mind.

"Sorry," Bill said, sounding contrite. "I shouldn't have brought that up. I just didn't want you thinking I was some sort of shrinking violet — a wuss, as the younger folks say."

"Never." I made a series of pleats in the dish towel I fiddled with. "Your reaction showed you have a sensitive, caring nature."

"Suppose the sheriff will ever discover who . . . *it* . . . belonged to?"

"Hmm . . ." I pondered the question. For all I knew, the sheriff hadn't made a lick of progress solving the case. If he had, news would have traveled throughout Serenity Cove with the speed of a California wildfire. In my humble opinion, the poor man could use some help. "I don't know," I said at last, deciding to cut the sheriff some slack. "At this point, it's probably hard to tell if . . . *it* . . . belonged to a man or a woman."

Bill turned to leave. "Don't think I'll ever forget that smell. First thing I did when I got home was take a hot shower. Not that it helped much."

"I know exactly what you mean," I admitted. And I did. Upon returning home from the course, I had debated whether to put the golf outfit I was wearing into the trash. At the last minute I decided against it. My shirt and shorts were practically brand-new. I ran them through an extra wash cycle instead.

"Guess I'd better be on my way." Halfway through the door, he stopped and turned. "Lowe's or Home Depot would be good places to start looking for a new fan. Then there's always Sears at the mall. Just call whenever you get it. I'll be right over to install it for you. Shouldn't take long."

I smiled when the door closed behind him. Golf course ranger, handyman, and widower. All wrapped up in one neat package. Quite a guy!

Chapter 11

After Bill left, I just couldn't seem to settle down. I couldn't stop thinking about . . . body parts. Not when Claudia and Vera were still absent without leave. And then there was the matter of Rosalie, who still hadn't returned. After agonizing over the situation for hours, I concluded extraordinary times called for extraordinary measures. Measures such as an emergency session of Bunco Babe Crime Solvers.

"I know it's late, Connie Sue." I glanced at the kitchen clock. It read nine p.m. Who goes to bed at that hour? Or should I rephrase? Who besides Thacker Brody and Earl Brubaker goes to bed at that hour? "I wouldn't call if this wasn't important."

I could hear Connie Sue sigh from Magnolia Lane two blocks away. "Out with it, sugar. What's so dad-blame important it couldn't wait till tomorrow?"

"I'm calling an emergency bunco game."

"Honey, tomorrow's Monday," Connie Sue quickly pointed out.

"I know that." Liar, liar, pants on fire. Actually I'd lost track what day of the week it was. With "arms" and "remains" cropping up all over the place, the days all seemed to run together.

"What's wrong with Monday?" I said, probably sounding a trifle defensive. "My place. Same time."

"Thacker expects pot roast Monday night."

My, my, Thacker was certainly a creature of habit. To bed at nine. Pot roast on Monday. It made me wonder what else in the Brody household was done according to schedule. Somehow I didn't want to go there.

Now it was my turn to sigh. "Use your imagination, Connie Sue. Tell Thacker the government just declared Tuesday National Pot Roast Day."

"Well, I don't know. . . ."

"Connie Sue, tell Thacker whatever you want. Just be there. I need you — the Babes need you."

"OK, sugar. No need to get your panties in a twist. See you tomorrow."

Rita was next on my list. "Emergency bunco? Kate McCall, you're going to have to tell me more than that if you expect me to cancel bridge."

Bridge is Rita's true passion. The fact that she plays bunco never ceases to amaze me. Rita used to be a branch manager of a bank in Cleveland. In other words, she's good with numbers. Bridge satisfies her talent for skill and strategy, but bunco . . . ? Bunco is purely a flip of the dice. Leave skill and strategy at the doorstep. But who knows? Maybe bunco is a nice change of pace. Gives those brain cells a night off.

"Trust me, Rita. It'll be worthwhile." I plucked a dead leaf off a plant on the windowsill. "Make sure to bring Tara along. The Babes and I need your shrewd minds to help get at the bottom of what's going on."

"*What's* going on?"

Next she'd be asking me, "Who's on first?" and that old Abbott and Costello routine would be off and running. It never fails to crack me up. "Just come, all right?" I hung up before she could bombard me with more questions. I knew she'd be there with her daughter-in-law. Rita simply couldn't resist a puzzle.

Pam was much easier. "Course I'll be there. Megan, too, since she doesn't have to work the next day."

"Great," I replied, grateful Pam didn't need a boatload of explanations. "And, Pam," I added just before hanging up, "don't forget the tiara."

Pam chuckled. "Monica's been biding her time for a chance to take it away from me. She's gunning for rhinestones."

I couldn't help but smile as I dialed Janine. As much as Monica wanted to wear the crown, Rita tended to be the Babes' high roller.

No answer at Janine's, so I left a message on the answering machine. I continued down the list. Monica and Diane readily agreed. Since Claudia was still off doing her thing with her mystery man, I phoned Nancy — whom I secretly refer to as Never-Say-No Nancy — and asked her to sub. She said yes, of course.

I saved Polly for last. She answered on the first ring. "What's up?"

"I'm calling an emergency bunco game for Monday night. My place, usual time."

"If I'm any judge of character, Kate McCall, you've got something up your sleeve. Can you give an old lady a hint?" Polly is the youngest "old lady" I've ever met. She's only "old" when it suits her.

"We need to discuss what's going on here in Serenity Cove. Help the sheriff figure things out."

"Gotcha. Gloria and I'll be there with bells on." I could picture her trotting down the breezeway separating her mother-in-law suite from the main house, to give her daughter the message. "Besides," Polly continued, "this'll give me a chance to show off my new outfit."

"I can hardly wait," I replied.

And that was the god-awful truth. Polly's choice of a wardrobe was a constant source of amazement. At the tender age of seventy-five, she exchanges fashion advice with Megan, who's barely out of her teens. And if that isn't enough to sustain her youthful image, Polly happens to be the resident authority on pop culture. According to Gloria, she subscribes to a slew of celebrity gossip rags. Want to know who's in rehab, who's out, who's dating whom, or who just broke up, Polly's your girl.

"Be there or be square," she chortled. "See you Monday."

I crossed her name off my list and sat back. Good, everyone was coming. An emergency bunco game seemed the best route. I didn't want to have to explain my plan eleven times when I could do it once. We needed to band together. Put our collective heads together and track down Vera and Claudia. I'd rest better, and so would all the Bunco Babes, once we knew our friends were accounted for.

Sheriff Wiggins was much too close-mouthed for my liking. He didn't seem to share my sense of urgency when I told him about Vera and Claudia. I know he's a busy man, but I didn't feel like waiting until he got around to it. I needed to know they were safe and sound. And I needed to know sooner as opposed to later. If he wasn't going to investigate, we'd do it ourselves.

I was wide-awake by this time. *Wired* is the term I hear used for this type of wakefulness. I decided to test the soothing power of chamomile tea one more time.

Once the tea was ready, I retreated to the library/den and turned on the computer. Nothing like surfing the Internet to while away an hour or two. My first stop on the World Wide Web was an Internet bookstore. Novel Nuts, the book club here in Serenity, was due to meet in two weeks, and I had yet to order the month's selection. That accomplished, I surfed awhile longer, checking this, checking that. On a whim, I typed *forensics* in the search field and clicked the mouse.

Wow! More than fifty thousand results popped up within seconds. Isn't the Internet grand? But I didn't need to peruse fifty thousand references to make my selection. Almost instantly, I spied exactly what I was looking for. *The Complete Idiot's Guide to Forensics.* Perfect! The title practically leaped off the page.

Fixed income or not, I splurged. A twitch of a finger, and it was done. *The Compete Idiot's Guide to Forensics* was slated for one-day shipping. With luck, it might even arrive in time for emergency bunco.

As I turned off the light and headed for the bedroom, I glanced out the kitchen window. A light still burned in the Brubaker house across the way.

Come Monday morning, word spread like crazy that Sheriff Wiggins had called a town hall meeting for two o'clock that afternoon. It was likely to be quite an event. The likes of which Serenity Cove Estates had never seen. What was he about to announce? Had they identified the victim?

My phone rang nonstop. I finally gave up trying to answer it, or I'd never get to Lowe's and back. As much as I wanted a new ceiling fan, I wanted a front-row seat even more. Most of the Bunco Babes planned to attend the meeting except for Diane, who's the town's librarian, and Tara, who teaches preschool. Janine said she'd try to make it, but it was her day to volunteer at the Habitat Store.

I headed for Augusta. I know, I know. Augusta is in Georgia, and Serenity Cove Estates is in South Carolina. A look at a map will show the two states are kissing kin. Brookdale might have all the necessities of life, but Augusta supplies the frills. Not that I consider a ceiling fan a frill, nevertheless . . .

I averted my gaze when I drove past Wal-Mart. Didn't like to think about the last time I had seen one of their bags. I kept going, straight to one of those large home-improvement stores. I passed boutiques, discount stores, and a pricey new strip mall, but refused to get diverted. I was on a mission.

Inside Lowe's, I wandered down aisles of plumbing and electrical gadgets, past appliances, paint, tile, and carpet. I was one of only a handful of women in the entire place. But men were everywhere, staring into bins of doodads with looks of pure rapture. Apparently home-improvement stores are to men what jewelry stores are to women. If I'd been looking to meet a fella, this place would top the list. Once word got out, it'd be mobbed by single women.

Focus, Kate, focus, I told myself. Buy a fan and get on with your life.

I found ceiling fans at last, and suppressed a groan. There were dozens from which to choose. A vast array hung overhead like a fleet of spaceships. The choice loomed more daunting than the fifty thousand forensics references. What size did I need, fifty-two or sixty inch? Then came blades. Oak, teak, or cherry? Nickel, pewter, or bronze? Remote control or no remote? Price? Warranty? My head was swimming. So I did what I always do when confronted with too much information, too many decisions. I closed my eyes and pointed.

"That one," I told the clerk.

When I opened my eyes again, I said hello to my new fan. It was white; it had blades that whirled around. It was perfect.

Then I heard the one word all shoppers fear: *backorder.*

A glance at my watch told me I was running late. I didn't have any more time to waste on a stupid fan, not with a town hall meeting in the offing. I left Lowe's fanless and headed home. I arrived with only minutes to spare before Sheriff Wiggins was scheduled to address the good citizens of Serenity Cove Estates.

The meeting was being held in the auditorium of the Recreation and Fitness Center. I was forced to park halfway on the grass at the end of the lot. The place was jammed just like I predicted. The custodian kept hauling extra chairs out of the storage room, but finally gave up. People were still filtering in, taking up spots along the walls and standing at the back of the room.

Connie Sue stood and waved when she saw me. I made my way to the front, ignoring the dirty looks some people sent my way. Except for Diane and Tara, the Babes were there in full force. Since we were the ones to find the arm, we had a vested interest in the proceedings.

"Saved a spot for you, sugar." Connie Sue indicated a seat smack-dab in the middle of the front row, between her and Rita. Polly winked and gave me a thumbs-up as I scooted past her and Gloria. I spied Pam along with Megan several rows back. Monica, looking none too happy, was there, too.

Rita and Connie Sue resumed their conversation where it had left off.

"What do you suppose the sheriff's going to tell us?"

"Probably about what the campers found in the woods."

"Why do you suppose he'd call a town meeting when we could just read about it in the paper?"

"I watched the noon news out of Augusta. Not a single word."

"Someone said the FBI's been called in."

Listening to the two of them go back and forth, I felt like a spectator at a tennis match.

Polly leaned forward and tapped me on the shoulder. "I heard the body's Jimmy Hoffa's."

"Mother, really . . . ," Gloria remonstrated, sending her large gold hoop earrings swaying.

Polly shrugged, nonplussed. "He's got to be found somewhere. Why not here?"

A hush started at the back of the room and worked its way forward like a tsunami. The time for speculation was over. Sheriff Wiggins strode into the room accompanied by the two deputies I had seen with him Saturday at the state park. I marveled at his effect over a crowd of people. He put me in mind of Tiger Woods. I had seen the same type of reaction when Jim and I watched Tiger stride up the fairway at the Masters the time we had been lucky enough to get tickets.

The room was so still you could've heard a clock tick.

Sheriff Sumter Wiggins went directly to the podium at the front. His coal black eyes swept over the assembled throng. I thought his gaze lingered a second or two longer on me, but then again I might be getting a little paranoid.

He didn't wait for an introduction, but started right in. "I'm glad to see such a good turnout. The purpose of this here meetin' is threefold: First of all, I hope to put an end to some of the wild rumors that have been circulatin' concernin' recent findings in and around Serenity Cove Estates."

"Does this rule out Jimmy Hoffa?" I heard Polly ask in a stage whisper.

"Shhh!" I recognized the sound as Gloria's.

Our sheriff is no dummy. If he overheard any of this, he wisely ignored it. "Second, I want to bring you up to speed on the ongoing investigation and, last but not least, ask for your cooperation in bringin' the perpetrator to justice."

A murmur passed through the crowd, followed once again by hushed silence.

"As some of y'all already know, human remains were discovered by campers on Saturday at the state park." His gaze flickered in my direction, then moved on. "Although we haven't yet been able to make a positive identification, I can tell you the victim was female."

Female? The victim *was* a woman! This time the murmurs rippling through the crowd were louder and more insistent. The sheriff waited them out.

"You were right, Kate," Connie Sue said in a low voice. "We need to make sure our friends are all in one piece."

I grimaced at her choice of words, but Connie Sue didn't seem to notice. "Thacker'll just have to wait till tomorrow for pot roast."

The sheriff waited until things quieted down. "Law-enforcement officials, myself included, believe this is an isolated incident of violence directed at one specific target."

One specific target? My hunch had been right. The arm and whatever else the campers found apparently belonged to the same person.

Bernie Mason, the jerk with the bad comb-over, jumped to his feet. "Sheriff, we could all be murdered in our beds. How do you propose to stop this crime wave?"

"One murder, sir, hardly constitutes a crime wave. My department is doin' everythin' possible to bring the killer to justice. Let me assure you, there is no need for panic."

No need to panic? Could he be a little more specific? Does this mean Shirley and

Bootsy, the ladies from the Piggly Wiggly, won't have to debate security systems versus guard dogs? Can Bootsy's husband stop locking doors? The possibilities were mind-boggling.

"Any more questions?"

Brave man, Sheriff Wiggins. My arm shot into the air like a rocket.

"Miz McCall . . . ," he dragged out my name.

"I heard you call for a sled on Saturday. I waited as long as I could, but never saw one arrive. Could you please explain why no one responded to your request?"

For the first time, I saw him crack a smile. His whole countenance seemed to change, to light from within. He seemed almost . . . human. "Ma'am, that might be because SLED isn't a sled. *SLED* is an acronym. It stands for *South Carolina Law Enforcement Division.* It's the official investigative arm of the governor and attorney general. Rest assured, SLED will, indeed, be assistin' in the investigation."

I could hear people in the audience titter at my inane question and the sheriff's response. Again he succeeded in putting me in my place. Rita, sensing my embarrassment, reached over and squeezed my hand.

"Next question."

This time it was Mort What's-His-Name, Bernie's golfing buddy, who stood up. "What can you tell us about the weapon?"

"Cause of death still hasn't been established. All I can say for now is that the perpetrator has access to power tools."

Power tools?

Sheriff Sumter Wiggins had just declared every man in Serenity Cove Estates a suspect.

Chapter 12

The appointed hour for the first-ever Bunco Babes Emergency Session was at hand.

"Nice outfit," Megan said, complimenting Polly on her stonewashed jeans and stretchy top.

"Thanks, sweetie." Polly preened, sticking out her modest bosom to emphasize the cherry red top adorned with sequins arranged in the shape of a heart. "Got it at that place you told me about at the mall. They have some really cool clothes." She sent a meaningful glance at her daughter's slacks. "I'm not ready for polyester."

Gloria rolled her eyes and refused to take the bait. Apparently mother and daughter had had this discussion before. "Where's Monica?" she asked, zeroing in on a table set for three instead of the usual four.

Monica was conspicuous for her absence. I could have cheerfully strangled her when she called half an hour ago to back out of tonight's game. How was I supposed to find a sub at the last minute? The Babes all turned to me, waiting for an answer.

"Don't shoot the messenger." I held up both hands palm out and shrugged. "Monica was afraid she'd get sick again if we started talking about . . . you know."

"What do you mean *if?*" Polly asked. "That's why we're here, isn't it?"

"Well, yes," I admitted. "I tried to assure Monica that we'd leave out all the gory details, but she hung up before I finished."

Polly wagged her head in disgust. "Never figured Monica for a weak stomach."

"Did you call Judy?" Diane asked. "She always likes to play."

"What about Barb?" Tara said, trying to be helpful.

I set out a bowl of foil-wrapped dark chocolate truffles. "Barb's packing for a cruise with a bunch of her sorority sisters. Judy has company from out of town."

"What about Rosalie?"

Never-Say-No Nancy's question just sort of hung there. Kind of like the ceiling fans at Lowe's.

When I didn't answer immediately, the women looked at me expectantly. "I did try Rosalie," I confessed, pouring cashews into a bowl. "Earl claims she's visiting grandkids in upstate New York."

"I can't remember the last time I saw Rosalie." Connie Sue picked up a chocolate truffle, then replaced it unopened. "I used to run into her all the time at the golf course."

Gloria helped herself to a handful of cashews, the ceiling light glinting off the collection of bangle bracelets she wore. "Seems like Rosalie was forever taking lessons from Brad."

"Brad?" Polly's ears practically perked up. "Who's Brad?"

"Brad Murphy," Pam explained. "He's the golf pro at the club."

"I know you ladies have the luxury of sleeping in, but I have to be at the preschool bright and early tomorrow." Tara took a place at the head table and picked up the dice. "Shall we start?"

Nancy slid into an adjacent chair. "Sleeping in is one of the perks of retirement, my dear. We've earned the right."

"Not me," Connie Sue said. "I go to water aerobics at seven a.m."

"I have yoga at eight," Rita added.

"And I'm volunteering at the food bank," Janine put in.

Good heavens! We're an energetic group for a bunch of old fogies. What would the

Babes take up next? Bungee jumping?

"The only time George and I set an alarm these days is to catch an early-morning flight when we leave on vacation," Nancy confessed.

Amen! You go, sista!

It was time to get the ball, or in this case the dice, rolling. "We've all played a player short in the past," I said. "Just remember, everyone at the table with only three players keeps their own score instead of combining scores with their partner. Piece of cake, right?"

Munchies and drinks in hand, we were ready to roll — quite literally, that is. Pam placed the tiara on her head, and we got down to business.

The first go-round we pretended to be serious bunco players. We rolled ones until Janine rang the bell and called bunco from the head table. I groaned. Diane and I had managed to accrue only six points between the two of us, which meant we switched partners, but stayed at the same table.

No sooner had the bell sounded for the next round than Rita, never one to beat about the bush, came straight to the point. "OK, Kate, put us out of our misery. Tell us what we're really doing here tonight."

"This better be good, sugar," Connie Sue

called from her seat. "Thacker didn't buy into the notion of Tuesday being National Pot Roast Day."

I tossed the dice before answering. Not a two in sight. "I was at the state park Saturday when the sheriff found *remains*."

Polly looked at me quizzically. "Since when did you start camping?"

"I didn't. I haven't."

The dice made the rounds. None of us seemed to be having much luck rolling twos.

"Kate, out with it." It was Rita again. Of course. "How did you just happen to be at the state park when the remains were found? And don't try to tell me it was coincidence."

"I was loading groceries into my car at the Piggly Wiggly when I heard the sirens. I looked up and saw the sheriff's cars racing past, so I decided to follow and find out what was going on."

"And then what?" Pam was so busy listening to me that Rita had to remind her she had rolled a baby bunco and scored another five points.

"And then," I continued as I watched Pam rack up even more points, "I hung around to see what was in the trash bag the dog had dug up."

Polly leaned so far off her chair at an adjoining table I was afraid she'd fall and break her scrawny neck. "Did you see a body?"

Finally it was my turn. Zip, nada, nil. Not a two in sight. At least the other ladies at my table weren't suffering from the same problem. "No body, just something zipped into a black vinyl bag."

"Cool," Polly said.

"Mother . . ."

"I mean how awful," Polly quickly amended, though she didn't sound the least bit remorseful.

"Bunco!" Janine's voice boomed out for the second time.

With my dismal score, I stayed where I was while others rotated tables and partners. Once everyone settled again, Rita attempted to get us back on track. "Kate, are you trying to say that the reason for this emergency bunco game is to tell us you were there when the sheriff found the remains?"

I gave up all pretense of concentrating on the game. So did the rest of the Babes as they turned to listen to what I had to say. "Actually, I called all of you together to elicit your help finding Claudia and Vera."

"Isn't that the sheriff's job?" Gloria asked.

"You heard Sheriff Wiggins this afternoon. He asked for our cooperation. Practically begged for our help."

Diane idly rolled the dice between her palms lest they grew cold in the interim. "What can we do?"

"All we know for sure is that the victim is female. I don't know about the rest of you, but I'm worried sick about Claudia and Vera. And if that isn't enough, Rosalie's been gone too long. I know I'll sleep easier knowing they're all OK."

"Amen," Pam murmured.

"Ladies, we have our work cut out for us." I stood. Suddenly I felt like a general rallying his troops to battle. Eisenhower on D-day. Patton at the Battle of the Bulge. Custer at Little Bighorn. "The sheriff probably has dozens, maybe hundreds, of missing persons to track down. It could be days, or even weeks, before he starts checking into Claudia, Vera, and Rosalie. I thought we might speed things along. See if we can track them down ourselves."

"How?" several of the Babes chorused in unison.

"We need to do an investigation of our own."

I could see some nods, some frowns.

"Where would we start?" Tara ventured.

I looked from one worried face to another. "By chance, does anyone know how we might contact Claudia's sons?"

"I know one's a surgeon in Chicago," Janine volunteered.

"The other's an engineer," Gloria said. "Seattle, I think."

"We could start there," Diane said in a burst of enthusiasm. "I worked the reference desk back in Florida. I'm good at research."

"I'm good with computers," Megan volunteered. "I'll help Diane."

"Great!" I wanted to clap my hands and applaud. Now who was behaving like a cheerleader? "That leaves Vera," I continued, warming to my role of general. "I found out Vera recently divorced an abusive husband. I also learned that Lisa, her daughter, is expecting her third child soon."

Tara looked thoughtful. "If her daughter has young children, maybe someone at the preschool knows her. I can ask around. Discreetly of course."

"And I'll take it upon myself to find out more about Rosalie — discreetly of course." I sank back down and picked up the dice. The Bunco Babes had come through again. I knew they wouldn't let me down.

The game resumed where we left off. We rolled our way through a series of fours, fives, and sixes. I eventually worked my way up to the head table along with Connie Sue,

Polly, and Megan.

"C'mon, baby. Mama needs a new pair of shoes." Connie Sue blew on the dice for luck. Megan grinned when she failed to score.

"Don't know about the rest of you, but I got the shivers when the sheriff said the perp had access to power tools. Yuck!" Polly grimaced.

"Hey, sugar, how about turning on the ceiling fan?" Connie Sue loosened a button on her blouse. "I'm having another of those hot flashes."

I got halfway out of my chair before I remembered. "Sorry, Connie Sue, but I can't. It's broken."

"Did you ever get hold of Bill?" Pam called from the neighboring table.

"He dropped by yesterday afternoon. Told me it was the motor. Said I needed to buy a new fan, and he'd install it for me."

"Bunco!" Megan rang the bell.

Nancy got up to refill her glass with soda. "Bill Lewis?"

"That's right." I noticed most of the girls were sticking with soft drinks tonight. The wine went mostly untouched. Shows how serious they were about finding our missing friends.

"Bill's in the Woodchucks with my husband," Rita commented. "Dave said he just got reelected president. Says he has every power tool known to man. Even more than Bob Vila on *This Old House.*"

Access to power tools? The sheriff's words flashed across my brain like a neon sign at a cheap motel. I glanced around the table, but no one made eye contact. The Babes didn't have to be psychic to read one another's minds. Not only Bill, but every man who owned so much as a simple saw, was suspect.

We were unusually silent as we played the final round and tallied scores. Janine was the night's big winner with over seven hundred points. She wore the tiara with queenly aplomb.

"Everyone'll be able to spot me two aisles away at the Piggly Wiggly," she said, winking at me as she left.

As the ladies began to file out, Megan, sweet little Megan, gave me a hug. "Love you, Kate."

Polly and Gloria were the last to leave. It might have been my imagination, but Polly's smile didn't beam its usual wattage. In fact, it seemed a bit strained. "Be careful, dear," she said as she lowered her voice and patted my arm. "There's a killer on the loose."

■ ■ ■ ■

Now that everyone had finally gone home, the house seemed unusually quiet. I jumped when the phone rang, and ran to pick it up. It always made me a little nervous when the phone rang at this hour.

"Mother, how are you?" It was Jennifer, our daughter (or should I say *my daughter* now that Jim's dead? I'm never quite sure) calling from California.

"I'm fine, dear." I used to be "Mom," but apparently got promoted to "Mother" after Jen's move to the West Coast. After Jim died, both Steven and Jennifer thought I should return to Ohio. Mind you, neither of the kids still lives in Ohio. No way. They couldn't wait to leave Toledo. Not even the lure of Tony Packo's famous Hungarian hot dogs could keep them there. From the time they entered college, they yearned for bigger and better. Somewhere more exciting. Big cities and sprawling suburbs beckoned with an appeal impossible to ignore.

"I forgot about the time difference," Jen said apologetically.

"It's always good to hear your voice, honey. Regardless of the time."

And I meant it.

After marrying her college sweetheart, Jason Jerrard, Jennifer moved to California. They have two little girls, Juliette and Jillian. The "Four Jays," as I refer to them, live in Brentwood, the same place O. J. Simpson used to live. Jennifer and Jason own a big house with an even bigger mortgage.

Personally I always thought Jason was somewhat of a geek. Not much to look at, but then I always told my girl not to judge people by appearances. Jennifer didn't. She's a smart girl, my Jen. She saw beyond the nerdy glasses, poor posture, and mismatched clothes. It's amazing what contact lenses, confidence, and Armani can do for a man. Jason is now a high-priced attorney with a long list of celebrities as clients. He spends his days creating contracts and clauses Hulk Hogan himself couldn't break.

"I hope you weren't asleep."

"No, your timing's perfect. The girls just left."

"The girls? Oh, you mean the women you gamble with."

Jen just couldn't seem to grasp the concept of a nonsensical dice game like bunco. I had tried to explain it on numerous occasions, but obviously my explanations fell short. "Bunco isn't gambling, dear. It's simply a . . . game."

"I'd hate to think you were gambling away your pension."

"There's no money involved, Jen. You make it sound almost illegal."

"Isn't bunco what the high rollers do in Vegas? Only there they have another name for it . . . craps, I think."

"Playing bunco with the girls is nothing at all like rolling craps in Vegas," I said with asperity. Actually I've never been to Vegas, so my knowledge is rather limited. But I do watch movies. And I've seen those tacky T-shirts that read WHAT HAPPENS IN VEGAS STAYS IN VEGAS. You can bet that slogan exists for a mighty good reason.

"Craps, bunco, whatever. It's nice you found a hobby. Jason and I worry you might be bored in a community with all those elderly people."

Elderly? I bit my tongue before correcting her distorted view of active adult communities. "People here in Serenity Cove Estates believe age is a state of mind, *not* a date on a driver's license."

Jen continued, nonplussed. "It's dangerous to become inactive. Studies show that mental exercise reduces the risk of getting dementia."

Dementia? As if *elderly* weren't insulting enough, now I'm getting senile? Oh! The arrogance of the young. "Jen, you must be the one who's bored if you're reading studies on aging. For heaven's sake, join a book club."

"Playing dice games may be fun, Mother, but you need mental stimuli to retard the aging process."

"Honey, there's too much happening in Serenity Cove Estates to ever get bored."

I heard Jen stifle a yawn. "Really?"

"Really," I replied, determined to set her straight. "Take right now, for instance. I bet I'm getting enough mental stimuli for a woman half my age."

"Mother, are you in some sort of trouble?"

From her sharper tone, I knew I had succeeded in grabbing her attention. *Elderly? Demented?* I'd show her. "I'm helping the sheriff solve a murder," I said, sounding a trifle smug.

"You're what!"

"You heard me, dear. Along with the rest of the Bunco Babes, I'm helping Sheriff Wiggins solve a murder."

"Murder? Whose murder?"

"I'm afraid we won't know that until we discover who the arm belongs to."

"Arm? What arm?"

"Who's on first; what's on second," I wanted to tell her. Once again that old

Abbott and Costello routine ran through my mind. I wanted to say "I-Don't-Know's on third," but was afraid Jen would fail to see the humor. Instead I said, "Relax, honey, there's nothing to worry about."

I heard her draw a calming breath. "Mother, I'm going to sit down now. Then I think you had better start from the beginning."

And so I did.

Dead silence followed my account of the last few days. The quality of long-distance calls has vastly improved since my youth, but still I never trust them a hundred percent not to lose the connection. "Jen, honey, are you still there?"

"Mother," she said, her voice shaky, "I take back everything I ever said about Serenity Cove being boring."

I smirked; I couldn't help it. I got a lot of satisfaction from hearing her admission.

"That . . . that place simply isn't safe. Pack your suitcase. As soon as we hang up, I'm going to call the airlines and book you a flight out of there first thing tomorrow."

Apparently I had smirked too soon. "There's no need to get upset, dear," I tried to placate her. "Serenity Cove is perfectly safe. Why, only today, Sheriff Wiggins reassured everyone at a town hall meeting.

He said law enforcement feels this was an 'isolated incidence of violence.' " I was proud of myself for using the sheriff's direct quote. Emboldened, I took my new acronym out for a stroll. "He's already called in SLED."

"Sled? Mother, you're not making any sense." Jen's voice was rising again. "Are you sure you're all right?"

Perhaps Jen lives too close to Hollywood for her own good. Even as a child she tended to overdramatize.

"I'm fine, dear," I assured her. "*SLED* stands for *South Carolina Law Enforcement Division.*" How could she not be impressed with that bit of information? That should prove beyond a doubt that my brain cells were getting plenty of stimuli.

Jennifer switched tactics. "Jason and I would both love to have you visit. And the girls would be delighted. You could drive them to all their activities. They both take ballet and tap. Just last week, I enrolled Jillian in soccer and gymnastics. Juliette started violin lessons and needs someone to listen to her practice. You'd love it."

Listening to an eight-year-old practice violin wasn't exactly my idea of a vacation. And though I'd dearly love to observe a dance class or soccer game, the thought of being a chauffeur in heavy California traffic didn't appeal to me. "Save your money, sweetheart. I don't need a plane ticket. I have no intention of going anywhere right now."

"I wish you'd reconsider, Mother. I worry about you in *that* place."

I assured her again I was perfectly all right in Serenity Cove Estates, then changed the subject. When the phone conversation ended fifteen minutes later, I made a mental note to be more careful of what I told my daughter in the future — no matter what the provocation.

CHAPTER 13

I thought about the previous evening as I waited for my bagel to toast. I was glad the Babes had agreed to pitch in with the investigation. I could hardly wait to do my part and grill — I think that's the term cops use — Earl about the disappearance of his wife. I'd look closely for beads of sweat to appear along his hairline — at least what was left of it. And I'd watch his eyes. Did they dart? Did they dilate? No detail, no matter how small, was going to escape my attention.

My bagel popped up, and I slathered it with cream cheese. The reduced-fat variety. In spite of what some might think, I do make healthy choices now and again. After pouring a cup of coffee, I plopped down in the nook and began planning my day.

I needed to drive into town to stock up on groceries. My cupboards were beginning to resemble Old Mother Hubbard's.

I took a bite of bagel and grimaced. Pain sharp as an ice pick stabbed my lower jaw. Gingerly I felt around the area with the tip of my tongue and encountered a rough edge that hadn't been there before. My molars were at it again. I tried a sip of coffee and winced. That dad-blamed tooth was also sensitive to heat. Time for a trip to the dentist. I had ignored similar symptoms once before and lived to regret it.

Problem was, I was picky when it came to dentists. The dentist I had been seeing had just retired to Hilton Head, and I hadn't gotten around to replacing him. As usual, I turned to my favorite go-to person for a recommendation and dialed Pam.

"Got a minute?"

"Sure. What's up?"

"Seems like I'm in need of a new dentist. I know Megan works part-time as a receptionist for one in Brookdale. Is he any good?" What I really wanted to know was if he was going to hurt me. I have a severe case of dental phobia dating back from childhood. I'm still waiting to grow out of it. Maybe by the time I hit eighty.

Pam laughed. "Kate, you're such a baby."

"Hmpph!" I sniffed. "Only when it comes to dentists. The rest of the time I'm big and brave."

"His name is Dr. Jeffrey Baxter. Megan says all his female patients are in love with him."

"I don't want to fall in love. I just want a dentist who believes in Novocain — and lots of it. Every time I hear that drill, I get flashbacks to a movie I saw years ago about an evil dentist torturing the good guy to find out where the diamonds are hidden."

"Oh, yeah," Pam murmured. "I vaguely recall a movie like that. What was the name again?"

"Was it *Man of La Mancha*?"

"That doesn't sound right."

"Could it have been *The Manchurian Candidate*?"

"That doesn't sound right either."

"Darn! I hate these senior moments." These sudden memory gaps make playing Trivial Pursuit next to impossible. I'll wake up with answers in the middle of the night, but by then can no longer remember the questions. Jennifer would think I'm demented for sure.

"Hey, I hate to cut you off," Pam said, "but I've got to run. I've got a hair appointment in twenty minutes." She rattled off the number for Dr. Jeffrey Baxter, and then disconnected.

No sense putting off the inevitable. I

refilled my coffee mug and took another swallow, careful to avoid the troublesome molar, then dialed the number Pam had just rattled off.

"Good morning. Dr. Baxter's office," Megan answered, her voice irritatingly cheerful.

"Hi, Megan. It's me, Kate."

"Hi, Kate. Sorry, but if this is about bunco, I can't talk right now. The office is hopping. We just got an emergency root canal."

"Wait, Megan, don't hang up." If she hung up on me now, it might take weeks, or an emergency root canal, to get me back on the line. "I need an appointment to see Dr. Baxter. Your mother said he's good."

"All the patients love him," Megan giggled.

Lordy! What in the world was going on? Women seemed to be falling in love all over the place. Good looks and a little charm turned women into putty. Where was their backbone? Where was their pride? Then I thought of Bill Lewis and shut up.

Megan cleared her throat and turned professional again. "Unless this is an emergency, Mrs. McCall, the doctor is booked solid for the next two weeks."

I reexplored the worrisome molar with my

tongue. No twinges, tingles, or stabbing pain. "No emergency," I said. "Just give me a date and time, and I'll be there."

I hung up, pleased at my bravery. And even more pleased that I had been granted a two-week reprieve. I said it before, and I'll say it again: I'm a dyed-in-the-wool procrastinator. Especially when it comes to dentists.

Dinner over, I tried to relax in front of the TV, but couldn't seem to concentrate. The sitcom seemed more silly than funny, the laugh track forced. I finally clicked off the remote and prowled the great room, rearranging a stack of magazines, plumping pillows that were already plump. All day I had dithered and dallied, trying to think of the right approach for my interrogation of Earl Brubaker. It certainly would be nice to cross at least one person off my missing-persons list — that is, if Rosalie was actually in Poughkeepsie.

I stopped prowling and stared out the window. The night was still young. Time to quit procrastinating. As long as I was in sleuth mode, I might as well check things out.

In spite of the Brubaker house being just across the way, I hadn't seen any activity there in days. Had Earl become as reclusive as Howard Hughes? Maybe he had fallen and couldn't get up. I had watched those commercials on TV where a little old lady lay helpless for countless hours until rescued by a kindly neighbor. What are neighbors for if they can't be helpful?

I was halfway to the door when I hesitated. What if Earl was his usually surly self? Or worse yet, what if he thought I'd developed the hots for him? I'd feel pretty foolish without a plausible excuse for another nocturnal visit. Then it came to me like that proverbial bolt out of the blue. I'd return the sugar I had borrowed. But this time I'd be fully clothed — not in my bathrobe.

Clutching the same half-empty bag in one hand, I set off to pay Earl a house call. I knocked on the door, once, twice, three times, then waited. Finally the porch light came on. I could sense an eyeball pressed against the peephole. Just for the heck of it, I wanted to press mine against it, too, but managed to restrain myself. The notion of being eyeball-to-eyeball with Earl Brubaker left a lot to be desired.

The inspection over, the door opened, and I found myself face-to-face with Earl. At least I assumed it was Earl. The eyes and nose looked the same as always, but it was the lower half of his face that gave me pause. Thick salt-and-pepper stubble covered his jaw and upper lip. A bumper crop of hair grew out of his various orifices. *Ee-yew!* I said to myself. *Gross!* Had I seen this face on a wanted poster? Or did it really belong to Earl Brubaker?

"Kate . . . ?" He scratched his head, which by the way was sorely in need of a barber.

"Hey, Earl," I said. "Growing a beard, eh." I'd bet my last dollar he was still wearing the same faded golf shirt and rumpled khakis that he had on the last time I'd seen him.

"Kate . . . I . . . er, I'm kind of busy right now."

He looked busy all right, busy being a slob. I shoved the bag of sugar at him. "Thought I'd better return this in case you decided to bake cupcakes."

"Unhh . . . ," he grunted.

I half turned as if to leave, then turned back. "By the way," I said with a studied casualness that would have made my high school drama coach proud, "I haven't seen Rosalie around the rec center lately. She still out of town?"

"Yeah, I guess."

"You guess?"

He shrugged. "We're not much for talking on the phone while she's away."

"So you haven't heard from her?" I persisted. My internal antennae along with a host of red flags were waving like mad.

"Nah, didn't expect to." He scratched his head again. His hair was so . . . unkempt, I wondered whether he had things living in it. Or maybe he was searching for a new style, dreadlocks à la Bob Marley.

"Why don't you expect to hear from her?" I asked.

"We had a little spat before she left." He scuffed the toe of his shoe against the doorsill. "I think she's mad at me."

I felt sorry for him. I couldn't help myself. I've always been a pushover for basset hounds with their big, sad brown eyes and that was precisely what Earl reminded me of. "Whatever you fought over, Earl, I'm sure she'll get over it by the time she gets home."

"Maybe," he mumbled, looking dejected. "Maybe not."

I didn't know what else to say so thought it might be a good time to make my exit. "Well, Earl, gotta be going. Tell Rosalie, whenever you talk to her, to give me a call. Maybe we can do lunch."

The door closed in my face before I finished speaking. I'm not sure whether he heard the part about doing lunch.

I walked home slowly. The night was beautiful, almost as bright as day thanks to a full moon. From the very first, Serenity Cove Estates had always seemed aptly named. Peaceful, serene, safe. It was hard to believe there was a killer on the loose. A sick pervert responsible for bringing murder and mayhem to our quiet little corner of the world. It was harder yet to imagine that a woman I knew might be the killer's victim.

I thought about the conversation I'd just had with Earl. He had admitted he and Rosalie had argued. Had the argument turned violent? Violent enough for him to kill her? Somehow, I couldn't imagine Earl guilty of that much passion. I just couldn't. Besides, I hadn't noted a single bead of sweat on his brow or a single dart of the eye.

So lost in thought was I that I nearly missed seeing a package tucked behind a pot of mums by the side door. I hoped it was the Sandman. I needed a fancy electronic device if I was ever going to get any sleep without worrying about friends disappearing. I picked up the package and brought it inside. After double-checking to make sure the doors were locked, I opened the box. It wasn't the Sandman, but the next-best thing. *The Complete Idiot's Guide to Forensics.* I could read myself to sleep.

I opened the book, and there it was: "An Investigator's Toolkit." A comprehensive checklist of items needed by crime-scene investigators. I got out paper and pencil and went to work.

Chapter 14

Tai Chi is purported to reduce stress. Just the ticket, I decided. I definitely needed to relax, unwind. I felt wound tighter than a child's top, ready to spin out of control. I was the last of the class to arrive. Marian acknowledged my presence with a nod as I slipped into place next to Pam at the back of the room.

Tai Chi is also supposed to improve concentration and focus. Problem was, I was concentrating and focusing on all the wrong things.

Things like body parts.

"You look tense," Pam whispered as she performed a series of warm-up exercises.

I swiveled my neck to the right, held it for a beat. I could hear my vertebrae go snap, crackle, pop. Rotated my neck back to the center. Then repeated the exercise to the left. "Tense? I look tense?" Was Pam deaf? Couldn't she hear my joints crackle like a bowl of breakfast cereal?

Marian glared at us from the front of the room. "Quiet, class," she instructed in a hushed tone. "Block out all external distractions. Clear your mind."

Easy for her to say, I thought grumpily. She didn't find an arm in a Wal-Mart bag. She didn't have three people she knew disappear without a trace. Marian pressed a button of the compact stereo, and the room filled with soft, hypnotic music. I followed Marian through a series of warm-up exercises. Gradually the popping in my joints subsided to a level where I was probably the only one who could hear them.

"Wave Hands like Heavenly Clouds," Marian murmured.

Raising my arms over my head, I swayed back and forth. I tried my best to let the flowing Chi flow. To listen to my inner self and block out everything else. "Pssst . . ."

I kept right on waving at those invisible clouds on the rec center's ceiling as if I hadn't heard Pam hiss. Marian would be pleased at my progress.

"Pssst . . ." Pam again, louder, more insistent. "What's wrong?"

"Nothing . . . everything," I muttered. I felt angry at myself and frustrated by my attempt to play detective. Would any detective worth his salt hand a possible murder suspect a bag of sugar and then walk away feeling sorry for him? I hadn't done my job last night. I was determined not to let the matter rest. There must be something more. . . .

Class over, I hefted my purse onto my shoulder. "I'm going to stop by the pro shop before I go home. I heard Brad Murphy was giving a putting clinic. I thought I'd sign up if it isn't too late. Besides, this will give me a chance to ask him if he knows anything about Rosalie."

"Fine, I'll go with you. I heard they're having an end-of-season sale on golf shoes. I could use a new pair."

We climbed into Pam's golf cart and zipped over to the pro shop. While Pam tried on shoes, I studied the bulletin board tacked near the entrance. Since there were still openings for the putting clinic, I added my name to the list.

Pam couldn't decide between a pair of tan and white saddle-shoe-style or a white pair with a black argyle pattern. I suppose a really good friend would have helped end the agony. My advice would have been to buy them both. Even on a fixed income, I know a bargain when I see one. Pam, however, is the model of frugality, so I kept my opinion to myself and perused the bulletin board instead. Looking at a listing of handicaps, I happened upon an announcement of an upcoming member-member tournament nearly hidden beneath it. I also noticed Rosalie Brubaker was the chairperson.

Just then, Brad Murphy, the golf pro, came out of his office at the rear. Now, let me tell you, Brad is a good-looking specimen. In my humble estimation, he looks the way a golf pro should look. Tall, broad shoulders, narrow hips, and a terrific tan. Short sun-bleached strawberry blond hair and nice brown eyes complete the picture. The way he fills out a golf shirt, he could model for an ad in *Golf Digest.*

"How's the game, Mrs. McCall?"

"It's still a work in progress, Brad. I just signed up for your putting clinic. Hope it'll help."

"That's the spirit. Saw you looking at the announcement for the ladies member-member. Thinking about giving it a shot?"

"No, not me." I laughed. "I'm not ready to subject a friend to that kind of torture."

"If you want some private lessons to tune up your game, just give me a call."

I remembered a comment someone had made about Rosalie perpetually taking golf lessons from Brad. I could see how she might be tempted. Just wait until she got a load of Earl's new beach-bum look. The driving range at the course would be getting more use than the range in her kitchen. Earl didn't stand a chance.

"I understand Rosalie Brubaker is chairing the committee," I added as casually as I could.

Brad ran a hand through his strawberry blond locks. "I'm on the verge of asking for another volunteer. The sign-up sheet should have been posted a week ago. The manager of the Watering Hole complained that Rosalie still hasn't sat down with her to discuss the luncheon menu."

"I'm sure Rosalie has a good reason why not." But the words, even to my own ears, lacked conviction. "I heard she's visiting grandkids in upstate New York."

"It's not like Rosalie," Brad said, moving off. "She's usually on top of things."

In my mind's eye, red flags fluttered in the breeze.

After an unscheduled trip to Wal-Mart to pick up a few items, I devoted the remainder of the afternoon to household chores. I dusted, ran the vacuum cleaner, and did a couple loads of laundry. It wasn't until after dinner — a Margherita pizza that I'd been hoarding in the freezer, saving it for a rainy day — that I remembered that tomorrow was trash pickup. I shuddered at the word. In my mind *trash* had become synonymous with *arm.* It's hard for me to comprehend that someone had ruthlessly killed another human being, then discarded the body like so much trash. Whoever did it needed to be caught. And punished.

I went room to room emptying wastebaskets. I dumped it all into a larger can under the kitchen sink and tossed the whole works into an even larger can in the garage. I grabbed the handle, tilted the can, and wheeled it to the curb. Taking out the trash always used to be Jim's job. There's something macho attached to taking out the garbage. Women could bring home the bacon and fry it up in a pan, but the man of the house hauled out the trash. Let me ask you, is that an equal division of labor?

I met Earl down at the curb. Even though the Brubakers' house sits on the corner of Loblolly Court and Shady Lane, both our driveways are entered off Loblolly Court. "Hey there, Earl," I greeted him.

He looked up and grunted.

"Nice night, isn't it?" How's that for a witty conversational gambit?

Earl parked the heavy trash container next to his mailbox. "Yeah, I guess."

I squinted, trying to see him better in the dim light. I really did new need glasses, or maybe LASIK surgery. But even in the moonlight, I could see he still hadn't bothered to shave. He looked more and more like a caveman each time I saw him. "How're things going?"

He mumbled something and turned to head up the drive.

"Heard from Rosalie?"

"Nah, not a word." He called back over his shoulder. "She's probably still mad."

I slowly walked back toward the house, closed the overhead garage door, and went inside, taking care to twist the dead bolt behind me. Next thing I'd be shopping at the Humane Society for a pit bull.

Home again, I brewed a cup of chamomile tea and sat down at the kitchen table. While waiting for it to cool, I flipped through *The Complete Idiot's Guide to Forensics.* Just out of curiosity, I turned to the section on human hair. I learned hair can be helpful in identifying a victim, but examiners need to match it to a specific individual.

I don't know exactly how long I sat there stockpiling tidbits of information I'll probably never use, but when I glanced across the cul-de-sac at the Brubakers', I noticed the house was dark. Earl must have gone to bed early for a change. I surely would have noticed if his car had backed out. Sitting where I was, I would've seen the flash of taillights. Earl had looked ready to drop with exhaustion. The bags under his eyes looked like the luggage variety. Not the little carry-on type either, but the hefty kind you check at the gate.

I stared across the way. Not a single light gleamed. I could barely make out the dark blur of trash cans parked along the curb. Although I hated the thought, Rosalie was still unaccounted for. Before I could talk myself out of it, I decided to test-drive my brand-new crime-scene-investigation kit.

I grabbed my fire-engine red tackle box — courtesy of Wal-Mart's sporting-goods department — from atop the washing machine and left by the side door. I'd been careful not to turn on any outside lights. I stopped, looked, and listened from the shadow of my Japanese maple. All was quiet at the junction of Loblolly Court and Shady Lane. Up and down Shady Lane, trash cans lined the curb like good little soldiers standing at attention. Lights from TV sets flickered in some windows. The good citizens of

Serenity Cove were all snug as bugs in their homes, resting up after another hectic day. Retirement, as I often tell anyone who'll listen, isn't for sissies.

It was now or never.

I gripped the tackle box, alias Tools of the Trade, tighter in my hot little hand and hustled across the street. At the end of the Brubakers' drive, I set Tools of the Trade on the ground and snapped open the lid. I tugged on a pair of latex gloves — also courtesy of Wal-Mart — and took out my spanking new, high-intensity LED flashlight, which had been horrendously priced for a widow on a fixed income. But I splurged and bought it anyway. It came in either yellow or black. Naturally I picked the yellow. I'd even e-mailed CBS about the type of flashlights used on *CSI: Crime Scene Investigation,* but I hadn't gotten a response. They probably thought I was some sort of nutcase.

I eased the lid off Earl's trash can and began rummaging through the detritus of his life. Soup cans, milk cartons, plastic trays from frozen dinners, an empty peanut butter jar. Earl needed to be lectured on the importance of recycling. He needed to "go green." Relearn the three Rs.

A rustling sound in the lantana at the base

of the mailbox startled me. I froze like a deer in the headlights. Could it be a snake? I hated snakes almost as much as I hated dentists. Or was I about to be mauled by a wild animal? Only last week, Ed Beckley reported seeing a coyote run across the golf course. I'm not exactly sure what a coyote looks like. The only ones I've seen have been on cartoons. I'd like to keep it that way.

When my worst fears failed to materialize, I resumed my search. I dug deeper, ripping open a bulging plastic trash bag. I stuck my hand inside and fished around. I was about to give up when I encountered something wet and sticky. I quickly withdrew my hand and stared at it. My latex glove was smeared with a dark substance. Wet, sticky, and dark . . . red.

Blood . . . ?

Now what? An anonymous call? I didn't want to make any foolish mistakes. What would Gil Grissom or Catherine Willows do in a situation like this? I closed my eyes and imagined a rerun from *CSI*. In it, Gil would frown, then nod sagely. Catherine would then ask, "Well, what do you think?" And Gil, ever the cool scientist, would raise his hand to his nose, sniff, and say . . .

Spaghetti sauce.

My eyes sprang open to find my gloved

fingers an inch from my nostrils. The wet, sticky, icky substance on my gloves was nothing more than plain old garden-variety spaghetti sauce. And judging from the smell, not even one of the premium brands. Earl also needed to be enlightened about the wonders of basil and oregano and garlic.

Just then something brushed against my leg. I stifled a scream and leaped back. My heart pounded like a trip-hammer. I glanced down at my feet to where a fat sassy raccoon systematically pawed through Tools of the Trade. Its tiny hands were absurdly human as it pulled out item after item. It gnawed the cover of my brand-new little black notebook, then flung it aside. My retractable tape measure was discarded in favor of the box of latex gloves.

"Shoo, shoo." I flapped my hands in a futile attempt to scare it off.

"Hssss . . ."

Its bright, beady eyes held a malevolent gleam as they stared up at me from its characteristic bandit's mask. Then, the annoying critter turned tail, running across Earl Brubaker's front lawn, leaving a trail of latex gloves in its wake.

I sighed as I bent to retrieve them. Crime solving wasn't all it was cracked up to be.

CHAPTER 15

I decided to swing by the sheriff's office after a stop at the Piggly Wiggly and check on his progress. Sheriff Wiggins needed a reminder that Rosalie was definitely MIA. Not to mention Claudia hadn't been heard from and there was still no sign of Vera. I didn't want to call on him empty-handed. My mother, God rest her soul, had drilled into me the nicety of always bringing your host, or hostess, a small gift. I tried to instill that same habit into my children and often wonder if I succeeded. I knew from past experience the sheriff wasn't a sweets eater, so that ruled out bakery items. With this in mind, I had backtracked to the produce department. I looked over the display of fresh flowers and houseplants. The man didn't strike me as the type to appreciate roses, so I decided on an ivy plant instead. Nothing like a little greenery to liven up a dreary office.

The same girl was at the front desk when I arrived. Same lank brown hair and too-large glasses. Same good features. Given half a chance, Connie Sue could turn this girl into a beauty pageant knockout.

I gave her my friendliest smile. "Tammy Lynn, isn't it?"

The girl looked up from her computer. "Miz McCall . . . ?"

I smiled wider at hearing my name. Clearly my last visit had left an impression. "I'm here to see the sheriff."

Tammy Lynn didn't return my smile. In fact, if anything, she looked — I searched for the word — uncomfortable. She looked decidedly uncomfortable. "Ah, um . . . ma'am, Sheriff Wiggins is kinda busy at the moment."

"No problem, dear." I plunked myself down in one of those molded plastic chairs best suited for pygmies. "I'll wait."

I glanced around the waiting room. The dog-eared magazines dating back three years were still piled on a corner table. I was pleased to note that no new felons had been added to the bulletin board. No need for more when there were already enough as it was. Yes, I thought, this place could stand a houseplant or two to liven it up. Next time I called on the sheriff, I'd bring a fresh supply of reading material, too. Maybe some recent issues of *Southern Living* or *Better Homes and Gardens.*

To help pass the time, I blew the dust from a three-year-old back issue of *Field & Stream* and settled in to learn the intricacies of bass fishing. As I perused a scholarly dissertation on fishing lures, I overheard Tammy Lynn inform the sheriff I was waiting to see him.

"Ma'am . . . ?"

"Yes, dear . . ."

Tammy Lynn held the phone against her chest, her expression anxious. "The sheriff said he's very busy right now."

"Well, of course he's busy," I agreed pleasantly. "He holds a very important office with a great deal of responsibility."

Tammy repeated my words into the phone in a hushed tone. "Sheriff Wiggins said to tell you he has a meeting with the mayor in ten minutes."

I was grateful I didn't have dairy products spoiling in the trunk of my car. "I'm in no rush. I can wait until after his meeting with the mayor."

She turned away, relayed my message, then turned back to me. "He said to ask you the nature of your business."

"Tell the sheriff I'm here to discuss our

case, but not to worry if he's in the middle of something. I'll just wait out here and keep you company. I have all afternoon." I went back to studying the colorful fishing lures guaranteed to attract the largest bass in the kingdom.

The he-said, she-said game between the sheriff and his receptionist had reached an impasse. Tammy Lynn spoke into the phone once again, then glanced over in my direction but seemed reluctant to meet my gaze. "Sheriff Wiggins asked me to send you in."

I didn't question my good fortune, but picked up the ivy and scurried down the short hallway and toward his office. Spending an afternoon in that dreary waiting room would have tested the disposition of a saint. Poor Tammy Lynn.

Sheriff Wiggins was ensconced behind his desk, appearing every bit as substantial as a giant redwood. Judging from the scowl he wore, he was none too happy to see me. An injection or two of Botox would smooth those lines right out.

"Have a seat, Miz McCall. I'm sure Tammy Lynn explained I'm very busy. I'd appreciate if you just stated your business and let me be about mine."

"Of course, Sheriff." I sat down in my usual seat without waiting for an invitation.

"Your dedication should be applauded. Come election time, I'll be sure to mention it to my friends."

"You do that, ma'am. I'm much obliged."

Funny, he didn't sound the least bit obliged. He needed to lighten up. Maybe my gift would do the trick. I plopped the ivy down on his desk. "Nothing like a houseplant to make an office a little less . . . institutional."

"Institutional . . . ?" He drew the word out in that melodious voice of his. "Sorry, ma'am, but most government offices tend to be . . . institutional."

"Yes," I agreed, "but does that mean they have to be quite so drab? Decor goes a long way to influence a person's state of mind."

He studied the plant I had brought him, then drilled me with a look from eyes like shiny black onyx. "Most folks that pass through here have more pressin' matters to worry about than the decor."

"Oh, I don't disagree, but those are the folks that would benefit most from a cheerful environment."

He sighed from way down deep. A sound that started in his toes and worked its way up. And let me tell you, that's a long trip for a man six feet two. "Suppose, Miz McCall, you just tell me what urgent business brought you here today."

"Very well." I could tell he was in no mood for chitchat, so I cut to the chase. "Three friends have disappeared without a trace. As long as I was in town, I thought I'd stop by and see if you made any progress on locating their whereabouts."

He arched a dark brow. I have to admit the overall look was quite effective. I'd have to give it a try. It's easy to raise both brows simultaneously, but to lift one and not the other required some practice.

I could read his mind. He was telling me to get on with it, so I did. "The Babes and I have taken it upon ourselves — as concerned citizens, naturally — to help you out."

"Exactly who are these Babes who have decided law enforcement is in need of their assistance?"

"We call ourselves the Bunco Babes." I squirmed a bit, discomfited by that stare of his. "We . . . er . . . play bunco."

"Bunco?"

"You know . . . the dice game." Clearly the sheriff's lack of knowledge about bunco was on par with his lack of knowledge about Nancy Drew. "There are twelve of us altogether including Claudia, but Nancy's been filling in as a sub till she gets back."

He glanced at his watch, a not-too-subtle reminder minutes were ticking away. "This Claudia . . . she's the one you said is missing?"

"The one and the same," I replied cheerily, grateful we were at last on the same page. "Diane, who happens to be the librarian here in Brookdale, is a whiz on the computer. She's trying to locate Claudia's sons to see if they've heard from their mother. Tara, who works at the day care center, is going to see if she can get a lead on Vera."

"Vera . . . ? Another of your missing ladies?"

I nodded my approval that he was keeping up with me. "And that brings us to Rosalie."

"Rosalie . . . ?"

"Rosalie Brubaker, my neighbor. She's been away an unusually long time. Supposedly she's visiting grandkids in upstate New York. Poughkeepsie to be exact. Her husband, Earl, admitted he hasn't heard a word from her since she left Serenity Cove."

"So . . ." He pursed his lips.

"I think it would be a good idea if you bumped Rosalie up a notch or two on your missing-persons list. I'm getting bad vibes about her. Brad Murphy, the pro at the club, told me she's chairperson of the member-member tournament and hasn't even posted a sign-up sheet yet. That isn't like Rosalie. She's very organized."

Those big thumbs of his began to circle each other. "Miz McCall, people, women in particular, visit grandbabies all the time. Nothin' unusual in that. To my way of thinkin', be more unusual if they didn't."

"Except . . ." I paused for effect. "Except," I began again, "her husband hasn't gotten so much as a single phone call. Earl claims they had some kind of argument before she left and —"

"An argument . . . ?"

He stopped twiddling his thumbs and sat up straighter. Something I said had actually piqued his interest. Finally. But before I finished congratulating myself, I wanted to take back my words. Good grief! What had I gone and done? Now the sheriff probably thought Earl had something to do with his wife's disappearance. Wasn't that how it usually went in these cases? The husband, or significant other, whichever, was always the prime suspect.

I tried to backpedal. "Their little spat was probably nothing at all. Earl wouldn't harm a flea."

"To the best of my recollection, it wasn't

a flea that got itself harmed."

I surged to my feet and slung my purse over my shoulder. "Well, I've already taken up too much of your time. I trust you'll keep Rosalie Brubaker on the list?"

Sheriff Wiggins made a show of jotting her name in his little black book. Just as I was about to leave his office, I detected a slight problem. At least I hoped the problem was slight. The ivy plant I'd brought to liven up his office had leaked. Water seeped from holes at the bottom of the plastic container. A tiny rivulet ran along the desk to pool near a neat stack of papers.

"Oops," I muttered.

The sheriff followed the direction of my stare.

"Oops," I muttered again for lack of a better word. I frantically dug through my purse for the packet of tissues I always carry. As luck would have it, it had settled in the nether regions of my shoulder bag, wedged beneath my checkbook and day planner. Grabbing a handful of tissues, I tried to mop up the mess.

Sheriff Wiggins reached for the intercom. "Tammy Lynn, would you please bring in some paper towels."

Glancing down at the wad of soggy tissues in my hand, I decided to cut my losses and get the heck out of Dodge.

In the outer office, Tammy Lynn stood with her back to me. She held a roll of paper towels in one hand and pressed the intercom button with the other. She was so intent on relaying a message into the speaker, she didn't notice me standing there. I eavesdropped shamelessly while I pretended to search my bag for car keys.

My curiosity was rewarded a minute later when Sheriff Sumter Wiggins barreled out of his office, issuing orders as he went. He never even noticed little ol' me standing off to the side, my head practically buried in my large handbag.

"Have Sam and Mitch meet me at the recyclin' center," he barked. "Notify SLED. Have 'em send their man down ASAP."

And then he disappeared out the door.

SLED? I was all ears. The car keys magically leaped into my hand. Before you could say *supercalifragilisticexpialidocious,* I was once again the caboose in a train of official-looking vehicles headed down the highway.

The recycling center was located behind a chain-link fence off a little-used county road not far out of town. Technically since the recycling center is outside Brookdale city limits, it falls under the sheriff's jurisdiction. I slowed as we approached, flipped on my turn signal, and followed the car ahead of me. Well, at least I attempted to follow the car ahead of me. The drive was blocked by Brookdale police, who I assumed were first to appear on the scene.

The Buick crunched to a stop on the gravel drive. I craned my head for a better look. Large metal bins, lined up like boxcars in a railroad yard, were marked with specific designations: PAPER, GLASS, PLASTIC, ALUMINUM CANS, CARDBOARD. I started to inch forward, but was stopped by a uniformed policeman barely old enough to shave.

"Ma'am, I'm afraid this is as far as you can go. The recycling center is closed."

"Closed?" I stared at a large sign hanging from the gate. I took a wild guess and assumed it contained the hours of operation. For all I knew, it could have been a recipe for oatmeal cookies. They really ought to make signs trifocal friendly. "But, Officer, doesn't that sign over there say the center is open nine to five, six days a week?"

"Sorry, ma'am. You'll have to come back another time."

"It'll only take a minute." I crossed my fingers and got creative. "I've got a big bag of aluminum cans in the trunk of my car. And a huge stack of newspapers," I added for good measure. It wasn't a total lie. I did have a bag of aluminum cans and a stack of newspapers, but they happened to be in my garage, not in the trunk of my car. A little white lie, not a big black one.

"It'll have to wait for another day, ma'am. Sheriff's orders."

I peered around the steering wheel, hoping to catch a glimpse of what was going on. It was hard to tell with a half dozen uniformed men blocking my view. I thought some idle small talk might buy me extra time before I was shooed away. "I'm going green," I announced.

The youthful policeman's eyes widened. He looked at me as though he expected me to change color right then and there. "Excuse me?"

"I'm going green," I repeated. "I think everyone should, don't you?"

"Hmm . . ." He looked a bit uncertain. Probably wondering if I was off my meds.

"It's up to us to save the planet, you know."

Before he could reply, the coroner's van pulled up behind me, and was motioned through. Something was up. Something was definitely up. Surely no one could expect me to leave just when things were starting to get interesting. I knew it wouldn't be long before the mean old sheriff evicted me, so I had to make the most of the time I had left.

"People need to become eco-friendly if we want to take stress off the planet," I said, expanding on my ecology lecture. "Personally I believe all of us should practice the three Rs."

He scratched his head. "Reading, writing, and 'rithmetic? If you don't mind my asking, how's that going to save the planet?"

"Son, get with it," I scolded. "This is the twenty-first century. The three Rs have changed since your grandmother's time." I said this with a straight face. Mind you, I'm well aware I'm a grandmother myself. This young man should thank me for updating his education. "The three Rs stand for reduce, reuse, and recycle."

"Is there a problem, Olsen?" one of the sheriff's deputies called over. He had probably noticed my Buick semipermanently parked at the entrance.

"No, sir," Olsen called over his shoulder. "This nice lady was just leaving."

At the mention of "nice lady," Sheriff Wiggins's head whipped around. I waggled my fingers at him. A friendly gesture, which, by the way, he didn't return.

"Olsen," he growled, "kindly review the meanin' of obstruction of justice for the 'nice lady.' She seems to have forgotten." After giving me the evil eye, he turned back to business.

Keeping my gaze fastened on the sea of uniforms, I shifted into reverse. I watched as a man in jeans, T-shirt, and ball cap gestured repeatedly at a large bin marked PLASTIC. I was about to ease my foot off the brake when I noticed the bottom of the bin had rotted away. A dark icky liquid oozed out of a hole in one corner. I squinted, trying to see what had captured the men's attention.

I couldn't be one hundred percent positive from this distance, but if I had to hazard a guess, I'd say it looked like string. Long, dark string mixed with gooey liquid. But why would string have the sheriff bringing in SLED? And the coroner?

I squinted so hard my eyes nearly crossed. I berated myself for not making an appointment for an eye exam. *String* wasn't quite the right word for what I was seeing. This was finer. More like thread — or hair.

"Ma'am? If you don't want to get on the sheriff's bad side, it's best that you leave."

I nodded absently, my mind busily computing. SLED wasn't called if someone accidentally dumped aluminum cans in a bin reserved for glass bottles. Or for improperly disposing of flashlight batteries. Body parts were another matter, however.

"Ma'am . . ."

It was time for me to go. I had seen enough.

CHAPTER 16

The following afternoon I went out to get my mail, stopping from time to time to pull weeds from the flower beds bordering the drive. I had just reached my hand inside the mailbox when the sheriff's car pulled into the Brubakers' driveway. I watched with interest as Sheriff Wiggins climbed out, then disappeared around the walkway leading to the front.

Now what? I wondered. Had the sheriff actually taken my worry about Rosalie seriously? Or was there another, more sinister reason for his visit? I hoped it had nothing to do with whatever had been found at the recycling center. I knew I should go inside, mind my own business, but my feet seemed to have a will of their own.

With each step toward the Brubakers', I wondered how I was going to explain my visit. I had already traveled the lamebrained borrow-a-cup-of-sugar route. I glanced downward and realized I still held a handful of mail. I leafed through it slowly as I walked along, needing time to form a plan. An electric bill, a Macy's ad, and the answer to my prayer — a mail-order garden catalog. Knowing Earl's penchant for growing things, I was sure he'd appreciate my loaning him a garden catalog. No hurry returning it, I'd tell him. Take all the time in the world.

Belatedly my conscience kicked in. I hesitated just as the walk curved toward the front porch. How rude of me to intrude on a private conversation. I hated nosy neighbors, and now I had become one.

"Mr. Brubaker?" The sheriff's voice carried loud and clear. "Your wife has been reported missin'."

Apparently I was out of sight, but not out of earshot. Should I go, or should I stay? My feet seemed encased in cement and unable to move of their own accord.

"Missing? Rosalie's not missing," Earl replied, sounding irate. "She's visiting the grandkids in upstate New York."

"Then you wouldn't mind givin' us a number where she can be reached."

"It's none of your damn business."

"Sorry, sir, but I'm afraid we need to verify her whereabouts."

"Why? What's wrong?"

"Nothin', I hope. We have the body of an unidentified female in the morgue. We're just tryin' to account for women in the area who have been gone two weeks or longer."

"Well, it's not my wife. Rosalie's at our daughter's in Poughkeepsie."

"If you could give us your daughter's number, we could clear this matter up with a phone call."

"Fine." Earl mumbled a number with an 845 area code. "Call her, you'll see."

" 'Preciate your cooperation. And, sir, one more thing. Would you be willin' to give us somethin' that belongs to your wife? For instance, a hairbrush or a toothbrush."

"What the hell you want that for?" Earl demanded.

"No need to get riled," Sheriff Wiggins soothed in that wonderful baritone of his. "Thing is, if we had an item we could use for DNA, it would help us exclude your wife as a possible victim — and eliminate you as a . . . person of interest."

"Me!" Earl squawked. "No frickin' way! Surely you don't think . . . ?"

"Of course, I could ask Judge Blanchard to sign a search warrant, but I hope that won't be necessary."

Could he really do that? I wondered.

Wasn't that against some constitutional amendment or other? But the sheriff was a shrewd one. He could be bluffing. Have to admit, he had me going for a minute. Sure wish he'd let me hang out with him so I could study his technique.

"Search warrants," the sheriff continued smoothly, "tend to draw a heap of unwanted attention. You know how nosy folks can be."

Humph! Nosy? Was he talking about me?

"Not that you have anythin' to hide, but some folks might jump to the wrong conclusion." The sheriff let the threat hang.

Earl finally relented. "Why the heck not? What've I got to lose?"

I could hear Earl's footsteps recede, then grow louder again as he returned. I knew I should make my getaway, but those darn feet of mine didn't want to budge.

"Here's her hairbrush. Take the darn thing. Now leave me alone."

The door slammed shut.

Before I could duck into the bushes, Sheriff Wiggins rounded the walkway, nearly knocking me off my feet. "Whoa," he said, catching my shoulders just before I toppled into the holly.

"Sheriff . . . um . . . fancy meeting you here."

The grim set of his mouth signaled he

wasn't in the mood for small talk. Didn't that man ever smile? Someone should tell him it takes fewer muscles to smile than it does to frown. But that someone wasn't going to be me. At least not today.

"I . . . ah . . . ," I stammered. "I was bringing Earl a garden catalog." I waved the Jackson & Perkins catalog under his nose to give my story credibility. "Did you know he grows orchids?"

"I didn't come here to discuss hobbies with Mr. Brubaker."

"I'm afraid I might have given you the wrong impression yesterday."

Sheriff Wiggins headed down the walk at a brisk pace. I practically had to run to keep up.

"I never meant to imply that Earl is guilty of any wrongdoing. I just wanted you to be aware that Rosalie's been gone a long time and no one's heard from her. I thought you could make a few calls, confirm that she's safe at her daughter's and that she'd be returning all in one piece."

I winced at my choice of words. All in one piece?

When he didn't reply, I forged ahead. "Where friends are concerned, the Babes and I only want peace of mind."

I wanted to clap my hand over my mouth.

There was that word again. *Piece* or *peace,* no matter which way you spell it, they both sound the same.

As we rounded the walk, he made a beeline for his cruiser. Soon he'd be gone and once again I'd be floundering with unanswered questions. I took a deep breath and blurted, "I see you have Rosalie's hairbrush. Is it true examiners can eliminate a person based on microspectrophotometry?"

Well, that certainly got his attention. He stopped so abruptly he almost left skid marks. "How do y'all come up with these questions?"

I shrugged, not wanting to brag. "I read."

"That Nancy woman again?"

"Uh-uh." I shook my head. "The Internet."

Hooking his thumbs in his belt, he glared down at me. "This is a murder investigation, ma'am. Best leave it to the professionals."

I have to admit, if he meant to intimidate me, it worked. But I didn't want to let him see that. I countered by tilting my head back until I heard vertebrae in my neck crackle and stared him in the eye. "Earl isn't a murderer."

"And you know this how?"

"I just do, that's all."

The sheriff wagged his head and, heaving a sigh, continued toward his car. I hustled to keep up. No easy task for a woman who used to be five feet three before she started shrinking. I make sure to take plenty of calcium. Can't afford to get any shorter.

I caught up with him just as he slid into his cruiser and started the engine. "If Earl *did* harm Rosalie, I probably would have found something when I went through his trash."

"You what!" He looked as if he wanted to throttle me. "What were you thinkin'?" He didn't wait for an answer, which turned out to be a good thing since I didn't have one. "You know, don't you, that I could arrest you for tamperin' with evidence?"

"Unless you want to consider a jar of spaghetti sauce evidence, there wasn't any *evidence* to be found. Besides, it isn't against the law to look through trash that's been left out on the street. Lennie and Ed do it all the time."

Sheriff Wiggins pinched the bridge of his nose. "Lennie and Ed who?"

"Detectives Lennie Briscoe and Ed Green. They're partners on *Law & Order.*" There! I had gone and done it again. How could I ever expect the man to take me seriously if I kept spouting TV trivia?

"Oh, yeah, right," he sighed. "*That* Lennie and Ed. I suppose they're best friends with the lady detective you talk about — Nancy somebody or other." He shifted into reverse and backed down the drive.

"You really ought to watch more TV," I called after him. "You can learn a lot."

I don't think he heard me. The man must think me a complete idiot. I swear my IQ drops to a new low each time we talk. At this rate, I'll soon have no brain cells left.

I stared after him until the patrol car disappeared from view. That man made me so mad that I wanted to stomp my foot like a two-year-old. It should be reassuring to know that by checking out Earl he was at least taking my concerns seriously. Small consolation, that. How hard could it be to track down three missing women? He had all sorts of resources at his command. He had SLED, for crying out loud. I bet I could do an equally good job with far less. And I had one resource he didn't have — I had the Babes.

CHAPTER 17

Megan phoned early Tuesday morning. "Lucky for you, Kate, Dr. Baxter just had a cancellation. Naturally I called you right away."

"Naturally." This is the kind of luck that keeps me from buying a lottery ticket.

"Can you come in this afternoon at two thirty?" Megan sounded so pleased, so proud. Poor girl, she probably harbored the delusion she was doing me a huge favor.

I explored the evil tooth with the tip of my tongue and felt a *zing.* "Sure," I replied, resigned to my fate. "Pencil me in."

"Great. We don't get many cancellations. Turn this one down, you'll have to wait till your scheduled appointment. If that tooth is bothering you, you really need to have the dentist look at it."

I groaned inwardly. Since when had sweet, precious Megan turned into my mother? Next, she'd be scolding me for eating too many sweets. "All right, all right, I'll be there."

"Don't be mad, Kate, but if you don't take care of it, it could abscess."

"Sorry, hon, I didn't mean to snap at you. It's not your fault I'm dental phobic." I had assumed everyone was aware of my little idiosyncrasy. Conceited of me, I know, but I had done everything short of taking out an ad in the *Serenity Sentinel* to advertise the fact.

"You'll see, Kate," Megan gushed. "All the ladies have a crush on him."

"I don't want to fall in love, Megan. I just don't want him to hurt me." I knew I sounded childish, but didn't care.

Megan laughed, obviously not taking my fear seriously. "Dr. Baxter doesn't believe in pain. You'll like him, I promise. Now I've got to go, someone's at the desk. See you this afternoon."

The rest of the morning, I took out my frustration on the kitchen floor, scrubbing the ceramic tile until it was antiseptically clean. Antiseptically clean? That phrase only reminded me of my looming appointment with the irresistible Dr. Baxter.

I had just put away the mop when the phone rang again. I crossed my fingers hoping it was Megan calling to say Dr. Baxter had been unexpectedly called to East Africa and wouldn't be available to see me after all. No such luck.

"Hey, Kate," Diane greeted me. "I wanted to let you know that book you had me order by interlibrary loan just came in. Thought if you happened to be in town this afternoon, you might want to swing by and pick it up."

"Well, that was quick." My appetite for forensics whetted, I'd asked Diane to see if she could find me a copy of forensics text I'd seen advertised.

"I'm not sure why you want this. I leafed through it, and it looks kind of technical."

"Curious is all. If nothing else, it might help put me to sleep. Heaven knows the Sandman, the electronic marvel I paid good money for, hasn't been much help."

"Book's at the front desk. Just ask for it if I'm not here."

"Thanks, Diane. I'll stop by after my dentist appointment."

"Sounds like a fun afternoon," Diane chuckled. "Don't worry, Dr. Baxter's a dream. Everyone loves him."

"So I've heard."

In spite of the ringing endorsements of my friends, I still had my doubts.

Megan, looking perky as could be in pink

dental scrubs with dancing green toothbrushes, handed me a clipboard. With her long hair pulled back into a ponytail, she could easily have passed for sixteen instead of twenty. "Since you're new here, Kate, would you mind filling these out?"

I dutifully filled out the forms, then plopped down in the waiting room and leafed through a magazine to keep from fidgeting. I had to give Dr. Baxter credit. Unlike the sheriff's, his office carried a huge variety of magazines that appealed to every taste and age group. And none more than a month old.

Sheriff Wiggins could also learn a thing or two from the good doctor about decor. The entire waiting room was devoted to golf. Not just ordinary golf, but the big daddy of golf itself — the Masters. As anyone in close proximity of Augusta, Georgia, knows, the Masters Tournament is the real deal. The first week of April, Augusta doesn't just hum; it buzzes. We feel that buzz all the way up the road at Serenity Cove Estates. Friends and relatives, some of whom we haven't heard from since kindergarten, converge in our homes and guest rooms looking for free room and board while scrambling for tickets.

Even nongolfers ooh and aah over the

banks of splashy pink azaleas and lacy white dogwood. It's truly a sight to behold.

An attractive young woman in scrubs identical to Megan's appeared in the doorway and called my name. Megan gave me a thumbs-up as I passed the office area and followed the dental assistant, who introduced herself as Caitlin, down a hallway lined with exam rooms. After I was seated, the young woman clipped a paper bib around my neck and informed me Dr. Baxter would be with me shortly.

Even the exam room carried out the golf motif. Mounted right next to a diagram depicting the ravages of gum disease was an autographed photo of Tiger Woods. Tiger's picture revealed an awesome display of perfect white teeth. The ideal choice for a dentist's office. Someone should tell Tiger that if he ever loses his golf endorsements, he'd make a fortune hawking dental floss. Along with legendary golf prowess, the man looked blessed with cavity-free choppers. Some things just aren't fair.

At precisely two forty-five, I found the reason why ladies took one look and promptly fell in lust with Dr. Jeffrey Baxter. When good looks were handed out, he must have been at the front of the line. He put Brad Murphy to shame. Movie-star handsome, he reminded me of a youthful Rock Hudson, or the more contemporary Ben Affleck.

"Afternoon, Mrs. McCall." He offered his hand. "It's a pleasure to meet you."

I wished I could say the same, but the sentiment stuck in my mouth like glue.

"Megan said you're a good friend of her mother and warned me to be on my best behavior."

His smile was dazzling. He could have been, hands down, the poster boy for every teeth-whitening product on the market. I returned the smile, and made a weak stab at witty repartee. "I see you're a golfer."

"Love everything about golf. Unfortunately my game isn't at a level to support the lifestyle to which I've grown accustomed. I still like to eat three squares a day and have a roof over my head." He gave me a self-deprecatory smile as he snapped on latex gloves.

A killer smile. And charm. A wicked combination.

"Now, what brings you here when you could be out on the course?"

I felt myself tense. Chitchat I could handle. What I didn't like was this getting-down-to-business stuff. "I have a sensitive area in one of my lower molars. On the right."

"Well, let's just take a look, shall we?" He slipped a mask in place and put on a pair of plastic goggles.

I gripped the arms of the chair as I felt it recline. Now, this is the part where I get *really* tense. The part when I have to open my mouth. I watched him pick up a sharp, pointy instrument and steeled myself for the worst. The elusive name of the movie about the evil dentist popped into mind: *Marathon Man,* in which a helpless Dustin Hoffman was tormented by a diabolical Sir Laurence Olivier.

"Don't be nervous. I'm not going to hurt you."

No sooner were the words spoken than I felt that familiar *zing.*

"Sorry about that," Dr. Ben-Affleck-Handsome apologized. He pulled down his mask, removed gloves and goggles. "Looks like you fractured an old filling. I'll know more after Caitlin takes a few X-rays. Afterwards I'll be back to discuss a treatment plan."

I shot the photo of Tiger Woods a resentful glance, then settled back to await my fate.

"How bad is it, Dr. Baxter?" I asked the second he returned carrying my X-rays.

"Call me Jeff." He gave me his megawatt

smile. “Just as I suspected, you’re going to need a crown on that tooth. Good thing, though, if you waited any longer, you’d need a root canal. Have Megan set up an appointment for next week. We’ll get the prep work done and get you fitted for a crown.”

“That sounds painful.” I sounded pitiful; I sounded whiny. I didn’t care. “I should’ve told you I’m dental phobic.”

He patted my shoulder. “Promise you, it won’t hurt a bit.”

“You’re sure?” I asked in a pathetic bid for reassurance.

“Don’t worry — do you mind if I call you Kate? — I’ll numb you up real good. If you like, I’ll give you a little gas just to help you relax.” He held out his hand again. “See you next week. In the meantime, if you have any questions, don’t hesitate to call the office.”

Good news. Bad news.

Good news: I needed a crown. Bad news: I needed a crown. Maybe I hadn’t fallen head over heels in love, but at the promise of no pain in a dentist’s chair, I could be smitten.

At the library, Diane had my book waiting for me on a shelf behind the checkout counter. The flyleaf promised to tell me everything I ever wanted to know about DNA and then some. Wouldn't Jim have been surprised to know my reading tastes have expanded beyond romance novels?

I spotted Janine, who works as a volunteer, industriously shelving books and waved at her. She waved back. I checked out my book and was about to leave when Diane motioned me aside.

"Have you heard the news?" she whispered.

"What news?" I asked. "The only news I've heard is that I need a crown on my back molar."

"The sheriff called a press conference on the courthouse steps for four o'clock."

"Press conference?" My stomach clenched. This sounded serious. I'm not a betting person, but I'd bet the bank this was big news. First the grisly find at the recycling center, then Rosalie's hairbrush. Two and two weren't adding up to coincidence.

"Think I'll stick around. I don't want to wait until the news at six to find out what's going on."

"Me either," Diane agreed. "I'm off at four. Janine and I will meet you there."

I checked my watch. It was only three thirty. Plenty of time to drive from Serenity

Cove to Brookdale. "I'll call Pam."

"I'll call Gloria." Diane was already pulling out her cell phone. "You know how Polly hates being the last one to find things out."

Some things might move slowly here in the South, but news isn't one of them. News or gossip, whichever the case may be, travels at the speed of sound. Both Brookdale and Serenity Cove Estates were well represented on the courthouse lawn.

A news crew from an affiliate station in Augusta had just finished setting up. I recognized several faces from the anchor desk of the nightly news but, since I was having another of those darn senior moments, couldn't put names with the faces. I'd remember, but probably at two in the morning. I also noticed a couple reporters and a photographer from the local paper. Shortly before four o'clock, Pam arrived slightly out of breath with Monica in tow. Polly and Gloria were close behind. Diane and Janine were the last to join our group of Bunco Babes clustered in the shade of a willow oak.

"Looks like we got here in the nick of time." Diane glanced around, taking in the crowd. "I was afraid we were going to be late."

"What do you think the sheriff's going to tell us?" Pam asked.

Gloria hitched the strap of her purse higher on her shoulder. I noticed in her haste she had forgotten to don her jewelry. "Do you suppose the murder victim's been identified?"

I shrugged. "Your guess is as good as mine."

"I wore my new outfit," Polly announced, resplendent in canary yellow pants and top. "You know — in case I get interviewed. Reporters are always on the lookout for eyewitness accounts. I heard bright colors show up best."

Janine smiled at her fondly and patted her arm. "You always look pretty, Polly, no matter what color you wear."

Monica hugged her arms around her body, her expression grim. "I only hope this isn't about body parts."

We didn't have long to speculate before the sheriff stepped out the front door and strode to the podium that had been set up for the occasion. In his hand, he held a prepared statement.

"Ladies and gentlemen," he began in that lovely voice of his. "I called y'all here this afternoon to end speculation and request help from the community in solvin' this case.

"The Brookdale County Sheriff's Department, assisted by the Brookdale Police Department and the South Carolina Law Enforcement Division, have been successful in ascertainin' the identity of a female victim of a homicide. DNA extracted from hair follicles match those of the victim, who has been positively identified as Rosalie Brubaker."

CHAPTER 18

Rosalie?

We were speechless.

I glanced into my friends' faces. Tears silently streamed down Janine's cheeks. Monica stood, arms wrapped around her middle, ghostly pale and tight-lipped. Polly seemed to have donned a wizened mask, for once looking every minute of her age. Gloria's face was drawn and worried as she placed her arm around her mother's shoulders. Pam wept quietly. Diane pressed a hand against her mouth to hold back sobs. As for me, I felt numb all over. As though my entire body had just received a megadose of Novocain. Reaction, I knew, would set in later. Just as it had when Jim died.

The voice of the news anchor from Augusta sliced through our shock. "Could you spell the victim's name for us, Sheriff?"

The sheriff complied. Hearing him do this made the situation all the more surreal. As of one accord, the Babes and I huddled together, our arms wrapped around one another for support, for comfort. We all knew Rosalie in varying degrees either as neighbors or friends or bunco partners. Regardless of how well or how little we knew her, all of us mourned her passing.

The rest of those assembled obviously didn't share our grief. Life went on. Hands flew upward. Questions demanded answers. A cacophony of sound rose from the crowd as reporters shouted questions at Sheriff Wiggins. I wanted to put my hands over my ears to block out the noise.

"One at a time!" The sheriff held up his hand for silence. "I'll take your questions one at a time."

"Sheriff . . . ?" a pert blonde in a navy blue pantsuit and too much makeup called out. "What can you tell us about the cause of death?"

"Sheriff, have you found the murder weapon?" asked a man with a receding hairline and an expensive sport coat. Apparently he hadn't fully grasped the concept of "one at a time" in journalism class.

"We're still lookin' for the murder weapon." Sheriff Wiggins waited a beat while reporters scribbled notes. "I can tell you this, however: The cause of death is listed as blunt-force trauma to the head."

The Babes and I stopped sniffling long enough to exchange puzzled glances. Rosalie had been killed by a blow to the head?

"Could you be more specific, Sheriff?" the man with the receding hairline persisted. "By blunt-force trauma you mean . . . ?"

Sheesh! Even I knew what blunt-force trauma meant. This reporter needed serious help.

"Blunt-force trauma occurs when death is caused by a blow from somethin' such as a pipe, hammer, or similar object."

"Do you have a suspect in custody?" I recognized this to come from a reporter from the weekly *Brookdale Sun.*

" 'Fraid not, Mr. Smythe. This is considered an ongoin' investigation."

"Is there a Mr. Brubaker?" the pert blonde asked.

"Yes, there is a Mr. Brubaker. Earl Brubaker was informed a short time ago of his wife's demise."

The blonde again: "Has he been arrested?"

"At present, no one's been placed under arrest."

"But is he considered a suspect?"

"Tenacious little thing, isn't she?" Polly whispered in my ear. "I can picture her scrapping with the big dogs. Guess that's what it takes."

I nodded absently, my mind on what the sheriff was saying.

"As many of you might already suspect, the spouse, or significant other, is always considered a prime suspect until such time he, or she, is cleared."

In my heart of hearts, I couldn't believe Earl had killed Rosalie. Call me crazy, call me naive, but I just couldn't.

"For the present time," the sheriff continued, "Earl Brubaker is considered a person of interest. And, as such, has been advised not to leave town. Ladies and gentlemen, I believe this concludes the press conference. I will continue to keep you apprised as new developments are brought to light."

With the majestic old courthouse in the background, the television crews did their final wrap-ups, then tucked away their handheld lights and sound equipment before hurrying back to the station in time for the six o'clock news. The rest of the crowd dispersed, heading toward their cars, eager for the relative safety of home and hearth. The Babes and I trailed behind, still stunned by the sheriff's revelation.

"I can't believe Rosalie's dead," Janine murmured.

"Me either," Gloria concurred as she guided her mother toward their parked car.

"Why would someone kill Rosalie?" Diane muttered, digging out her car keys. "It just doesn't make sense."

For me, however, it did make sense in some strange, macabre way. Rosalie had been gone far too long. It was out of character for her to neglect her responsibilities. And neglecting them was just what she had been doing. First, as chairperson of the member-member tournament. Second, and more important, neglecting her husband. But whether it made sense was irrelevant. Knowing the arm we had found on the golf course belonged to a woman we knew and liked made my stomach churn.

And what about Claudia and Vera? I couldn't bring myself to voice the question out loud.

Innocent until proven guilty.

Deserves the benefit of a doubt. The American way.

Rita, as usual, had been the voice of reason when some of the Babes wanted nothing to do with a "person of interest."

We debated what to do in a series of telephone exchanges and a flurry of e-mails. In the end, we did what women through the ages have done in times of death and crises. We baked. Cakes, cookies, and casseroles. We did this more for Rosalie's sake than Earl's, but we did it all the same.

One question, however, needed little debate. None of us wanted to deliver our culinary masterpieces alone. In the end, we agreed to meet at my house and go together to the Brubakers'.

"Ready, ladies?" I asked at promptly four thirty the following afternoon.

"Ready," the Babes chorused.

United, we marched across Loblolly Court bearing gifts of ham, macaroni, and cake.

I rang the bell, and we waited. When that failed, I pounded on the door, and we waited some more.

"Do y'all suppose he's not home?" Connie Sue asked, looking worried.

"I didn't see his car pull out." I knocked again, harder this time.

"The sheriff warned him against leaving town," Rita reminded us.

Before we could turn and march back the way we had come, Earl cracked open the door. Frowning in suspicion, he looked from one of us to the other.

"Earl," I said, assuming the lead, "we wanted to extend our condolences. We wanted you to know how terribly sorry we are about Rosalie."

Considering the wear and tear of the last twenty-four hours, Earl looked both better and worse than the last time I'd seen him. Though still in desperate need of a barber, he'd at least shaved and donned clean clothing. But his basset hound face seemed even more droopy than usual with jowls sagging nearly to his shirt collar. His brown eyes were bloodshot and red-rimmed, but whether from grief or lack of sleep, I had no way of knowing.

"I made you a pot roast." Ever the consummate Southern hostess, Connie Sue held out her aluminum foil–wrapped offering. "It's Thacker's favorite."

Rita handed over a Tupperware container. "Tara, my daughter-in-law, and I fixed you some ham and scalloped potatoes."

Janine took pity on Earl, who looked dumbfounded at being confronted with more choices than Billy's Buffet Barn. "Why don't you invite us in so we can find a place in your refrigerator for all this food?"

He stepped aside, and the parade of women sailed past the dining room and into the kitchen. I paused on the threshold. The kitchen had undergone a remarkable transformation since my late-night visit. Thoroughly cleaned and polished, it was ready for the white-glove test. The granite countertops were free of clutter and shone prettily. The stainless steel sink didn't host a single water spot much less a dirty coffee mug. Even the hardwood floor gleamed. All this elbow grease would have made Rosalie proud.

"Will your daughter be coming down to lend a hand?" I asked, tucking my dish of macaroni and cheese onto a refrigerator shelf next to Connie Sue's pot roast.

"Nah." Earl shook his head. "She said one of the kids has an ear infection. Said she can't get away."

"Is there anyone we can call?" Janine slid her pan of veggie lasagna onto the bottom rack of the fridge. "Anyone at all?"

"Nice of you ladies to ask, but all I got is a brother in Phoenix. The two of us aren't on good terms."

Pam set her trademark carrot cake on the counter. "Rosalie was our favorite bunco sub. She never turned us down — even on short notice."

"She was at the top of our list. We'll miss her." Gloria put the sticky buns next to the carrot cake. "Just zap these in the microwave for fifteen seconds."

Monica placed her take-and-go container of oatmeal raisin cookies alongside the rest of the baked goods. She shook her head sadly. "Rosalie was always so lucky at bunco. Seems every time she subbed, she took home the tiara."

Our supply of small talk depleted, we just stood around the kitchen, none of us looking at anything in particular.

The awkward silence spun out before it was finally broken by Earl. "Can't believe the sheriff actually thinks I might have done something to hurt Rosalie."

I was tempted to remind him that Rosalie had been more than hurt. *Murdered* and *dismembered* were the words that sprang to mind.

The doorbell rang then, sparing us the need for a reply.

"I'll get it," I volunteered, eager to remove myself from the quandary of trying to converse with a "person of interest." As willing as I had been seconds ago to answer the door, I now found myself in no particular hurry to discover who was on the other side of it. I hoped, whoever it was, it wasn't some nosy reporter. I just wasn't in the mood.

My pace slowed until my feet were still moving but just barely. I took in the details of Rosalie's living room as I passed. Rosalie's love for golf was evident everywhere. Plaques and small trophies filling shelves of a glass and chrome wall unit testified to her skill. Photos taken at various golfing events covered several end tables. I stepped inside for a closer look, praying that whoever had been on the front step had grown tired of waiting and left. I recognized most of the people in the photos as living right here in Serenity Cove.

One partner in particular — movie-star handsome — stood out. Dr. Jeffrey Baxter. While, by his own admission, he might not be ready for the pro tour, he acquitted himself admirably among other amateurs. I continued to study the photos. I spotted Dr. Handsome again. This time with Rosalie and Earl as well as an attractive brunette who I assumed was Mrs. Baxter. The caption underneath proclaimed them winners of the His and Hers Classic.

The doorbell pealed twice more in quick succession. I reluctantly stopped perusing photographs of Rosalie, triumphant and smiling, and went to answer the door. "I'm coming, I'm coming," I grumbled under my breath.

I swung open the door and was surprised to find myself face-to-face with Sheriff Sumter Wiggins. He looked equally surprised to see me.

"Miz McCall . . . ?" he drawled. "Didn't

know you and Mr. Brubaker were close."

"Close?" I practiced one of those single-eyebrow lifts at which he excelled. "That, Sheriff, would depend on your definition of close. As it happens, I live catty-corner from the Brubakers. Guess that qualifies us as *close* neighbors. Now" — I kept my tone all prim and proper — "was Mr. Brubaker expecting you?"

He huffed out a breath. "Kindly tell Mr. Brubaker I'm here on official business."

"Very well," I said, still in prim-and-proper mode, "since that's the case, Sheriff, please follow me." I led the way to the kitchen.

Sheriff Wiggins stopped dead in his tracks when he saw the Babes gathered. His eyes swept the assortment of covered dishes and take-and-go containers. His expression lightened a fraction as the reason for my — for our — visit became apparent.

"Ladies . . . ," he greeted the group.

"I don't believe you've met all of the Bunco Babes." Still acting as hostess-at-large, I proceeded to introduce Rita, Janine, and Gloria. "You've already met Connie Sue, Monica, and Pam the day we found . . . *it.*"

He dipped his head in acknowledgment. "How do you do, ladies?"

I marveled to myself. That inbred Southern politeness surfaces every time, even in rough and tough sheriffs who are about to skewer a "person of interest."

"Perhaps we'd best be on our way," Rita offered.

"No!" Earl practically shouted. "I want you ladies to stay. No reason for you to leave. I don't have any secrets."

Fine by me, I thought. I was as curious as the next person to hear what the sheriff had to say. I pulled out a chair from the kitchen table and plunked myself down. Pam followed suit. Connie Sue and Monica did likewise, while Gloria and Rita leaned against the counter, arms folded.

The sheriff frowned, evidently none too pleased at having seven extra sets of ears present. Since it didn't appear we were about to budge, he pulled out his little black notebook, prepared to do business.

"I suppose I need an alibi?" Earl asked, his voice not quite steady.

"Not yet. Time of death hasn't been determined."

"Establishing time of death isn't an exact art," I whispered to Pam, proud I had done my homework and read chapter thirteen.

The sheriff gave me one of his looks, and I lapsed into silence.

"I came by to ask if your wife had any enemies. Anyone who might want her dead?"

"Hell, no," Earl exploded. He ran his hand over his shaggy hair. "Unless she pissed someone off at the golf course . . ."

Sheriff Wiggins shifted his considerable bulk. For the first time in our brief acquaintance, he looked uncomfortable. "The next subject is of a rather personal nature, Mr. Brubaker. If you'd rather these ladies leave . . ."

Earl threw up his hands. "How many times do I have to tell you I've nothing to hide? Ask away."

"How would you describe your relationship with your wife?"

"The same as any married couple who's been married thirty years. She does her thing, I do mine."

Was that how it was supposed to be after thirty years? I hoped not. Call me a romantic, but I believe in togetherness. Growing older, growing closer. That had been my hope for Jim and me.

"Do you think your wife might have been seeing someone?"

"If you mean 'Was Rosalie having an affair?' the answer's no."

"Help me out here, Mr. Brubaker. If

you're as innocent as you claim, give me something to go on. Think, man, is there anyone your wife showed an unusual interest in?"

The seconds ticked by. The Babes and I looked from one to another, scarcely making a sound. Earl scrubbed his hand over his jaw, looking vaguely perplexed at finding it clean-shaven. I could almost hear little gears grinding inside his head.

"Yeah," he said at last, "there is this one guy Rosalie was always calling over."

The sheriff's ballpoint hovered over a page in his little black book. "And who might that person be?"

"The guy's name is Bill. Bill Lewis."

Chapter 19

My jaw dropped, nearly hitting the table, when I heard Earl mention Bill Lewis. A collective gasp rose from the Babes.

Earl was on a roll now. "Yeah, that's right. Bill Lewis. He's a part-time ranger on the golf course, part-time handyman. Rosalie was forever calling him to come over to fix this or that around the house. She'd always arrange for him to come when she was damn well sure I wouldn't be home."

Sheriff Wiggins dutifully recorded the information in his little book. "By any chance, does Bill Lewis live in Serenity Cove Estates?"

I couldn't believe my ears. Call me crazy, call me besotted, but to my way of thinking, Bill Lewis was an even less likely candidate to kill Rosalie than Earl. I felt, rather than saw, Pam's sympathetic glance slide my way.

Earl nodded vigorously. "He not only lives here, but he's president of the Woodchucks."

The sheriff did his one-eyebrow-lift thing. "The woodchucks?"

Gloria cleared her throat to draw the sheriff's attention. "Woodchucks is the name of the woodworking club here in Serenity Cove."

Earl rubbed beads of sweat from his forehead with the back of his hand. "Bill Lewis either owns or has access to every power tool on the planet. Who's better equipped to dismember a body?"

Monica pressed a hand against her mouth, her skin that nasty olive green. Connie Sue draped an arm around her shoulders. "Gentlemen, if y'all excuse us. I think we've overstayed our welcome."

One look at Monica's face, and Janine flanked her other side. "Our friend needs some air," she explained. Together with Connie Sue, Janine herded Monica toward the door.

"B-but . . . ?" I protested. I don't know which I hated more, not knowing the outcome of the sheriff's questioning or watching Monica barf.

"Say good-bye, Kate," Gloria ordered, her voice stern.

Pam took one of my arms, Rita, the other, and they escorted me from the house. I had been cleverly outmaneuvered.

Once outside, I sputtered, "Imagine! Earl practically accused Bill of killing Rosalie."

"Calm down, Kate." Pam patted my back as we walked down the Brubaker drive and crossed the street heading toward my house. "Emotions are running a bit high right now. People are bound to say and do all kinds of crazy things."

"Just because a man owns power tools, saws, and such doesn't mean a thing," I fired back. "Like we said before, if that was the case, practically every man in the world would be a suspect."

Monica's normal color was gradually returning. "Why would Earl say such a thing if it wasn't true?"

"Maybe Earl's the jealous type," Connie Sue suggested. "You never know with men."

Rita reached her Honda Accord parked in my driveway and paused, her hand on the door. "Rosalie used to complain at bridge that when it came to doing things around the house, Earl would either be on the golf course or puttering in his garden."

"Bill can fix just about anything," Gloria agreed. "Rosalie probably had him on speed dial."

Connie Sue smoothed her honey blond bob. "Y'all, I said it once, I'll say it again. Could be Earl's the jealous type."

"Think about it, ladies," Janine said with a wicked grin. "Picture Bill Lewis in a tool belt — then picture Earl."

"Janine!" Gloria pretended to be shocked.

Connie Sue giggled. "Earl doesn't even come in a close last."

The phone rang just as I was about to prepare dinner. It was our son, Steven — there I go again — is it our son, or my son, since Jim died?

"Hope I'm not interrupting anything important."

Who was he kidding? Was he trying to be funny? A widow's life in a retirement community — even one for "active" adults — isn't filled with activities so important they can't come to a screeching halt for her to take an occasional phone call from her only son.

"Of course you're not interrupting, dear. How are you?"

"I'm fine. How about yourself?"

"Everything's fine. I can't complain."

"Great. Good to hear it."

"I haven't heard from you in a while." I try not to sound whiny and clingy, but I ask you, how hard is it to call a poor widowed mother once a week? How many times did I have to remind the boy that I was in labor with him for eighteen hours?

"Been busy, Mom." I could hear the babble of voices in the background. "I'm getting ready to go on another buying trip."

"Where to this time?"

"Sri Lanka."

My geography of that part of the world is a bit fuzzy. I'd have to look up Sri Lanka on the Internet later. "Mmm. Sounds . . . interesting."

"Yeah, I'm looking forward to it. I leave day after tomorrow."

I twisted the phone cord around my finger. I felt a little wistful. Steven and I used to be close, but since his move to New York I feel like I'm slowly being phased out of his life. Exciting job, exciting city, boring mother. "How long will you be gone?"

"A couple weeks, I guess. The company is looking to expand one of its product lines and wants me to scout out the situation. You know, do a preliminary report. Take a look around. Bring back samples."

"That's wonderful, Steven. I'm proud of you." And I was. I could feel my chest swell with maternal pride and affection. I was happy to learn that the company he worked for recognized his talent. "Our boy is a winning combination," Jim used to say, "my brains and your good looks." Hearing that always made me smile.

"Listen, Mom . . ." He hesitated.

"Yes, dear, go ahead," I encouraged. It was good to hear him call me *Mom* and not the more formal *Mother* that Jennifer prefers to call me.

"I'll cut to the chase. I talked to Jen this morning."

"Ohh . . ." I braced myself for what I feared would come next.

"She wants you to come out to LA and stay with her and Jason."

I stopped twisting the phone cord, pulled out a kitchen chair, and sat down. "Yes, dear, I remember the conversation."

"I just wanted to let you know that I disagree with her."

"Attaboy!" I said, smiling. Maybe Steven and I were still on the same wavelength after all.

"You'd end up being Jen's live-in, unpaid nanny to her girls," he continued. "I told her you were too old for that kind of stuff."

Too old? I felt myself deflate like a balloon after the Macy's Thanksgiving Day Parade. "Steven, it's not a matter of being too old to keep up with Jillian and Juliette," I hastened to correct his misconception. "The fact is I'm very happy where I am."

"You mean in Serenity Cave?"

I huffed out a breath. "*Cove,* Steven, not cave. Serenity *Cove* Estates." To Steven's way of thinking, if it wasn't Manhattan, one might as well be in Siberia. Sometimes I wonder if he even remembers how to spell *Toledo.*

"Jen told me what's going on down there. Is it true someone was chopped into little pieces and scattered all over the golf course?"

"You know how your sister tends to be a drama queen." I picked up a pencil and started to doodle on a notepad I kept by the phone. "It's not as bad as you make it sound."

"Then it's not true?"

"I didn't say that. It's just, well, not exactly the way you described it."

"Mom, I don't have time for word games. Define 'not exactly.' "

"There weren't body parts all over the golf course. There was only an arm — and it wasn't scattered. It was in a Wal-Mart bag."

There was a long pause, followed by the tinkle of what sounded like ice in a glass. I could use a drink myself about now. I had survived the teen years, but now that my children were adults, I wasn't so sure I'd make it without hitting the bottle.

"Oh, well" — Steven found his voice at

last — "the Wal-Mart bag does add a certain touch of class." I could almost hear the sarcasm bounce from satellite to satellite all the way from Manhattan to Serenity Cove. "One arm, or a dozen, still means there's a maniac on the loose."

I couldn't very well deny this, but forged ahead. "It's not quite as bad as you make it sound, dear," I said, trying to sugarcoat the grisly facts. I wanted to see for myself if a spoonful of sugar really did help the medicine go down — in a most delightful way, of course. "Sheriff Wiggins called it an isolated incidence of violence."

"That place isn't safe, Mother."

I noticed he'd switched from the less-formal *Mom* to the more-formal *Mother.* Went to show how upset he was. Sweet of him to worry — even though it wasn't warranted.

"What do *you* think I should do, Steven?" I asked. "Come to New York and stay with you?" There! I had tossed out the challenge just to hear his reaction. I didn't have long to wait.

"No, of course not, Mother. Coming to New York and living with me wouldn't be practical for either one of us."

That's my boy. Smart like I said.

"I was thinking of something more along

the lines of an assisted-living facility."

I gasped at the notion. *Assisted-living?* The instant I recovered from my shock, I dug into my bag of righteous indignation, and let him have it with both barrels. "Steven James McCall! Bite your tongue."

By the time I finished telling him exactly what I thought of his idea, I doubted the words *assisted-living facility* were still in his vocabulary.

"Have a safe trip to Sri Lanka, dear," I managed to say pleasantly enough at the end of my diatribe, and disconnected.

I sat at the kitchen table for a long time afterward staring out the window at nothing in particular. I suppose, in his own way, Steven meant well. I wish he'd come down for a visit. Then he'd see that I was happy, healthy, and active. And not elderly or demented, as Jen feared. Or ready for assisted living, as he suggested. Didn't either of the children read the newspapers? Didn't they know that sixty was the new fifty?

CHAPTER 20

Bill Lewis had said he'd be over at four to replace my broken ceiling fan with the one that was no longer back-ordered. I'd driven to Lowe's in the morning to pick it up. Just as I suspected, Bill pulled into the driveway a full ten minutes ahead of schedule. I watched him climb out of his Ford pickup and come around to the side door.

"Am I too early?" he said by way of a greeting.

"Not a bit." One glance into those Paul Newman baby blues, and I was glad I had remembered to put on lipstick. I held the door wide to allow him and the big metal toolbox he carried to pass through.

"What kind of fan did you end up with?" he asked as he followed me into the kitchen.

"A white one," I answered promptly, pleased with my purchase.

"White, eh?"

There it was again. That smile . . . and

that tool belt. How lucky could a girl get? He nodded his approval. "Can't go wrong with white."

"I know." I choked back a giggle. I couldn't help it. He had that kind of effect on me. "White goes with everything."

"Never know what I might need to get the job done," Bill explained, setting a toolbox the size of a steamer trunk on my kitchen floor. "Guess I'd better get started. I'll have you up and running in no time."

I was already up and running, but I couldn't very well tell him that. He'd turn tail and run. Suddenly I was faced with the same dilemma as before. Should I make myself scarce? Or stick around . . . just in case?

And once again I decided to stick around — just in case.

I looked about the kitchen for a project, something to keep me busy while he worked on the fan. I wanted to stay close without being obvious. My eyes rested on the houseplants on the sill. They were starting to look in need of attention. Translation: They were in dire need of water and a little TLC.

I set out to impress Bill with my green thumb. I rummaged under the sink and pulled out supplies. Watering can, plant fertilizer, mister, and moisture meter. While on my way through the garden center at Lowe's, I'd picked up one of those moisture-meter gadgets. I had been meaning to get one for years, but never got around to it. The cost would be negligible compared with that of replacing ferns and ficus on a regular basis.

"I'll need that stepladder of yours out in the garage," he said, then went off to get it.

While he was gone, I carefully measured liquid fertilizer into a watering can, then added the prescribed amount of water. At least I'd look like I was an expert in the houseplant department. Bill didn't have to know I'm a regular Dr. Kevorkian when it comes to growing things.

Wish I would have thought to have a pie in the oven. Apple pie. Nothing like the aroma of fresh-baked apple pie to go straight to a man's heart. Belatedly, I remembered apple pie was the culprit that brought Bill and me together in the first place. If the juices from my pie hadn't baked over, causing the kitchen to fill with smoke, it might've taken weeks, or even months, to discover the ceiling fan was broken.

Bill returned with the stepladder and positioned it under the defunct fan. Next he opened the box containing the new fan and proceeded to read the directions. I watched, amazed. A man who actually read directions! My earlier impression was confirmed. Bill was, indeed, quite a guy.

"Simple yet practical." He gave me a thumbs-up. "Looks as though this will do nicely. Some folks go for all that fancy stuff, but I tend to think in the long run simple is better. Fewer things to go wrong."

Hmm . . . ? Maybe I had made the wrong choice after all. Things going haywire would have been the perfect excuse to have him make another house call. I stifled my disappointment, and asked, "Can I get you something to drink? Water or iced tea?"

I could use a little something myself — a cold shower perhaps? The man had me babbling like a teenager.

"No thanks, Kate. Maybe when I'm finished."

Just then I heard a knock. I answered the door and found Pam on my doorstep, a book in her hand and a phony smile on her face. "Hope I'm not interrupting anything important. Mind if I come in?"

In the blink of an eye, she was seated at my kitchen table. "Hi, Bill," she said, giving him that same insincere kind of smile. "Don't mind me."

"No problem." Bill went about the task of attaching blades to my new fan.

"What brings you here at this hour?"

"I came to return this." Pam tapped the cover of the book she had brought with her. "I found it while I was cleaning this afternoon and thought I'd better bring it back."

I frowned when I read the title. "That's not mine."

"Really?" Now it was Pam's turn to frown. "Are you sure? I could have sworn this was yours."

"You know I never read science fiction."

It wasn't like Pam to just drop in for no particular reason. And it certainly wasn't like her to drop by to return a book she'd never borrowed. Come to think of it, Pam seldom borrowed books.

"Can I get you something to drink?" I offered to be polite, yet hoped she'd refuse.

"Sure. Iced tea would be great."

I got two glasses from the cupboard, took the pitcher of iced tea from the fridge, and poured us each a glass. "I'm surprised you're not at home fixing dinner."

"Dinner's cooking in the Crock-Pot. I started it this morning." Pam leaned back and crossed her legs. "This way I've got all afternoon to do as I please."

"Great." But was it? As much as I always enjoy Pam's company, I had hoped to use this time to get to know Bill better while he worked. But a glance at Pam's relaxed pose told me she planned to "sit a spell," as they say in the South.

For the next half hour, we chatted about this and that before moving on to more important issues. Such as the character changes in our favorite TV series. Pam liked the new actor who replaced a longtime lead, but I wasn't so sure. "Give him time," Pam counseled. "He'll grow on you."

Out of the corner of my eye, I could see work on the ceiling fan was progressing nicely. It was clear this wasn't the first one Bill had installed. Reluctantly I swung my attention back to my guest. "More tea?" I asked, noticing Pam's glass was empty.

Before she could respond, the front doorbell chimed. "Excuse me," I said to Pam as I got up to answer the door. I was surprised to see Connie Sue standing on the porch.

"Connie Sue! What brings you here?"

She gave me an apologetic smile. "I need to borrow your springform pan."

I stood aside. "Sure, come on in."

Connie Sue headed straight for the kitchen, where she stood, head cocked to one side, hands on hips, and studied the ceiling fan Bill had just finished assembling. "White?"

"You have something against white?" I

said, feeling somewhat put off by her tone. "White goes with everything. You can't go wrong with white."

"Don't get me wrong, sugar. It's nice, but . . . awfully plain. I thought you might go for something a little more . . . high-tech. Stainless steel, maybe with a remote."

"Simple and practical are more my style. Fewer things to go wrong," I said, parroting Bill's words.

Connie Sue and Pam exchanged glances. Pam rose. "Well, guess I'd better go home and stir the Crock-Pot."

Connie Sue plunked herself down in the chair Pam had just vacated, and looked like she intended to stay awhile. Without asking, I poured her a glass of iced tea.

"Don't think we've met." She smiled at the man on the stepladder. "You must be Bill. After hearing so much about you, it's a pleasure to meet you. I'm Connie Sue Brody."

"Bill Lewis." Bill returned the smile. "How do you do?"

No fancy speech from Bill, just a plain old Midwestern perfunctory response. Seemed like simple and practical could describe more than ceiling fans.

Connie Sue turned her attention back to me. "I thought I'd surprise Thacker and make his favorite dessert — praline cheese-cake."

I glanced pointedly at the kitchen clock. At this rate I'd never get in a word or two with Bill before he finished installing the fan. "Isn't it rather late to start making a cheesecake?"

"Of course it is, silly. I'll make it first thing tomorrow morning, right after tennis."

Of course, I thought as I started rummaging through a cabinet for my springform pan. Don't use the darn thing much anymore. Maybe I should just give it to Connie Sue in case she's tempted to show up next time I entertain a blue-eyed devil.

"I could swear you had one of these," I said when I finally extracted the pan from the bottom of a stack of baking tins of various shapes and sizes.

"I do, sugar, and I looked high and low for it. For some strange reason, I can't seem to find it."

I set the pan on the counter. "Shouldn't you be home tending Thacker's dinner?"

"You're a sweetie to worry about Thacker, but never you mind, I turned the oven down low before coming over. I thought it'd be nice to sit a spell."

I listened to Connie Sue ramble on with half an ear. Trying not to be too obvious, I kept shooting glances in Bill's direction. He had the old fan down, and was getting ready to put the new one up.

The doorbell rang again. "S'cuse me," I muttered as I rose to answer the door.

"Rita!" Who next? A vacuum cleaner salesman?

Rita held up a brown paper bag. "Surprise!"

"It certainly is," I said, making no move to stand aside. Rude, I know, but I felt as if my foyer had suddenly become Grand Central Station.

"Mind if I come in for a minute?"

"No, of course not." With a sigh of surrender, I stepped aside. Where were my manners? Usually I'm pleased as punch when one of my friends happens to drop by. But not today. Today I needed to be available — in case Bill needed my help.

I led the way into the kitchen. Connie Sue stood the minute she spied Rita. "Well, sugar," she said to me, "gotta run. I need to check on that nice pork loin I'm fixing. Thacker complains if it gets too dry."

Connie Sue departed as abruptly as she had arrived. It wasn't until I heard her pull out of the drive that I noticed the springform pan still sitting on the table. I shook my head and reached for the pitcher of tea.

"Care for some?" I asked, already knowing the answer.

"You never asked what's in the bag," Rita scolded.

"I haven't a clue."

"Rhizomes."

"What am I supposed to do with rhizomes?" I asked. "Eat them?"

"No, no, you plant them." She reached into the bag and pulled out a brown thing. "Next spring, you'll have beautiful iris growing in your flower beds."

I took a sip of my tea, noting as I did so that all the ice had melted. "Thanks, Rita, but you know I don't exactly have a green thumb." By this time, I didn't care whether Bill knew that. My thumb wasn't green. It was brown. Brown, brown, brown!

"Nothing to it, Kate. September or October are the best months to plant here in the South."

Rita was on a roll. Along with bridge, gardening was her passion. It didn't seem to bother her that it wasn't mine. She talked nonstop for the next half hour. Bill seemed to tune out the sound of Rita droning on and on and just went about his task.

Rhizome became a new word in my vocabulary. I learned gypsum is an excellent soil conditioner and improves clay soil such as we have here in South Carolina. Rita also introduced the term *vernalization.* I promised myself I'd try to use it next time I played Scrabble with the grandkids. Rita also warned me against the dangers of overwatering, and cautioned against the common mistake of planting irises too deeply.

By the time she finished, or perhaps ran out of breath — I'm not sure which — the new ceiling fan had been installed, and the old one hauled out to the trash. I watched in dismay as Bill gathered up his tools. We had barely exchanged a handful of words.

He snapped his giant tool chest shut. "All done," he said. "This ought to last a good long time, but call me if you have any problems."

I felt a moment's panic as he stared to leave. I might see him again only across a crowded golf course. I needed to say something before he walked out of my life, maybe for good. Needed to say something preferably witty or clever. "How much do I owe you?" I asked.

I groaned inwardly. Witty and clever, I wasn't.

"Don't worry about it. Glad to be of help." He nodded to Rita, then left.

Rita waited until the sound of Bill's pickup truck faded, then calmly finished her tea and rose to her feet. "Guess you know all you need to about irises."

"Rita, would you kindly explain what the heck is going on?" I demanded. "First Pam tries to return a book that doesn't belong to me. Next Connie Sue asks to borrow a springform pan, but leaves without taking it with her. And last but not least, you show up on my doorstep to give me a tutorial on growing iris."

Rita pursed her lips. "Kate, you're forgetting what the sheriff said earlier about power tools."

"What has *that* got to do with it?"

"Everything. Sheriff Wiggins said the killer has access to power tools. Bill Lewis has more power tools than all the rest of the men in Serenity Cove Estates put together. And don't totally disregard Earl Brubaker's accusations that Bill and Rosalie might have been an item."

Appalled, I stared at her. "Surely you aren't suggesting . . ."

Rita shrugged. "A woman can't be too careful."

Long after Rita left, I sat at the kitchen table idly watching the blades of my new fan whirl around and around. I didn't know whether to be angry with my friends or to hug them. In the end, hugs won out. Instead of me rallying the troops, they had rallied around me in an all-out, albeit misguided, attempt to protect me from the Bill, the nicest and best-looking tool guy in Serenity Cove.

Chapter 21

I sat bolt upright in bed. My heart pounded like a jackhammer inside my chest. Had I been dreaming? Or had it been real? Had a shrill bloodcurdling scream awakened me from a dead sleep?

Then I heard it again.

An unmistakable cry of pain. An eerie, high-pitched howl that made the tiny hairs at the nape of my neck stand at attention. A sound that filled me with terror. And seemed to be coming from just outside my bedroom.

What was it? Who was it?

Not stopping to weigh the consequences, I bounded out of bed and flung open the French doors that opened onto the deck that ran along the back of the house. I stood there in my nightclothes, shivering in the chill night air, trying to see through the murky darkness into the fringe of woods beyond. The only sound I heard now was the rustle of wind through the boughs of the trees.

I took a half step forward and recoiled when my bare foot encountered something hard and cold. I peered down at it — and sucked in a breath. Not believing what I was seeing, I stooped down to examine the object more closely.

A bone.

Long, pale, but undeniably a bone.

Part of a leg? Part of an . . . *it?* My mind refused to go there. I stared at the object as though it might disappear if I as much as blinked. I stretched out a hand to touch it, but stopped myself in time. Who had brought this grisly offering to my doorstep? And why?

Even more important, who had screamed in such anguish?

The thought sent goose bumps chasing up and down my spine. What if the person who brought the bone was still present, watching, hidden deep in the woods? I straightened slowly, wrapping my arms around my body for warmth. Keeping my eyes fastened on the woods beyond, I retreated backward step by cautious step until my feet were firmly planted on thick carpet. My hands shook as I turned the lock. I rattled the door a final time to make sure it was securely fastened, then reached for the phone and punched in 911.

My teeth were chattering so hard I had to repeat myself twice but finally managed to stammer the words *scream* and *bone.* The dispatcher on the other end of the line promised to send an officer to the scene.

"H-hurry," I stuttered.

"Do you want me to stay on the line until someone gets there?" the disembodied voice inquired.

I thought of how I had charged out of the bedroom barefoot and in my nightgown without a thought to my own safety. How dumb can you get? I berated myself. Staying on the line now with the dispatcher would be a little like closing the barn door after the horse ran off. "Thank you, but no. I'll be fine," I said, then hung up.

I threw on a pair of sweats while waiting for a deputy to arrive. For good measure I pulled a pair of woolen socks over feet that felt like blocks of ice. I'm not a particularly patient person. The minutes ticked by with frustrating slowness. I went about the house turning on every light in every room, and finally when the house blazed like a Christmas tree, I put on the kettle for tea. After what I had just been through, there was no chance in hell I was going to get any more sleep tonight.

A cruiser from the Brookdale County Sheriff's Department arrived within ten minutes. Ten minutes that seemed more like an hour. I recognized Deputy Preston from our encounter at the campground the moment he stepped out of the car. I was disappointed he hadn't deemed lights and siren appropriate for the occasion. I thought sadly of *Law & Order* and my beloved *CSI*, and realized life doesn't often imitate art.

I watched from the kitchen window as he walked toward the house, and answered the door before he had a chance to ring the bell. "Did you bring backup?" I asked, looking up and down the street for reinforcements.

"Ah . . . no, ma'am," he replied. "This is a Code Two."

I stared at him uncomprehendingly. Obviously I was the one who wasn't up to code. Something else I'd have to look up in *The Complete Idiot's Guide to Forensics.* "Did the dispatcher tell you I heard someone scream?" I shuddered at the memory of that horrible sound.

Preston scratched his head. "Didn't say anything about a scream. Said the caller mumbled something about being out of cream and claimed she found a bone. Told me I better come check things out."

"I'm not out of cream — in fact, I never even use cream. Too many calories." I digressed, but who could blame me after what I'd just been through? "I called because I heard a scream."

"Did you see anyone?"

"No, I went outside for a look around, but it's too dark to see much."

Preston's thick black brows drew together in a frown. "Let me warn you, ma'am, going out like that probably wasn't a good idea. There's a killer on the loose, you know."

As if I needed a reminder. I was, after all, one of the original discoverers of that sad fact.

Excusing himself, he switched on the industrial-size Maglite he carried, and proceeded to inspect the premises. I could hear his radio crackle as he made his way around the perimeter of the house, and felt comforted he could call for backup if need be. His inspection finally over, he returned to the door where I stood waiting.

"Didn't find anything that looked suspicious, ma'am. Whoever, or whatever, didn't leave any trace behind. Now show me this bone you found."

I led the way. French doors opened onto the deck from both the master bedroom as well as the great room. Since the great room was closer, I chose those. "There," I said, pointing to the offending discovery I'd made earlier.

"It's a bone all right," he agreed, squatting down on his haunches much as I'd done earlier to examine it.

Duh! I didn't need an anthropology degree to know a bone when I saw one. I kept my comments to myself, saying instead, "Well, aren't you going to photograph it?"

He looked at me blankly.

"You know, snap pictures like they always do on TV."

"Yeah, sure, I was just about to do that." He left and returned with a camera, then took a photo from two different angles.

"Good," I said, nodding approval. "What's next?"

"I'll take it back and have it sent to the lab in Columbia for proper identification." He started to reach for it, but froze when he heard my sharp intake of breath.

"You can't do that!" I cried, aghast at his technique — or lack thereof. "Where are your latex gloves? Where's the evidence bag?"

"Right," he muttered. "Be back in a flash."

Good as his word, he returned promptly, snapped on a pair of gloves, and dropped the bone into a bag marked EVIDENCE. "Guess that about does it."

"Guess so." I rubbed my arms, feeling a bit let down now that the adrenaline rush had subsided. I trailed after him through the house.

His studied me with kind, dark eyes before he turned to go. "Go back to bed, ma'am. Try to get some sleep."

Fat chance of that happening, I wanted to snap. Instead, I mustered a smile and thanked him.

"You did what?"

"Kate McCall, what were you thinking?"

"You could have been killed."

"Weren't you scared?"

I was being bombarded with questions after telling my friends about my latest escapade. The four of us, Connie Sue, Pam, Monica, and me, were gathered around our usual table at the Cove Café. Pam and I had just finished Tai Chi; Connie Sue and Monica had come straight from land aerobics.

"Once your kids find out what you've been up to, they'll have you out of here in a New York minute," Pam cautioned. "It'll be Assisted Living 'R Us."

Monica shuddered. "What if you had

found a . . . a . . . ?"

"But I didn't," I said. "What I did find, however, was a new theory. A really scary new theory."

Connie Sue speared the remaining grape at the bottom of her fruit cup. "Sugar, I'm not sure I want to hear this."

I glanced around the restaurant, but no one seemed to be paying us any mind. "I think there's a serial killer on the loose."

My announcement was met with stunned silence.

Pam was the first to regain her speech. She leaned closer and lowered her voice. "Surely, Kate, you can't be serious."

"I'm dead serious." I winced at the poor choice of words, but continued undaunted. "We still have no clue where Vera and Claudia have disappeared. What about the scream I heard last night? What about the bone I found literally on my doorstep? What if the killer is escalating?"

"Escalating? What the devil does that mean?" Monica looked more angry than confused.

"They use that term on that TV show *Criminal Minds* all the time," Pam said, taking pity on her. "It means things are speeding up."

"Ohh."

"It means *we* have to speed things up. We can't just sit back and wait for the sheriff to figure out who killed Rosalie. We need to think about Vera and Claudia. What if the sheriff is so focused on Rosalie's murder, he isn't trying to find *them?* What if that bone I found is *theirs?*" I paused, waiting for this to sink in.

Monica's face took on a mulish expression. "Things like that just don't happen here in Serenity Cove Estates."

Connie Sue shifted uncomfortably. "I don't cotton to the notion of a serial killer literally right here in our own backyards."

"Then prove me wrong." I tossed my napkin down, a symbolic gesture, since gauntlets were scarce here at the Cove Café. "Let's find Vera and Claudia and show the sheriff what the Bunco Babes can do."

Chapter 22

SERIAL KILLER STALKS SERENITY. Or perhaps KILLER IN THE COVE. I could see the lurid headlines already. Granted, a serial killer here in Serenity Cove was just a theory, but with two women still unaccounted for, in my mind at least, it was a very plausible one. I'd been awakened from a deep sleep by a scream that sounded human. If that weren't bad enough, someone had left a bone — a bone — on my doorstep!

I had been sorely tempted to call the sheriff and discuss my serial-killer theory with him. My fingers had actually been poised to dial his number when I'd changed my mind. Though it had taken a while to get it through my thick skull, I finally accepted the fact that the sheriff preferred to work alone. He obviously didn't appreciate the insights that I'd so generously provided. He had offered nothing in return. No,

Sheriff Sumter Wiggins didn't strike me as the sharing sort. Maybe he had been an only child. I decided I'd keep my theories to myself for the time being.

And the first order of business was to show the man the Babes could triumph where he faltered. We'd launch a no-holds-barred search for our friends. If this failed to produce results, we'd raise a hue and cry the likes of which had never been heard in Serenity Cove and vicinity.

With this at the top of my to-do list, I called Diane. She said she had a lead on contacting Claudia's sons, but needed a little more time. Next I talked to Tara, who had been trying to find out anything she could about Vera's daughter, hoping it would lead to Vera's whereabouts. Nancy Drew wouldn't sit around and twiddle her thumbs. And neither would I.

I took it upon myself to do a little sleuthing. And I'd start at the Cove Café.

This would be a perfect time to kill two birds, so to speak, with one stone. I'd have dinner there and, at the same time, do some investigating. With a bit of luck, I'd be able to wheedle more information out of Beverly. Hopefully she'd be feeling chatty after the generous tip I'd left on my last visit.

The café was busy, but not too busy. Only

about a third of the tables were occupied. A chalkboard announced liver and onions as the night's early-bird special. I know liver is good for you. Monica, or maybe it was Connie Sue, had lectured me on its benefits. She stressed how it was a good source of iron and loaded with B vitamins. Onions aside, my observation is that a person either loves or hates liver and onions. File me in the latter category.

I spied a table for two in what I hoped was Beverly's section and sat down. I guessed right, because Beverly headed in my direction and greeted me with a warm smile. "Back again, I see."

"It was either dinner here or frozen chicken potpie."

She handed me a menu. "Funny, somehow I didn't take you for a liver and onions fan."

"I'm not," I admitted, glanced over the menu. No sense flirting with fat grams and carbs on a night when lettuce would do just as well. "I'll have a chef's salad, ranch dressing on the side."

"What can I get you to drink?"

"Just water."

Waiting for my meal to arrive gave me time to think about how best to approach Beverly with my questions about Vera without seeming obvious. I wondered if there was a text titled *The Complete Idiot's Guide to Interrogation.*

"There you go, hon." Beverly set my salad in front of me along with a water glass. "I'll check back in a few."

I took my sweet old time, daintily cutting strips of turkey and slicing wedges of tomato into bite-size pieces. Poured a little ranch dressing here, poured a little ranch dressing there. I chewed slowly, stopping frequently to take sips of water. My ploy evidently worked, because the café began to empty.

"More water?" Beverly asked.

"Sure, fill it up." At this rate I'd be running relay races all night between bed and bathroom. But no sacrifice was too great. On *Law & Order* reruns, Detectives Lennie Briscoe and Ed Green were my role models. If they could sit through numerous stakeouts without complaining about full bladders, who was I to complain?

"How's it going, Beverly?" I asked.

"I'm getting too old for this kinda work. Should've listened to my mother years ago and learned to type. All I've got to show for years on the job are bunions and varicose veins."

I wanted to say, "Sit down, take a load off." A phrase I heard in those old James Cagney and Humphrey Bogart movies.

Instead I said, "Still no Vera?"

"Nope, and I'm still pulling doubles." Beverly wandered off to clear a nearby table.

I speared a cherry tomato and sent it skittering across the table and onto the floor. My interrogation technique definitely needed fine-tuning. I still hadn't learned anything of value. I wasn't about to leave until I found out something — anything. Even if it meant sitting here until Beverly kicked me out. It dawned on me I didn't even know Vera's last name. Once I knew that, I could find out where she lived, then do a drive-by of her home. Maybe find a clue or two.

I picked up my water glass, drained it, and signaled for more. Sacrifices had to be made. By my count I'd downed three glasses thus far. Hello, bathroom, I said to myself.

But my bladder had limits. Time to quit procrastinating and get down to business. I gathered my meager supply of technique, and appealed to Beverly's vanity. "You're much too young, Beverly, to have 'senior' moments like us older folk, but for the life of me, I can't seem to recall Vera's last name."

"It's MacGillicudy. Vera MacGillicudy."

"MacGillicudy! Of course! How silly of me to have forgotten." I pretended to laugh at my stupidity, but secretly toasted my success. "With a name like that, I don't suppose there are too many around."

Beverly picked up my empty salad plate. "Nope. Vera used to joke she's the only MacGillicudy in the phone book."

Feeling generous for someone on a pension, I left Beverly a hefty tip. Like Jim used to say, you get what you pay for.

My need for a phone book superseded my need for a restroom. As much as I was tempted, I couldn't very well ask Beverly for Vera's address. Especially not on the heels of all my questions about her. Then the answer dawned on me.

The rec center.

I jumped in the Buick and drove the short distance. Fortunately the rec center was still open for late-in-the-day exercise junkies. I practically ran inside and asked the girl at the front desk if I could borrow a phone book. She looked at me rather strangely, but managed to produce one. I thumbed through the *M*s, and there it was, staring me smack-dab in the face: M. MacGillicudy, 248 Jenkins Road. I committed the number to memory, thanked the girl at the desk, who, by the way, was still looking at me rather strangely, and hopped back into the Buick.

I knew I'd seen Jenkins Road somewhere in my travels in and around Brookdale, but wasn't exactly sure where. A county map would've come in handy, but I didn't have one. Map or no map, I was determined to find Vera's house if it took all night. Leaving Serenity Cove Estates behind, I drove sedately along the highway.

A couple miles outside Brookdale, I passed a white clapboard Baptist church. The marquee out front read WAL-MART IS NOT THE ONLY SAVING PLACE. Another Wal-Mart connection. I took this as an omen and continued down the road. Another half mile or so and cattle grazed in a farmer's field. Shadows were lengthening. A reminder I didn't have much time before dark. I slowed as I came to a crossroads and squinted at the street sign. JENKINS ROAD. I had found it. When you're good, you're good.

I turned left onto a narrow county road. The few houses and double-wide trailers I passed were widely spaced, each sitting on a large tract of land. I slowed to a crawl in order to read the weatherworn numbers posted on the mailbox at the end of each drive.

At last I found 248. Scraggly stands of pampas grass stood on either side of the driveway. I turned in and bumped my way down the dirt and gravel rut-filled drive. With each jolt, my bladder felt ready to burst. At the end of the drive was a modest ranch-style home with dingy vinyl siding. Two cheap plastic lawn chairs sat on a porch that ran the width of the house. Porches, I had observed since my move South, usually came equipped with chairs of one variety or another.

I shut off the engine and sat staring at the house. I really hadn't given much thought as to what I was going to do next. I pondered my choices. Should I march up to the front door and ring the bell? And then what? Claim I was a census taker? Tell Vera I was taking some sort of survey to see who was minus an arm?

Or should I be more subtle?

The longer I sat there, the more I realized the dingy little house with its weed-choked yard had a deserted, closed-up air. Feeling braver by the minute, I got out of the car for a better look. If Vera was home, I'd simply tell her I was in the neighborhood and stopped by to use her bathroom. As one woman to another, she'd understand the havoc time wreaks on female bladders.

Impatiens drooped in pots near the front steps, their leaves withered and brown. I interpreted the dead flowers as a clue that Vera MacGillicudy was still MIA. When I got one of those little black notebooks like Sheriff Wiggins, I intended to jot this down with a big star in front of it. Stars in my little black book would be synonymous with *CLUE.*

My heart raced as suspense built. What would I find? Miscellaneous body parts? Bloodstains? Footprints? I approached the porch cautiously, all my senses alert. I realized then I had left Tools of the Trade at home. I had none of the necessary paraphernalia with me that was required for my career as a detective. Just goes to show I was a rank amateur in the sleuth department.

Climbing the steps, I tiptoed across the porch. One of the floorboards creaked under my weight, and I jumped at the sound. My heart danced a tango inside my chest. I knocked on the door, not really expecting anyone to answer, so wasn't disappointed when no one did. The blinds were drawn in all the windows, but I didn't let that impede my investigation. Cupping my hands, I pressed my nose against the glass and peered inside.

"Can't see a darn thing," I muttered out loud.

Not to be deterred, I went around the rear of the house. A small concrete slab with wrought iron rails served as a back porch. Loropetalum bushes in dire need of pruning nearly obscured the steps. I pushed the bushes aside and went up the stairs for a better look. Just to be on the safe side, I knocked again — and again, no answer. No surprise there. Using the same technique as before, I cupped my hands around my eyes, pressed my nose to the glass door, and peered between a slit in the curtains. I could make out light-colored smudges of a washer and dryer, but nothing else. No body parts, no bloodstains, nothing.

Feeling bolder, I turned the door handle and found it locked. Again, no surprise. I had secretly hoped the door would have opened. Not only could I have gone in search of clues, but I could have found the bathroom as well. Surely Vera wouldn't have minded.

Don't know why I guzzled all that water back at the café, then bolted out of there without making a pit stop. I still had much to learn about crime solving. If I ever had to sit for hours on a stakeout, I'd need a Porta Potti close by.

Undecided what to do next, I looked around. The woods behind the house cast long shadows. My gaze swept over the yard and settled on a rusty metal storage shed at the edge of the property. My pulse picked up a beat. I had come this far, and couldn't turn back unless I checked this out, too. Nothing ventured, nothing gained, right? I picked my way across the weed-choked yard. If I found anything incriminating, I'd call the sheriff. Matter of fact, I wished I had his number programmed into my cell phone this very minute — just in case.

A length of chain was woven through the door handles of the storage shed and secured with a sturdy padlock. I went around the side. Junk surrounded the shed. A beat-up wheelbarrow with a broken handle, an old push-type lawn mower — and a plastic trash bin. I couldn't resist. I had to know what was inside the bin. Gingerly, I raised the lid and peered into the depths.

"Ee-yew!" I cried. A noxious smell assaulted my senses, making me reel. It was the same sickeningly sweet odor I associated with decay.

Dropping the lid back on the bin, I beat an undignified retreat. This was a job for the sheriff's department. The instant I was safely inside the Buick, I locked the doors and fumbled through my purse for my cell phone. My fingers hesitated before dialing.

How was I going to explain why I was snooping through Vera MacGillicudy's trash can? Would that make me guilty of trespassing? Could I be arrested? If so, and Jennifer found out, I'd be deported from Serenity Cove Estates to babysit in Brentwood. There, I'd spend the rest of my days chauffeuring young children to soccer, ballet, tap, gymnastics, and violin lessons. I shuddered at the thought.

I knew I had to be careful. Very, very careful. I put the car in reverse and backed down the drive. It wasn't until I turned off Jenkins Road and onto the highway leading back to Brookdale that I formed a plan. I don't know if cell phone calls can be traced, but didn't want to take the chance.

I soon discovered finding a pay phone is even trickier than finding a phone book. I drove all the way to Brookdale before spotting one outside a convenience store a block from the sheriff's office. Lowering my voice in an attempt at disguise, I told the dispatcher she had better get a man out to check the trash can near the storage shed at 248 Jenkins Road. I hung up when she asked my name, then, for good measure, wiped the phone clean with a crumpled tissue I found in my pocket. I made a note to add alcohol wipes to my growing list of detective supplies.

Nothing more to do than get back in the car and wait. Mother Nature chose that moment to remind me of other urgent matters that needed attention. I squirmed in my seat like a toddler who hasn't quite mastered potty training. Luckily my wait was brief. Minutes later, I watched a sheriff's cruiser speed down the road, lights flashing. I pulled away from the convenience store, proud I hadn't shirked my civic duty.

Chapter 23

"Bunco? Tomorrow?"

I was so surprised by the request I nearly dropped the phone. This time it wasn't me but Diane who summoned the emergency session. My internal radar beeped so loud, it nearly deafened me. Did this have anything to do with my serial-killer theory? Claudia and Vera were still missing. And not a single word from the sheriff's department about the bone I had found. "Fess up, Diane. What's going on?"

"No way, Kate." Diane is a calm, methodical person, not usually given to theatrics. But she sounded more animated than I'd ever heard her. "Besides, I won't get the real lowdown until tomorrow afternoon. Just say you'll be there."

"Wouldn't miss it for the world." How was I supposed to catch a wink of sleep tonight wondering about Diane's big secret?

"We can meet at my house," Diane continued. "Norm's working the four-to-midnight shift again, so we'll have the place to ourselves."

"Great. Can I bring anything?" I knew Diane worked a forty-hour week at the library. It wasn't always easy rushing home to get ready for bunco.

"Thanks, but I've got it under control. There is one thing, though. . . ."

"Sure, just name it."

"Do you suppose we could split the call list? The football game's about to start. The Jaguars are playing the Texans. Norm and I like to watch it together."

"No problem." I squeezed my phone between ear and shoulder while I dug through my junk drawer for pad and pencil.

"Think you could call Connie Sue, Monica, Janine, and Nancy?"

"Consider it done."

"Good. I'll call Gloria, Rita, and Pam. Seven o'clock sharp. My place."

"Gotcha."

And she had gotten me. Gotten me good. Diane had conveniently chosen what I refer to as the two-for-ones. Call Pam and she'd bring Megan. Call Rita, she'd tell Tara. Call Gloria, and Polly would be planning what outfit to wear. Oh well, I thought, not much else to do on a Sunday afternoon. Unless I wanted to watch two teams I'd never heard of pummel the living daylights out of each other on the gridiron.

I started with Janine.

"No, Diane wouldn't say what it was about," I explained in answer to the first words out of her mouth. "My gut feeling is that Diane wants to tell us something she found out about either Claudia or Vera."

"Did Tara ever learn how to contact Vera's daughter?"

"Not that I know of, but we can ask her tomorrow night."

"OK, see you then."

Never-Say-No Nancy was next on my list. "Sure, I'll sub," she agreed the instant she heard the *b* word. "You know me. I'm always up for bunco. Why don't I pick you up?"

"Fine," I said. "See you then."

Monica was a harder sell. "You're not going to talk about body parts, are you? My stomach can't stand any more talk about body parts."

I rolled my eyes. "No, Monica. Think of it as a committee meeting of sorts where Diane gives us an update on locating two friends. And, naturally, a chance to play bunco."

"Oh, all right. I would like to win the tiara.

Want me to drive?"

"Nancy said she'd drive. I'll ask her to swing by and pick you up. While she's at it, we might as well pick up Connie Sue and Janine." Diane lives in an old farmhouse set on five acres of land halfway between Serenity Cove Estates and Brookdale. Not far, but far enough to warrant carpooling.

"Sure she won't mind . . . ?"

"If she does, we'll offer to chip in for gas."

"Remind Janine not to forget the tiara," Monica added lest I suffer one of those annoying senior moments. "And before I hang up, Kate, I want your solemn promise there will be *no* mention of body parts."

I crossed my fingers. "Promise."

Connie Sue was last on my list. I wasn't looking forward to breaking the news that Diane had called an emergency gathering of Bunco Babes Crime Fighters. I knew Mondays were pot roast nights at the Brody home, and I was once again about to upset the applecart.

"Well, I don't know," Connie Sue drawled when I explained the reason for my call. "Thacker's a creature of habit. He gets upset with changes in his routine."

I heaved a sigh. Did Thacker know something the rest of the world didn't? Did pot roast really taste better on Mondays? "Look,

Connie Sue, Thacker's eaten pot roast on Tuesday and lived to tell the tale."

"I'm not sure. . . ."

"Connie Sue, it's time to take a stand." I was close to losing patience. "Which is more important? The lives of two friends — or a slab of beef?"

"Since you put it that way, sugar, deal me in. Want me to drive?"

"No, that's OK. We'll pick you up."

What was it with everyone wanting to drive? I never should have told the girls about my last speeding ticket. I suppose I should have noticed the police car parked behind that McDonald's billboard, but no one's perfect.

My phone calls completed, I flopped down on the sofa in the great room and flipped through a magazine. Tomorrow's bunco would also be a good time to tell the Babes about my little excursion to Vera's the other night. I had kept my ear to the ground, so to speak, and combed the local papers, but the grapevine had grown dormant.

So far, not a single solitary word about any unusual findings on Jenkins Road had leaked out. And so far, to my knowledge, no more women had been reported missing.

And Rosalie's murder wasn't any closer to being solved.

We all converged on Diane's doorstep at the same time. The decibel level in that old clapboard house went straight through the roof. Good thing Norm's working the afternoon shift at the mill and doesn't have to put up with the commotion. Most husbands are smart enough to clear the premises when the Babes gather. On bunco nights, they band together like castaways on Gilligan's Island to play poker or shoot pool.

The kitchen and dining room tables as well as a card table in the converted bedroom/den had been readied for play. A tray of fresh fruit — strawberries, kiwi, and pineapple — along with a yummy dip sat on the kitchen counter. Next to this was a frosty pitcher of some tropical drink that tasted so good it was downright sinful. Usually Diane doesn't fuss when it's her turn to host bunco. I took the fact that she had gone all out as an omen of important things to come.

For all intents and purposes, it seemed like a typical bunco night. Except for a certain tension in the air. This was, after all, a covert meeting of Bunco Babes — Crime Fighters.

As seemed to be our pattern, we filled our plates, filled our glasses, and found ourselves a place at one of the tables.

"Let the game begin," I announced from my seat at the head table.

Rita rang the bell. Play commenced. We rolled for ones till she rang the bell a second time, signaling the end of the first round.

We rearranged ourselves and settled down to shake, rattle, and roll those dice. I was eager to get down to the real reason for tonight's game. Not even Diane's fortified tropical drink could take the edge off my nerves. But if the rest of the Babes could keep their cool, who was I to quibble?

Twos were scarcer than hens' teeth. How did that cliché originate? Who makes up these things? What does it matter if hens' teeth are scarce or cheaper by the dozen? I corralled my wayward thoughts and tried to concentrate on the game. Out of the corner of my eye, I caught Monica eyeing Janine's tiara. No question where her thoughts were.

"Come on, Kate. I need some help here," Monica urged plaintively. "Roll some twos."

A friend in need is a friend indeed. Right? Apparently I'm alive and thriving here in Clichéville. I picked up the dice, shook them till the spots nearly fell off, and let them fly. One, six, and a three equal no score. I passed the dice to Rita.

Gloria's bracelets jingled merrily as she gave a little flip of the wrist and a careless toss. Lo and behold three twos magically appeared. "Bunco!"

Monica shot me a look, clearly indicating I'd let her down. Well, to paraphrase a once-popular country-western song, I never promised her a bunco. I promised only not to discuss body parts — and did that with my fingers crossed.

I held my head high as Monica and I made the transition from head table to lowly table three. From the way Monica carried on, we might as well have had *LOSER* tattooed on our foreheads. Along the way, I stopped to fortify myself with more of Diane's delicious tropical punch. Apparently I wasn't the only one in need of fortification. The pitcher was half empty.

Play resumed, this time everyone hoping to roll threes. Rita, I noticed, was still seated in the very same spot at the head table. From the smile on her face, she was obviously enjoying a run of good luck.

"I don't know about the rest of you," Polly piped up, "but if Diane doesn't hurry up and tell us why she called an emergency bunco, I'm going to explode."

"Me, too," Tara called from the kitchen.

Instantly, the dice ceased rattling. All heads turned toward Diane, who along with Megan sat with Polly and Nancy at table two.

"Let's make that unanimous," I said. "C'mon, Diane, stop torturing us. Haven't we been patient long enough?"

Diane stood so we could all see her and hear what she had to say. "I asked you here tonight to tell you that I finally contacted one of Claudia's sons."

"Well, why didn't you just say so?" Indignant, Polly shook her head hard enough to make her dangly earrings dance.

Diane held out her hands, palm up. "Just be patient. I think I'd better start at the beginning."

Polly squirmed in anticipation. "Hurry up, girl. I'm already on Medicare and not getting any younger."

Gloria sent her mother a reproving look. "Take your time, Diane."

Diane and Megan exchanged meaningful glances. "Do you want to start or do you want me to?" Diane asked Megan.

Megan nodded her encouragement. "Go ahead."

"If you recall, Megan and I agreed we'd try to locate Claudia's sons. This turned out to be a lot more difficult than we first thought, since no one seemed to know their real first names."

"Claudia," Megan interrupted, "always referred to the son who's an engineer as Butch."

"And," Diane continued, "she called her son the surgeon Bubba."

"What's so strange about that?" Connie Sue asked. "Most folks have at least one Bubba in the family. Bubba is a perfectly fine name."

"Perfectly fine for someone born south of the Mason-Dixon Line," Pam pointed out.

"I wasn't in South Carolina twenty-four hours when I met my very first Bubba," Gloria reminisced. "He came to read the water meter."

"I met my first Bubba at the hardware store," Janine volunteered.

Rita rapped sharply on the table, making the dice dance in place. "Ladies, ladies! I'm sure we all remember our first Bubbas, but let's stay on point."

"Rita's right," I agreed. "Get on with your story, Diane."

"I searched and searched, but couldn't find a single surgeon named Bubba Connors in Chicago, or, for that matter, the entire state of Illinois. So I expanded my parameters. The only Dr. Bubba Connors I managed to find turned out to be a vet in Alabama who specialized in rare bovine diseases."

"How udderly awful," Polly quipped.

Everyone groaned, including Diane.

Megan spoke, her face flushed, making her look even younger than her years. "I tried every which way, but couldn't find a Butch Connors who works as an engineer in Seattle."

"So if neither of you could locate her sons, how will I explain to Thacker that he missed pot roast for nothing?" Connie Sue whined.

Megan and Diane exchanged conspiratorial smiles.

Diane's smile turned into a grin. "We hit pay dirt."

"Pay dirt?" My voice rose a notch. "What kind of pay dirt?"

"I narrowed my search to surgeons with the surname of Connors in the Chicago area between the ages of thirty and forty and started making calls. Naturally, only office numbers were listed. When I called Friday, the doctors were all in the ORs, so I asked to speak with the office managers. I asked if any of them happened to know the name of the doctor's mother. Finally one admitted she thought the mother's name was Claudia and that she lived somewhere in the Carolinas."

By now the Babes were hanging on to Diane's every word. I was no exception.

"Bubba Connors, whose real name happens to be Charles, was at a surgical conference in Baltimore and not expected back till late Sunday. His office manager went on to say Dr. Connors had a full day of surgery scheduled Monday, but she would have him call me at the end of the day." Diane paused for effect, then continued. "Seems like Charles, aka Bubba, Connors is Claudia's son, all right."

Questions popped up like dandelions.

"What did he say?"

"Don't keep us in suspense."

"Is Claudia OK?"

"How can you be so calm at a time like this?"

"Did you ask Bubba if he's heard from his mother?"

Diane held up her hands for silence. Working in a library like she does, she probably gets plenty of practice asking people to hush. And, I must admit, she's good at it, since the house became so still you could have heard a pin drop.

"Oh, he's heard from her all right." *Smile* is too mild a word to describe Diane's ear-to-ear grin. "Claudia called him a couple nights ago with the news he has a new daddy. Seems like Claudia and this guy she met on the Internet eloped to Las Vegas."

You could have knocked me over with a feather. "Claudia ran off and got married?"

"Yep." Diane nodded. "Told Bubba they got married at one of those wedding chapels by an Elvis impersonator."

Polly shook her head, making the galaxy of purple stars in her ears sway. "Well, don't that beat all?"

And that about summed it up.

CHAPTER 24

One missing person down, one to go. And Rosalie's killer still unaccounted for.

After Diane's bombshell last night, bunco was abandoned in favor of a celebration. Claudia was not only safe and sound but married! Goodness! That had come as a shock. Next time I see her, I'm giving her a piece of my mind for worrying us half to death. Then, I'm going to give her a great big hug.

Lord knows Claudia deserves some happiness. Her auto-exec husband had left her for a floozy in a short skirt when their sons were barely out of diapers. Claudia had gotten her real-estate license and raised those two boys all on her own. This was her time to enjoy life. And no one enjoyed life better than Claudia. She was quite a character.

Diane must have shared those thoughts, too, because she brought out a sheet cake decorated with a plastic figure of a bride and groom. While the rest of us put away the dice and tossed away the scorecards, she whipped up another batch of her special blend, which, by the way, packed quite a wallop. By the time the evening ended, everyone — even Monica, who had fussed a bit that Janine still retained the tiara — was in high spirits.

Over cake and punch, I had recounted my experience at 248 Jenkins Road. I endured a lecture from Rita on the folly of going there alone and unprotected — a repeat of Pam's previous sermon. Polly, not surprisingly, begged me to take her along next time. All in all, it had been a great evening.

As I waited for my bagel to toast, I planned my day. I needed to stock up on groceries. I debated whether to drop by the sheriff's office afterward. Of course, the sheriff didn't think he needed our help, but I knew otherwise.

He needed to be told about Claudia. And I needed to be told about The Bone, as I had come to think of it. Surely he should have gotten a report back from the lab in Columbia by now. I wondered how much scientists could determine from the specimen I'd provided. Could they even be certain if it belonged to a man or a woman?

My bagel popped up, and I smeared it

with cream cheese. While I ate, I kept wondering who could've possibly killed Rosalie. The sheriff had called it an "isolated" incident. But was it? I wish I could be as certain as he seemed to be.

Breakfast over, I did a few chores around the house, then headed off to the Piggly Wiggly with shopping list in hand.

I hit the produce aisle first. I selected lettuce, a couple zucchini, and a small bunch of green bananas and placed them in my shopping cart. I said it before and I'll say it again: I'll never get used to calling it a buggy like they do here in the South. Say "buggy" and I immediately think baby carriage.

I was wandering through the frozen-food section when I happened to glance toward a woman who was rounding the corner at the far end. If I didn't know better, it could have been Vera's younger, more attractive sister. I shook my head to clear it. I was spending so much time thinking about the woman that my eyes had started to play tricks on me.

Canned goods were next on my list. Now that October was almost here, a nice pot of chili sounded like a good idea. But if I intended to make chili, I needed tomatoes. Sauced, pureed, or stewed? Whole or diced? These days picking the right can was almost as complicated as choosing a ripe melon. I reached for a can of each. A pantry can never have too many tomatoes. Now I needed to backtrack to the produce. Chili called for a green pepper. I whipped my cart — er, buggy — around and collided with Vera MacGillicudy's look-alike.

I stared. I simply couldn't help myself. This woman looked years younger than the one who served me hash browns and scrambled eggs. Her hairstyle was different, too, the cut stylish with blond highlights and low lights. Nary a single trace of salt-and-pepper gray. Instead of the polyester that I associated with Vera, this woman had on cotton Capris and a striped V-neck top.

"Mercy, Miz McCall. You look like you've seen a ghost."

Aptly put. That's exactly how I felt. "Vera . . . ?"

"The one and only."

I tried to collect myself. "Vera . . . you look, well, you look wonderful. I hardly recognized you."

And I meant this — both figuratively and literally. Vera looked better than I've ever seen her look. Well rested . . . and pretty. From the smile on her face, she was obviously pleased with my reaction. At close range, I could see fading bruises hidden beneath skillfully applied makeup. The new and vastly improved Vera had had some work done. A tweak here, an eyelid lift there. The results were truly amazing. She looked a good ten years younger. I was tempted to ask the name of her plastic surgeon.

"All the girls have been worried sick about you. Marcy said you just up and left. No one seemed to know where you were."

"It's sweet of y'all to worry, but as you can see, I'm fit as a fiddle."

"Yes, I can see that." Fit as a fiddle? Hell's bells. She was as fit as the entire string section of the Augusta Symphony. "I can't tell you what a relief it is to know you're safe. Considering everything that's been going on around here, the Babes and I have been scared silly thinking about what might have happened to you."

"Didn't mean to worry nobody. I had sick time coming and decided to take it. I let the manager know what was going on and when I'd be back. I asked him not to breathe a word to the rest of the girls." Vera gave me a sheepish smile. "I wanted to watch their reactions when they saw me."

I'd like to be there myself. It would be worth the cost of admission. "Well, I'm sure you won't be disappointed. You look like a different person."

"My aunt died a couple months back and named me beneficiary of her insurance policy. I had a hard time making up my mind between a vacation in Hawaii or having plastic surgery. In the end, I decided the surgery lasts longer than two weeks on Maui."

"Good thinking." I started to untangle my cart from hers.

Vera appeared unconcerned and in no particular hurry. "I feel like a different person. I've got a whole new lease on life. It's high time I live a little. Make some changes. Life's too short, and I've already wasted a good share on a no-account husband."

"I hope your plans don't include leaving the Cove Café?" Visions of Marcy raced through my head. In my imagination, she bore a close resemblance to the Wicked Witch of the West.

"Time will tell." Vera smiled, then lowered her voice. "There's a new man in my life."

Aha! A new man? Well, that certainly explained the hairstyle, the clothes, and the nip and tuck.

"Never thought I'd want a man after living with Mel all those years, but . . ."

"I heard your ex has a temper. Don't you worry about him?"

"I would if he was close, but Mel's brother offered him a job in construction once he got off probation. Last I heard, Mel packed his pickup and headed for Dallas."

"We — the Bunco Babes and I — are just glad you're safe, that's all."

"You ladies are so sweet to worry about me. Next time you're in the café, the coffee's on me."

"It's a deal."

"Gotta run." Vera started on down the aisle. "I promised my daughter I'd stop by and drop off bread and milk. Baby's due soon. Poor girl, her feet are swollen to the size of water balloons."

I watched Vera disappear around a corner. Scratch one more name off the missing-persons list, I thought. And then there were none. Unless the bone left on my deck proved otherwise, this marked the demise of my serial-killer theory.

Chapter 25

I was still mad as a wet hen by the time I returned from town. The sheriff had gone and done it again. Made me feel like a bumbling fool. And I didn't like being made to feel like a bumbling fool! He had even worn a condescending smirk when I casually mentioned my serial-killer theory. "Miz McCall," he had drawled in that velvety baritone that was beginning to grate on my nerves, "it's kind of you to take an interest in law enforcement, but best all around if you leave crime solvin' to the professionals."

The nerve of the man! He might as well have told me to stay home and take up knitting.

"My department was able to locate Ms. Claudia Connors's next of kin. We learned she was alive and well at a blackjack table at Caesars Palace. As for your other missin' person, Vera MacGillicudy, the manager of the Cove Café told us she had scheduled time off. We left a message for her to call us when she got back to town. Which she did, by the way — last night."

Well, those little snippets had certainly taken the wind out of my sails. Then, suddenly, a fresh gust had filled them up again. "But what about the bone I found?"

"Ah, yes, the bone." He'd leaned back in his chair, folded his hands on the desk, and interlaced his fingers. "The lab confirmed what Deputy Preston suspected all along. It's an animal bone, not a human one — deer most likely."

"I heard a scream. It woke me up."

He shrugged his linebacker-size shoulders. "Most likely an animal . . . or maybe one of your neighbors havin' a wild party."

"Most likely," I said, not trying to hide my sarcasm as I rose to leave his office.

"Don't suppose you know anythin' about an anonymous call to my department a few nights back?"

About to leave, I'd frozen with my hand on the knob.

When I didn't answer immediately, he went on. "Seems like some concerned citizen took it upon themselves to report a suspicious-smellin' trash can at the MacGillicudy residence."

"Mmm . . . uh . . . ," I'd stalled. Seemed like the sheriff was missing the whole point of an anonymous call.

"That call had my deputy siftin' through a trash can full of rottin' compost. Deputy Preston sustained serious grass stains on his brand-new uniform pants. He's none too pleased."

I forced a smile. "Be sure to have him check the Piggly Wiggly. I hear there are some marvelous new products on the market for getting out stains."

And that's the gist of our entire conversation. No one can say I didn't try to go through proper channels and cooperate with the sheriff's department. And where had it gotten me? Exactly nowhere! From now on, he was on his own.

But that doesn't mean for one minute, I'm going to stop trying to figure out who killed Rosalie. No, sirree. The monster needed to be brought to justice.

Hours later I was still fuming. My last meeting with Sheriff Wiggins had left me little choice but to resort to drastic measures. Drastic measures for me sometimes took the form of comfort food. Tuna noodle casserole has always been one of my favorites. Jim never cared much for casseroles, so I used to make it for the kids and myself when he was off on one of his business trips. Now that he's gone, I have it often. Sometimes I pretend he's off on one of his trips and will be home in a day or two. We had a good life together, and I miss him. I wonder what he'd think about the kids trying to ship me off to someplace "safe." Probably we'd share a good laugh, then threaten to disinherit the both of them.

I had just finished loading my dinner dishes into the dishwasher when the front doorbell rang. I wiped my hands on a dish towel and went to see who it could be.

"Bill . . . ?" I said, unable to keep the surprise from my voice at finding Bill Lewis, sans tool belt, on my front step. "What brings you here?"

He looked a bit sheepish. "Thought I'd drop by and make sure that new ceiling fan of yours is working OK."

"Come in." I stepped back to let him in. "Glad you came by."

"Hope I'm not interrupting your dinner."

"I just finished," I said, leading the way from the foyer.

Bill stood for a moment in the kitchen doorway and sniffed. "Mmm. Something smells good. Reminds me of my favorite — tuna noodle casserole."

"You like tuna noodle casserole?"

"I like most casseroles, but that's always been my favorite. My wife used to make it all the time."

"Jim never cared much for casseroles, so I'd only make them when he was out of town." Talk of casseroles faded into an uncomfortable silence. What next, I wondered, swap recipes? I wasn't used to entertaining men. I fell back on the tried-and-true, "Care to join me for a cup of coffee? It's decaf," I added as extra enticement.

"I'd love a cup, but first let me check this baby out." Bill switched on the ceiling fan and put it through its paces: high, medium, and low. It performed perfectly.

While the blades whirled overhead, I went to the cupboard and pulled down two coffee mugs. "I have some lemon bars left over from the church bake sale."

Bill smiled that sweet shy smile of his. "Lemon bars are right up there on my list alongside tuna noodle casserole."

Tuna casserole and lemon bars. Why weren't all men this easy to please? I wondered as I poured coffee. "How do you take yours? Cream, sugar?"

"Black is fine."

Mercy! We even liked our coffee the same way. Weren't we a pair? I studied Bill over the rim of my coffee mug. He wore khakis with a blue polo shirt that matched the color of his eyes. He was one fine-looking gentleman — and nice as could be. The kids had tried their darnedest to make me feel old and decrepit, but Bill seemed to have just the opposite effect. He made me feel young. Don't get me wrong, not the young and foolish type, but young in a good sense of the word. Young as in attractive and interesting.

"Did you work today?" I asked when he pulled out the chair opposite me at the kitchen table. "I thought I spotted you at the pro shop the other day."

"Thought I saw you, too, talking to Brad."

"I signed up for the putting clinic he's giving beginner golfers. I need all the help I can get."

"Brad's a good instructor all right. He's especially good with the ladies."

I looked at him sharply.

Bill flushed. "I didn't mean that exactly the way it came out. What I should have said was, Brad's good at instructing the ladies."

Curiosity killed the cat, but right this very minute, I could identify with that nosy feline. I wondered just how friendly Rosalie was with the handsome pro. Nothing ventured, nothing gained, right?

I gave Bill a smile. "I understand that my neighbor Rosalie Brubaker took a lot of lessons from him."

"Yeah, she did. I used to see her and Brad on the driving range quite a bit." Bill sipped his coffee and looked thoughtful.

I decided right then and there, this would be a good time to practice my interrogation skills. "From what I gather, Brad was none too happy that Rosalie was falling behind in organizing the member-member tournament."

"Don't know anything about that, but I wouldn't want to get on Brad Murphy's bad side."

All my instincts went on full alert. If I were a hound, you could even say my ears perked up. "Why's that?"

Bill shrugged. "I'm not one for gossip, but I hear Brad's got a real short fuse. I saw him lay into one of the groundskeepers once. Thought I'd have to step in before it came to blows."

Bill's words were a revelation. They made me view Brad Murphy in a whole new light. I had never seen that side of his personality. At the course and in the pro shop, he was Mr. Congeniality. But Bill had just warned me not to get on his bad side. Did that make

Brad Murphy a Dr. Jekyll and Mr. Hyde?

I felt a stab of disappointment when Bill finished his coffee and rose to leave. It had been nice to have someone to talk to in the evening. It was easy to fill the days with activities, but the nights could be . . . well, they could be lonely.

"Guess I'd better be going." He walked over to the sink, rinsed out his mug. "Did you mean what you said about giving that cradle I'm making a final inspection? I sure would appreciate a woman's opinion."

"I'd love to see it." And I would. Seeing the cradle meant seeing Bill again.

"Good. I was hoping you'd say that. I'll have the coffeepot on, but I can't promise anything as good as your lemon bars. Might have to settle for Oreos."

"Oreos are right up there with tuna noodle casserole and lemon bars," I said, following him to the door.

He paused on the front step and, turning, looked back at me, his expression uncharacteristically serious. "Be sure to lock up at night. A woman living alone can't be too careful when there's a killer on the prowl."

"I don't scare easily," I replied, touched by his concern.

"Well, if you ever are scared, all you have to do is call me. I'll be here in a flash with my Louisville Slugger."

I watched him back out of the drive, then closed the door and turned the dead bolt. I smiled to myself at the image of Bill Lewis coming to a damsel's distress armed with his trusty baseball bat, a Louisville Slugger.

Chapter 26

"What can I get you ladies?"

Vera had sneaked up on us unawares. Other than Pam, I hadn't told any of the girls about Vera's nip and tuck. Didn't have the heart to spoil the woman's surprise. The wait had been well worth it as I watched heads swivel, eyes widen, and mouths gape. I sat back and enjoyed the show. Only thing I regretted was not having a camera handy.

"Vera . . . ?" Pam squeaked.

"Ohmigawd . . . ," Connie Sue drawled. "Honey lamb, you look fabulous!"

I had to agree with Connie Sue. Vera did indeed look fabulous. In addition to highlights, a new hairstyle, and a firmer, prettier face, she must've lost ten pounds while she was away. I could stand to lose a pound or two myself. Tone up some. Maybe time had come to sign up for a session with that new fitness trainer at the rec center.

"Out with it, girl. Who's your plastic surgeon?"

"Connie Sue!" Monica scolded. "Shame on you. That's rude. You're going to embarrass Vera."

Vera, however, didn't look a teensy bit embarrassed. In fact, she looked pleased as punch.

"I'd be happy to give you his card, Miz Brody," Vera said, smiling. "In the meantime, let me take your orders."

Vera, bless her heart, was her usual efficient self. Without being asked, she brought Connie Sue water, lemon, no ice, and Earl Grey tea for Monica. She filled my cup and Pam's to the brim with coffee and kept them filled. I let out a blissful sigh. The Cove Café was back to normal.

"Whatever happened to Marcy?" I asked Vera when she delivered my Belgian waffle to the table.

"Marcy's given up on being a waitress. Said it was too hard on the nerves — and the feet."

"What's she going to do instead?" Monica asked, forking into her egg white omelet.

Vera placed an order of wheat toast — unbuttered — and a fruit cup in front of Connie Sue. "She decided to become a manicurist."

We, the four of us girls, exchanged looks. "Good choice," we said in unison.

I chose the first lull in the conversation to tell the girls about Bill's unexpected visit the night before and his invitation to view the baby cradle.

"I think he's sweet on you," Pam teased.

A warm sensation started in my chest and crept up to my cheeks. Not a blush, but a flush. Probably another of those power surges. "He just wants a woman's opinion before he ships it up to Ohio."

"Uh-huh."

"Stop making it into something it isn't," I scolded, trying to camouflage the fact I was secretly flattered at the notion of Bill being sweet on me. "I'm only going to his place to see the cradle, then have a cup of coffee and some Oreos."

"Uh-huh."

"He's just a very nice man." I hid my smile behind my coffee mug. "He made me promise to lock up tight at night. He said a woman living alone can't be too careful."

Monica nodded. "Sound advice, if you ask me."

"If I get nervous, Bill said all I had to do was call him. He'd rush over with his Louisville Slugger and bean the bad guy over the head. How's that for coming to the defense of a damsel in distress?"

I rambled on about Bill's virtues, oblivious of the looks my friends exchanged, until Vera approached with more coffee.

We were almost finished eating when Brad Murphy sauntered in. Heads turned to watch. Brad had that sort of effect on women. For a man close to forty, he was what you'd call "hot." A lemon yellow golf shirt bearing the Serenity Cove Estates logo molded broad shoulders and muscular arms. And my, oh my, those khakis! They hugged a set of buns that made old women sit up and take notice.

"Ladies," he greeted us with a warm smile. "How y'all doin'?"

While we babbled answers, Vera came by with our checks. Brad turned to greet her with his patented grin and his jaw dropped. "Vera MacGillicudy!" he exclaimed. "Is that you? Or is this your baby sister?"

Vera turned rosy pink. "Aw, Brad, stop. You're making me blush."

Brad slung his arm around her shoulders and gave them a squeeze. "Honey, you're lookin' fine. Mighty fine."

Of course we echoed Brad's sentiments. And left Vera generous tips. It was just our way of showing her how happy we were that she was "mighty fine."

It wasn't until I was in the Buick and driving home that I replayed the scene between Vera and Brad in my mind. In retrospect, their familiarity with each other seemed a bit out of place. Vera had positively glowed at hearing Brad's compliments. And Brad had had a certain gleam in his eye when he hugged her.

Hadn't Vera mentioned a new man in her life the other day at the Piggly Wiggly? I wondered if that new man could possibly be Brad Murphy. Brad had to be a good five years younger than Vera. But so what? Polly was always going on about all the older women/younger men that she read about in the Hollywood gossip rags. Said the women who hunted younger prey were called "cougars." Who's to say it couldn't happen right here at the Cove Café?

Only one fly in the ointment far as I could tell. Bill had said Brad harbored quite a temper under that pretty-boy face and sit-up-and-take-notice body.

Another thought struck me as I turned into my drive. Was Rosalie as enamored with Brad as Vera appeared to be? Was there more to their relationship than instructor and student?

I sat down to enjoy a cup of chamomile tea

before bedtime. Much to my amazement, I had acquired a taste for it. While waiting for my tea to cool, I stared out the window at the Brubaker house, all dark and broody, across the street.

What had Earl been up to all those nights when the house blazed with light? Earl, I knew from listening to Rosalie complain, was not a night owl by nature. According to her, he turned in to bed at nine every evening, not even staying awake long enough for the early news. Why the sudden change in his sleep habits? A nasty thought occurred to me. Had he used those long evening hours to obliterate traces of murder?

Absently I took a sip of tea. And promptly burned my tongue. I put the cup down and folded my arms on the kitchen table. Earl was the logical suspect in his wife's death, I grudgingly conceded. His story that Rosalie was away visiting grandkids in Poughkeepsie was plausible until various body parts — quite literally — surfaced.

The million-dollar question still remained: If Earl was innocent, who killed Rosalie?

My tea forgotten, I hauled Tools of the Trade out of a cupboard. Opening it, I took out the black spiral notebook that I'd recently purchased and scanned my notes — which I had to admit were pretty sparse.

Undaunted, I picked up a pen and flipped to a blank page. I needed to make a list. Lists were wonderful things. Don't know how people manage to accomplish anything without them.

I headed my first list *Possible Suspects.* Earl's name was the first one I entered. Under his name, I wrote Bill Lewis's only because of Earl's earlier accusations and because of Bill's association with power tools. Even though I believed wholeheartedly in his innocence, I needed to stay objective. After all, this wasn't the time to rely on women's intuition or consult the Psychic Hotline. I frowned at my list — my very short list.

Trying a different approach, I turned to yet another blank page and headed it *Facts.* Since Rosalie's body had been dismembered, I could safely assume the killer had access to power tools or at least to some wicked saws. At his press conference, Sheriff Wiggins stated Rosalie had been killed by a blow to the head. Last, but not least, was the question of whether Rosalie had been seeing someone. And if so, who? Under *Facts,* I scribbled down, *Power tools, golf, possible lover.*

I took a sip of tea and grimaced. Tepid chamomile tea left much to be desired. I focused on the word *golf* until the letters danced before my eyes. Brad Murphy was a ladies' man. He and Rosalie spent an inordinate amount of time together. Off the course as well as on? I wondered.

I flipped back to my list of suspects and added Brad Murphy's name. My list of possible suspects was growing. I now had three names. How hard could it be to whittle three down to one? Simply apply the process of elimination, and voilà!

But a single problem remained. Bill was on the list.

CHAPTER 27

I hummed to myself as I primped. Timing was everything. Just yesterday I had had my hair cut and the color — a nice ash blond — touched up. I even treated myself to a manicure. Something I almost never do. I chose a pretty rose pink nail polish, then went all out and had a pedicure, too.

Then later that day, Bill had called and asked me over. I felt like I was going to the prom. I had almost forgotten that excited, fluttery feeling. I took one last look in the mirror. My hair looked good — stylish and short, but not too short. I hinted to Jac, my hairdresser, that I might have a man in my life. Jac outdid himself, giving me a tousled look that he claimed was all the rage at a hair show in Atlanta.

I gave myself a final once-over in the mirror and sucked in my stomach. I had decided to wear an almost-new pair of black Capris. Black is thinning, right? I could stand to lose a few, but no way that was about to happen in the next fifteen minutes. I promised myself I'd swear off M&M's and eat more salmon. I'd give up chocolate-chip cookies and buy low-fat yogurt. Just don't ask me to give up pizza. I admit it, I'm bad. Really bad.

Along with the Capris, I wore a soft sage green boatneck sweater that Connie Sue said brought out the green of my eyes. I snapped a chunky silver bracelet around my wrist, and I was good to go.

I recognized Bill's Ford pickup parked in the drive. I pulled in next to it and got out. Bill must have been watching for me because he opened the door before I had a chance to ring the bell.

"Kate!" he cried. "Don't you look pretty tonight! Come in, come in."

He stood aside as I entered the foyer and handed him a plate of lemon bars I had made especially for him. "I brought you a little something."

"You shouldn't have." A smile spread across his face, forming cute little laugh lines at the corners of his baby blues. "But I'm glad you did. We can have these later over coffee."

Sheriff Wiggins could stand to learn a thing or two from Bill Lewis on how to graciously accept a small gift. “I can’t wait to see this cradle you’ve told me so much about,” I gushed, hoping I didn’t sound as nervous as I felt.

“Soon as I set these down in the kitchen. Right this way.”

I trailed after him, trying to take in as much of the house as I could without seeming obvious. The dining room to my left was empty except for a card table and four chairs. Bill must have seen my frown.

“Don’t do much entertaining,” he explained, “except for a poker game now and then. I’m not much of a gambler.”

“Toss in some dice and score sheets, this room would be perfect for bunco.”

“Never played the game. Is it high stakes?”

“Hardly.” I laughed. “Bunco’s more about having a good time with friends. The dice only make it look serious.”

I caught a glimpse of the great room as we turned down a short hallway. This, too, was sparsely furnished with a leather sofa, La-Z-Boy recliner, and flat-screen TV. A glass-topped coffee table held a neat stack of books. No pictures on the walls, no knickknacks, no houseplants. Everything — walls, carpet, tile — neutral and safe. A home in dire need of a woman’s touch.

Bill deposited the lemon bars on the

counter in the kitchen. "Just around the corner," he said, motioning me to follow.

Swinging open a door, he flipped a switch and fluorescent light flooded what was formerly a three-car garage. Two of the bays had been converted into a workroom worthy of HGTV. Tools were displayed on the walls like prized family portraits, everything grouped and labeled. The room smelled of sawdust and varnish and was neat as a pin. Even the gunmetal gray floor looked as though it had been recently vacuumed.

"Don't like to brag, but this place even has its own separate heating and cooling system." He pointed to a contraption mounted in the ceiling. "You're looking at the best dust-collection unit on the market today."

"I'm impressed," said she who can't tell pliers from a wrench. Bill owned enough equipment to dismantle the *Queen Mary* and put it back together again.

"The cradle's over here." Bill led me to a sheet-draped object near one of the overhead doors. He whisked the covering off, and I caught my breath. He beamed ear to ear at my gasp of delight.

"It's beautiful, Bill! Absolutely beautiful." And that was no exaggeration. A row of intricate spindles wrapped around the ends and sides of a basket suspended from sturdy but graceful supports that bore a single delicately carved rose.

"It's made from loblolly pine grown right here in South Carolina. I wanted the baby to feel close to its grandfather even though we're eight hundred miles apart."

Call me sentimental, but I felt a lump form in my throat. I knelt down and ran my hand over wood smoother than a newborn's bottom. "I'm sure this will be a gift that's cherished for generations."

"I was going to use polyurethane for the finish, but after some research decided against it. I went with pure beeswax instead. It's one hundred percent nontoxic biological wax."

"That sounds like an environmentally friendly decision." Chalk up more points for Bill Lewis. "I bet you don't need a lecture on going green."

"Reduce, reuse, recycle, right?"

"Right." I traced the carved rose with the tip of my finger. "Do your son and his wife know whether the baby will be a boy or a girl?"

He shook his head. "Said they want to be surprised."

"Boy or girl, he or she will be one lucky child to know they have a grandfather who loves it as much as you."

Bill tucked his hands into his pockets and rocked back on his heels. "My son said if it's a girl, they're going to name it after my wife, Margaret, and call her Maggie."

I was about to reply when my cell phone jangled. "S'cuse me." I rummaged through my handbag, which I had set on the floor while admiring the crib.

It was Diane. "Hey, Kate. What's up?"

"Hey, Diane, can't really talk now. I'll call you back later."

"Wait, don't hang up. I wanted to let you know that new mystery you've been talking about just came into the library this afternoon."

"Great." I glanced at Bill out of the corner of my eye. He was carefully replacing the sheet over the cradle.

"Want me to set it aside for you?"

"Sure. Thanks, Diane. I'll stop by to pick it up." I snapped the phone shut and dropped it back into my purse. "Sorry for the interruption."

"No problem. How about some coffee to go with those lemon bars you brought?"

The doorbell pealed as soon as we reached the kitchen.

"Be just a minute," he said as he hurried off.

I heard a soft murmur of voices in the distance. Familiar-sounding voices. Gloria and Polly? Impossible! What would they be doing here at this hour? I waited until I heard Bill tell his callers he'd fetch something from his workshop, then decided to take a peek for myself.

Polly spotted me about the same time I spotted her. She waggled her fingers and grinned. "Thought that looked like your car out front."

Gloria, dressed in her favorite polyester pantsuit and lots of gold chains, smiled, too, but her smile seemed forced. "Bill promised to donate an item to the Humane Society Auction. We thought we'd stop by to collect it."

Bill returned from his workshop carrying a handsome pair of wooden candlesticks and presented them to Gloria. "Here you go."

"Thanks, Bill. They're lovely." She dug through her purse and pulled out a pad. "Let me give you a receipt. Remember, this is a tax-deductible donation."

"I was planning to drop them off," Bill said. "The auction's still a month away."

"No problem. We were in the neighborhood." Gloria scribbled down the information, then handed him a receipt.

"Guess that's it," Polly chirped, giving me another of her finger waggles. "Bye, Kate. See you at bunco."

Bill closed the door on his unexpected guests. "Now it's my turn to apologize for the interruption. If memory serves, you take your coffee black."

"Same as you — if memory serves."

Bill turned on the coffeemaker and got out mugs while I peeled the plastic wrap from the lemon bars. We had just sat down to enjoy coffee and conversation when my blasted cell phone shrilled. I was tempted to turn it off without answering, but thought better of it when I saw Connie Sue's name on the display.

"Hey, sugar. Hope I'm not interrupting anything important."

"Actually, Connie Sue, this isn't a good time." I stared out the window of the breakfast nook, but it was dark outside and all I could see was my own reflection in the glass.

"Since when are y'all too busy to spare a minute for a friend?"

I mouthed, *I'm sorry* to Bill. Bill, in return, gave me one of those unassuming smiles that had first attracted me to him.

"It's just that I'm not home right now."

"Anywhere interesting?"

"Bill invited me over to see the beautiful cradle he made for his son and daughter-in-law. They're expecting their first baby this spring."

"Promise you'll call me the minute you step foot in the door. I need your chicken scaloppine recipe for the church potluck."

"Promise." I would have promised a kidney at this point. I turned off the phone, which I should have done an hour ago. "Sorry . . . again."

"Seems to me, your friends are just looking out for you." He took a sip of coffee, then smiled at me over the rim of his mug. "Can't say as I blame them with everything going on around here."

"Good coffee. Is it one of those special blends?" I said, taking a sip, but really trying to change the subject.

"No, just something I picked up at Wal-Mart." Bill broke apart the lemon bar on his plate, but stared at it like a bug under a microscope. "The way news travels in Serenity Cove, I suppose you know Sheriff Wiggins dropped by to question me about Rosalie Brubaker."

"No, I hadn't heard, but I'm not surprised. I was at the Brubakers' when Earl pointed a finger in your direction. The sheriff is just doing his job. No one in their right mind would believe you had anything to do with killing Rosalie."

"Have to admit it shook me up. Haven't gotten as much as a traffic ticket in the last twenty years. Next thing I know, the sheriff's asking me about a murder. Even asked to see my woodworking shop. I told him to go right ahead. He seemed really interested in my tools, especially my saws."

"Saws?" My voice sounded like a croak.

"Yeah, I've got a radial-arm saw, a table saw, and a band saw. I don't know what he was expecting to find."

I dearly wanted to ask Bill if the sheriff had spritzed chemicals on the saws to detect blood like they did on *CSI*. I bit my tongue instead.

Bill took a small bite of his lemon bar. "I admit Rosalie called me all the time. She was always after me to fix this or that. Complained all Earl did was putter with his orchids. Said things would never get done if she waited for him."

"Don't let it get you down, Bill. The sheriff seems like a competent man. He'll get things sorted out. Earl probably pointed at you in order to draw attention away from himself."

Bill looked relieved to have unburdened himself. "Thanks for listening, Kate. You've been a friend. I have to confess I nearly called tonight to cancel, but I'm glad I didn't."

"I'm glad, too."

We talked a little more; then it was time for me to go. Bill walked me to the door and waved as I pulled out of the drive. I hadn't gone more than half a block when I glanced into my rearview mirror and, for the first time, noticed headlights close behind me.

A little too close.

Chapter 28

Panic fluttered like a moth in the pit of my stomach. I had stayed at Bill's longer than planned. And later. Traffic was nonexistent at this hour — not that it was ever heavy to begin with. Another of retirement's perks. Everyone was home. Safe behind locked doors.

I turned right. So did the car behind me. Coincidence, I told myself.

I took a left. The car behind me did the same. Worry ratcheted up a notch. I drove with both hands on the wheel, at two o'clock and ten o'clock, just the way I had been taught, but seldom practiced. I kept one eye on the road, the other on the rear-view mirror.

I turned off Oleander Avenue and onto Shady Lane. The other car did, too. It had followed me ever since I left Bill's. Almost as if it had been . . . waiting.

A killer was loose.

The perils of a woman living alone sang in my head like a chorus of angry voices. Each second the notes seemed to gather urgency. Soon they would resound like the reprise from *Les Misérables.* I gave myself a lecture on coincidence. I demanded my fluttering stomach to quiet. I ordered my racing heart to slow. Neither stomach nor heart obeyed.

The true test to see if I was being followed was yet to come. My house sits in the center of a cul-de-sac with a vacant lot on either side. Normally I prize my privacy, but tonight I wished for neighbors. Neighbors with floodlights and barking dogs. In another minute, I'd turn off Shady Lane and into Loblolly Court. If the car behind turned as well, I was in deep doo-doo.

I needed a plan of action. I needed a weapon. What if whoever was behind me forced me out of my car? Tried to kidnap me — or worse? What if my serial-killer theory wasn't as far-fetched as the sheriff seemed to think? I swept the interior of my car with a glance. I didn't have a weapon. Maybe I should get a gun, I thought, stifling a hysterical bubble of mirth. But I hate guns, I reminded myself in the next breath. A person can get seriously hurt with a gun.

Now what? I wondered. Dial 911? Frantically I pawed through my handbag trying to find my darn cell phone. Duh! I realized I should've done that sooner. But even as my fingers closed around the phone, I knew why I hadn't called in the troops. I couldn't very well call the sheriff's office to report a car behind me on a public thoroughfare. After all, I didn't own the road. Nowhere in the Serenity Cove Estates bylaws did it state only Kate McCall could drive down Shady Lane at precisely 9:35 in the evening.

I reached the corner, the point of no return. Deliberately ignoring my turn signal, I jerked the steering wheel hard to the right and took the turn on two wheels. I had seen this move done somewhere with modest success, maybe on reruns of *Starsky and Hutch* or *Dukes of Hazzard.* I felt a stab of apprehension when a glance in the rearview mirror showed I still had company. My technique, it seemed, needed practice.

Beep! Beep! The quiet night was broken by a series of sharp staccato blasts of a horn.

As I circled the cul-de-sac pondering my next move, I thought I heard my name called. The car horn blared again. This time the driver flashed the headlights. I finally slowed to a stop when I heard what sounded like Pam's voice yelling my name. But that didn't make sense. Why would Pam be following me and blowing her horn? She was usually home with Jack at this hour watching TV.

I rolled down my driver's-side window a crack. The car behind me braked to a stop. Two figures emerged and approached the Buick. I squinted against the glare of headlights, but finally recognized the pair as Pam and Rita.

"Kate McCall, the crazy way you drive, you ought to have your license revoked!"

If I had been standing, my knees would have buckled in sheer relief at hearing Rita scold. When my nerves steadied a bit, I opened my car door and eased out from behind the wheel. The lights from Rita's Honda dimmed and shut off automatically.

"Are you auditioning for NASCAR?" Pam demanded.

Rita stopped in front of me, size tens firmly planted, arms crossed over 40 DDs. "The way you rounded that corner, you nearly mowed down Earl's mailbox."

"If you two hadn't scared me half to death, I wouldn't have to drive like a maniac. Hasn't anyone told you there's a killer roaming the streets?" I fired back. Imitating Rita's stance, I glared at my friends. "Now, will one of you kindly explain why you're following me? And why you ruined a perfectly good evening with your stupid phone calls? You can't really expect me to believe Polly and Gloria's story they *just* happened to be in Bill's neighborhood and decided to stop."

"Don't be mad, Kate," Pam said. "The Babes and I only wanted to make sure you got home safely."

"That's right." Rita gave a brisk nod. "And to give you a good talking-to. Someone has to knock some sense into you."

"Why?" I looked from one to the other, perplexed. "What did I do now?"

Rita jerked her thumb in the direction of the Brubaker house. "The woman across the street — your friend and mine — was hit over the head hard enough to kill her, and her body cut into little pieces. Her husband, as you well know, happens to be the prime suspect in her murder."

"Earl wouldn't hurt a flea." I huffed out a breath. "He grows orchids, for goodness' sake. He's not a cold-blooded killer."

"And then there's Bill," Rita pointed out succinctly. "Earl sounded pretty positive Bill Lewis could be, as the sheriff would say, a 'person of interest.' God only knows what might've been going on between Bill and Rosalie."

"Bill . . . ?"

"Yes, Bill." Pam laid her hand on my arm and gave it a squeeze. "A woman can't be too careful. I know he's sweet on you, Kate, but don't ignore the facts."

"Facts? What facts?" My mind struggled to take in the remote possibility of Bill being a vicious murderer.

"It's common knowledge Bill owns more power tools than Home Depot. Rosalie's arm didn't fall off by itself. It was cut off," Rita reminded me, her tone matter-of-fact.

"And, Kate, remember what you told us about Bill rushing to your defense with a Louisville Slugger?" Even in the dim light, Pam's face looked pinched and anxious. "You even thought it was cute. During his press conference, Sheriff Wiggins said the cause of death was a blow to the head with a blunt object."

Rita nodded like one of those annoying bobble-head dolls.

"A baseball bat could be translated as a blunt object," Pam concluded.

I felt nauseous at the thought of Bill being a suspect. I liked to boast I was a good judge of character, but right now felt I was on shaky ground. It didn't make me feel any better to know I had just spent an entire evening alone with the man. Not just any man, but a "person of interest."

Rita stepped closer, her voice hushed. "Did you happen to notice what Bill's house backs up against?"

I shook my head. My mouth was too dry to speak.

"Not just the golf course, Kate, but the eighth hole. The infamous eighth hole where we found . . . *it.*"

At this point in the conversation, I could have informed Pam and Rita that Bill also shopped at Wal-Mart. That he probably had access to bags galore — a convenient place to store a severed arm. But I couldn't heap any more suspicion on a plate that was already overflowing. I wondered if a woodworking shop, a Louisville Slugger, a house on the eighth fairway, and access to Wal-Mart bags constituted circumstantial evidence.

Suddenly it wasn't looking good for Bill. Didn't baby blue eyes and a bashful smile count for something? Or had Rosalie found them just as endearing as I did?

"We're not saying we think Bill is guilty." Pam adopted a conciliatory tone worthy of a UN ambassador trying to broker world peace. "I like the man nearly as much as you do, Kate, but the Babes and I just want you to be careful who you trust. Until this terrible thing is over, it might be best for you to play it . . . cool . . . where Bill is concerned."

But I don't want to play it cool. "I am careful," I muttered. "Granted, Bill has more saws than I can remember the names of, but I didn't completely forget what Earl had implied."

Rita's grim expression melted somewhat. "Glad to hear that."

I felt the need to prove I wasn't a total idiot. "I gave Bill's workshop a good looking over while I was there. The place was immaculate. I didn't notice any telltale signs that a body" — I shuddered — "had been dismembered. No blood spatter on either the walls or the floor."

Pam leaned against the Buick and frowned. "I watch nearly as many crime and punishment shows on TV as you do. We both know he's had time to scrub them down, repaint."

I leaned on the car next to her, closed my eyes, and imagined myself back in Bill's shop. *Concentrate, Kate. Concentrate.* The floor had been a serviceable gray, but it bore scuff marks and showed signs of wear. The walls had been white, but the paint hadn't looked fresh.

"I don't think so," I replied at last. "The place smelled more like varnish and sawdust rather than bleach and fresh paint." I looked from Pam to Rita, my look steady, unblinking. "You're wrong about Bill . . . just as you're wrong about Earl."

No sooner were the words out of my mouth than flashing red and blue lights lit up the night sky. The three of us turned as a stream of police cruisers pulled up across the street. Some blocked the Brubakers' driveway, while others screeched to a halt near the front curb. Uniformed men leaped out, too preoccupied to notice three women standing in the dark of a drive across the way.

Sheriff Sumter Wiggins issued commands in a quiet voice. Several police officers took up stations around the perimeter while he led a small procession around to the front door.

Pam, Rita, and I swapped meaningful glances. I felt the hair at the nape of my neck prickle. Something was up. Something huge.

I leaned over and said sotto voce, "Looks like the posse's got the place surrounded."

"What do you suppose is happening?" Pam whispered.

"I don't know," I whispered back, "but I'm not budging until I find out."

This time I intended to hold my ground.

No way was I going to allow Sheriff Wiggins to bully me with threats of obstruction of justice. I had every right to stand in my own driveway till dawn if that's what I wanted.

I counted a total of six police cars. Both the sheriff's office and Brookdale Police Department were represented. The red and blue flashing lights had attracted a lot of attention. Porch lights flickered on up and down Shady Lane. Neighbors poked their heads out of doors, or pressed their noses against windowpanes, trying to figure out what all the fuss was about. Gradually people emerged from their homes and stood in small clusters in one or another's yards to talk and gossip and speculate.

"Hey, gang, what's up?" Janine asked as she jogged around the corner to join us. Janine lived only a couple doors down from the Brubakers', but knew the best viewing was from my driveway. In her haste to get the skinny on what was going on, she had flung a sweater over the lime green T-shirt she had paired with pink plaid PJ bottoms.

"We're not sure . . . yet," Rita told her.

I motioned at the police cruisers, front and side. "Whatever it is, it must be pretty important to bring out the cavalry."

Janine ran her hand through short-cropped silver hair, making it stand up in tufts around her head. "Do you think they're here to arrest Earl?"

"They can't just do that, can they?" Pam asked. "At least not without a good reason, or evidence, or something."

The four of us leaned against the back bumper of my Buick and waited for the main feature to begin.

We didn't have to wait long.

Deputy Preston, the young officer I had come to know from my various exploits, escorted a dejected-looking Earl Brubaker around the walk and toward the cruiser parked in the Brubakers' drive.

"This is crazy. You're making a big mistake," Earl protested. "I would never hurt Rosalie. I loved her."

The deputy ignored him. Giving Earl's head a firm downward push, he eased Earl into the cruiser's rear seat and slammed the door shut. The deputy then came around to the driver's side, hopped in, and proceeded to back down the drive. I caught a final glimpse of Earl's expression as the car sped off. He bore the look of a trapped animal. A trapped animal with no way out.

"Well . . ." Pam let out a pent-up breath.

"Poor Earl." I shook my head in sympathy.

"Poor Earl!" Rita exclaimed loudly. "Right now it looks as if 'poor Earl' might've murdered Rosalie. The police don't haul someone away just for the heck of it."

"What about giving him the benefit of a doubt?" I rallied to Earl's defense, for no better reason than I felt sorry for the guy. "What about innocent until proven guilty?"

"Now, now, girls," Janine cautioned, playing peacemaker. "Let's not rush to judgment before hearing all the facts."

"Most of the police are still inside," Pam noted absently. "I wonder what's keeping them."

Once again we fell silent. And waited.

I hugged my arms around myself to keep warm. The October night air had a bite to it. I envied Janine her warm woolly sweater. I debated going inside for one of my own, but at the thought of missing some of the action decided against it. Better freeze than miss out.

"Found it!" Sheriff Wiggins's voice boomed out, bringing us all to attention.

"Cordon off the house," he shouted to another of his deputies. "At first light, we'll have the crime-scene unit do a thorough search — inside and out."

I shoved away from the Buick's bumper and walked to the edge of my drive. I was careful not to go any farther lest the sheriff shoo me away. Pam, Rita, and Janine followed, nipping at my heels. The moon was playing hide-and-seek behind the clouds, but by now my eyes had adjusted to the dark. I waited with bated breath while Sheriff Wiggins came around the bend of the Brubakers' front walk carrying what appeared to be a long object of some sort encased in plastic.

"What is it?" Janine whispered, standing so close her breath tickled my ear.

"Looks like a stick," Pam offered from my other side.

"Uh-uh," I disagreed. "More like a golf club."

Rita leaned forward and squinted. "From the shape and size, my guess would be a sand wedge."

"The murder weapon . . . ?" I murmured. Even a rank amateur such as me knows a sand wedge is the heaviest iron in a golfer's arsenal. The weighted club could do considerable damage against a human skull if swung with any force. I shuddered at the thought.

Janine's thoughts must have run parallel with mine because she drew her sweater tighter around her shoulders. "If that sand wedge turns out to be the murder weapon, Earl's going to have a hard time convincing people he's innocent."

The sheriff carefully placed the golf club/murder weapon in the trunk of his cruiser, then climbed in and drove off. The four of us stood at the end of the drive while police wound a spool of yellow crime-scene tape around the Brubakers' house and yard. Eventually only one police cruiser remained to stand guard. Or, in police jargon, to keep it under surveillance.

"Guess the excitement's over for the night." Rita turned toward Pam. "I'm ready to leave if you are. Dave probably fell asleep on the sofa and missed the last half of the ball game."

"Night, everyone." Janine gave us a final salute as she trotted toward home.

"Don't lose any sleep worrying about Earl," Pam said, giving me a quick hug. "Think positive. If the murder weapon turns out to be a sand wedge instead of a Louisville Slugger, Bill's in the clear."

I watched Pam and Rita drive away, then turned and walked slowly up the drive. I was having a hard time wrapping my mind around the fact that Earl might have killed Rosalie. Something didn't quite make sense, but I couldn't put my finger on what. One thing I did know for sure, however. As far as I was concerned, Bill was and always had been a person of interest — but not as a murder suspect.

Chapter 29

"Ladies, it's all about reading the green," Brad Murphy said to the group gathered on the practice green.

Personally, when it comes to reading, I'll take a good mystery over a putting green any day of the week. But I had an ulterior motive for coming today. I wanted to size up Brad Murphy. He remained a "person of interest" in my little black book. I needed to know whether to cross his name off my list or bump it up a notch. So I'd come to the putting clinic with my game face on. Not to be outdone by the rest of the ladies, I squatted down on my haunches and frowned at that smooth green surface until I thought my eyes would cross. If I stayed in this position any length of time, it would take a construction crane to get me upright.

"Try to imagine which way your ball is going to break. By 'break,' ladies, I mean, is the ball going to curve left or right?"

Whose bright idea was it to make putting greens undulate? Why couldn't they be flat? Wasn't golf challenging enough? If you want my opinion, putting on a flat surface would speed up the game considerably and eliminate the need for rangers having to hurry folks along. But that might mean Bill losing his job. Maybe flat putting greens weren't such a great idea after all.

"Allow me to demonstrate."

Ten pairs of eyes fastened on Brad's ball as it made a perfect arc and landed in the cup with a satisfying *plink.* He made it look effortless when I knew from experience that it wasn't. Guess that's why golf pros get paid the big bucks.

"See how easy it is."

I tried my best to follow Brad's advice, but my ball seemed to develop a mind of its own. Wasn't this darn clinic ever going to end? I wondered irritably as I watched my ball sail past its target and roll off the green. After talking on the phone yesterday with Connie Sue and Monica, I discovered they'd finish playing golf about the same time my putting clinic ended. We'd agreed to meet for a drink afterward at the Watering Hole. Right now, a cold drink held far more appeal than chasing a stupid golf ball.

Twenty minutes later, Brad glanced at his

wristwatch. "Now, ladies, remember what I told you. I want to see y'all out here practicing. You can't expect to play a good round without first putting a few balls to see what the greens are like. Class dismissed."

Finally! I was hot, thirsty, and cranky after another night of tossing and turning. I was tempted to box up the Sandman and send it packing. It certainly failed to live up to its promise of a blissful night's rest.

Half the group started toward the clubhouse, while the other half remained, determined to follow Brad's pithy advice and practice, practice, practice. Two women I knew only casually rushed up to him, flanking him on either side, while I lagged behind.

"Brad, I've been meaning to call you," said the shorter of the pair, a shapely blonde I knew only as Trixie. "I need to sign up for a private lesson. I'm not following through on my swing."

I smiled to myself as I trudged along. I'd like to point out that, from the exaggerated sway of Trixie's hips, she had at least one swing that didn't need work.

"Sure thing." Brad flashed his patented smile. "Soon as we get back to the pro shop, I'll check my schedule."

"Brad," Betty, the taller, thinner brunette,

purred, "I need my sand wedge regripped."

Sand wedge? After last night, I didn't like the sound of that word. In my mind, the term *sand wedge* was in the same category as *Wal-Mart bag.*

"No problem." This time Betty was the recipient of Brad's practiced charm. "Just got in a new order of grips you might want to take a look at."

I followed the trio, fascinated at watching Brad Murphy in action. He was quite a flirt, and the ladies seemed to eat it up with a spoon. If Vera was seriously interested in winning Brad's affection, she better consider taking up the game of golf.

"I remember Rosalie mentioning you re-gripped some of her clubs," Trixie said. "She said you did a terrific job."

Betty shook her head sorrowfully. "Isn't it just awful about Rosalie?"

"Terrible," Brad murmured. "Just terrible."

I'd heard enough. A cool drink sounded more inviting than ever. I veered away from the pro shop and headed for the Watering Hole. Connie Sue and Monica had gotten there ahead of me and waved me over to a table. I noticed Connie Sue munching on a celery stick from a small veggie platter. No potato skins or nachos for that girl. I always wished her self-control would rub off on me, but it never did.

I thought about ordering a glass of wine, but needed to quench my thirst, so ordered unsweet tea with lemon instead. "How'd you guys do?" I asked after the waitress left.

"I parred the eighth hole," Monica volunteered. "It's the first time I've played since, uh, you know."

"As if I could forget."

"I swear, we must be the only ones in this entire place discussing golf," Connie Sue noted, taking a ladylike sip of her pinot grigio.

Monica removed her visor and fluffed her dark hair. "We've been here fifteen minutes, and I haven't heard birdies, eagles, or bogeys mentioned even once."

"Weird," I agreed. "So what's the hot topic?" I asked, playing dumb.

Connie Sue smiled at me over the rim of her wineglass. "Earl Brubaker. What else?"

I was beginning to think I should have ordered something stronger than iced tea. Mind you, I'm no saint. I enjoy gossip as much as the next person, but Poor Earl, as I had come to think of him, was getting more than his fair share. My iced tea arrived, and I guzzled half of it before asking, "What's the word on the street?"

Connie Sue leaned forward and lowered her voice. "Folks around here are mighty unhappy."

"Seems like Earl was only taken in for questioning last night, then released," Monica elaborated.

"Really?" That came as a surprise, especially after seeing him hustled off last night by a sheriff's deputy. "The authorities don't think he's guilty?"

"The husband of my hairdresser's niece has a friend who works in the county clerk's office." Monica inspected the veggie platter, chose a cherry tomato, and popped it into her mouth. "Rumor at the courthouse is that the sheriff doesn't have a strong enough case for an arrest warrant."

"I heard the same thing," Connie Sue said, relaxing back in her chair. "Our landscaper dropped by this morning to check on the Leyland Cypress. We got to talking, of course, and he mentioned his brother-in-law told him that the golf club found at the Brubakers' was sent to Columbia for testing."

Monica nodded. "The clerk at the post office said she heard there were traces of blood on it."

I dredged a carrot stick through a puddle of low-cal ranch dressing and pretended it was a potato chip. "It's probably going to be examined for trace evidence."

Connie Sue frowned at me. "No offense, sugar, but you need to find yourself a new hobby. All this law-and-order stuff is beginning to affect your brain. You're starting to scare me."

I chewed slowly, considering Connie Sue's advice. If I was brutally honest, I had to acknowledge there were times I scared myself. "I can't totally disagree," I confessed halfheartedly. "I may have gotten a *little* carried away with all this."

"A *little . . . ?*" Monica asked.

"Well, perhaps a little more than I should have." I looked from one concerned face to another and held my hands up in a gesture of surrender. "I admit I got caught up in all this, but I can't seem to let go."

"Take a step back, sugar, and let the sheriff do his job," Connie Sue advised, reaching for another celery stick.

"She's right, you know." Monica wagged a strip of green pepper in my direction. "That's why the man keeps getting re-elected."

I know their advice was sound. I've given myself this same counsel a time or two. But to no avail. I wouldn't have peace of mind until Rosalie's killer was caught and brought to justice. I've said it before, and I'll say it again. I just wasn't convinced Earl was that person.

CHAPTER 30

All this thinking was giving me a headache. I tapped the pen against the table and stared out the window. The Brubaker house remained dark and still. The premises were still festooned in yellow crime-scene tape like a sloppily wrapped birthday gift. A giant cockroach of a patrol car sat at the curb. There was no sign of Earl. The grapevine had it, he had taken up temporary residence in a sleazy motel on the outskirts of town.

I kept asking myself, if Earl had killed Rosalie, why leave the murder weapon practically in plain sight? And why would he have been not only willing but eager to give the sheriff Rosalie's hairbrush for a DNA match? It just didn't make sense.

Problem was, not everyone viewed the situation the same way I did. In the minds of most people, if the sand wedge proved to be the murder weapon, Earl might as well phone the South Carolina Department of

Corrections and reserve a cell.

I looked away, then back again. Nothing had changed at the Brubakers'. The squad car hadn't budged an inch. Surveillance can't be easy work. Having to stay awake while the rest of the world sleeps. How did one occupy one's time cooped up in a car hour after hour? Read, work crosswords, write a novel? But all these activities would distract one's attention from the original purpose, which was to watch. How boring!

This in mind, I went to the pantry, pried the lid off a large Tupperware container, and filled a Ziploc bag with chocolate-chip cookies. A little sugar might be just the ticket along with the thermos of coffee — which I assumed was standard-issue on a stakeout. A sugar buzz might help whoever guarded the Brubaker house to stay alert. No one could say I wasn't civic-minded.

I slipped on the gray zip-up-the-front sweatshirt I reserve for gardening and trotted across the street. The young officer inside the cruiser jumped as if he'd been shot when I knocked on the passenger window. Automatically, his hand reached for his holster.

I nearly dropped the cookies right then and there. "Don't shoot! Don't shoot!"

Officer Olsen, the young policeman I had instructed on the three Rs of recycling, scowled back in a pretty fair imitation of Sheriff Wiggins. I wondered if he was practicing the one-eyebrow lift as well.

He lowered the window, obviously feeling no threat from a nosy senior citizen. "Ma'am?"

I held up the bag of cookies. "I brought you a treat."

Confusion replaced the scowl. "Uh, that's mighty kind of you, ma'am, but, uh . . ."

Clearly the receipt of baked goods wasn't a topic covered in the police procedural. "If you're hungry, Sergeant" — he seemed such a nice young man; I thought he might like a promotion — "I'd be happy to bring you a sandwich."

"That's real thoughtful, ma'am, but —"

"Kate." I cut him off. "Just call me Kate."

All this ma'am stuff was making me feel older than Grandma Moses. Poor kid. He appeared to be in his early twenties, not much older than Megan. He looked more discomfited now than he had when he first spotted the cookies. "I live just catty-corner from here. The house on the cul-de-sac. I saw you sitting out here all alone and felt sorry for you. I thought some cookies would taste good with your coffee."

His face relaxed into a smile as he reached for the cookies. Then, just as suddenly, his demeanor changed. "Ma'am . . . Kate . . . please step to the rear of the vehicle. Stay there until I tell you it's safe."

Right before my eyes, boy morphed into man. I didn't argue, but backed up until I was even with the rear bumper of the cruiser. I narrowed my eyes to see what had captured Olsen's attention. In the light of a half-moon, I could see a figure emerge from the shadows and start across the Brubakers' lawn.

Olsen quietly opened the car door and stepped out, his right hand resting on the butt of his pistol. "Halt! Identify yourself!"

"Don't shoot. I'm unarmed," Earl Brubaker shouted.

Olsen approached cautiously, his hand still on his gun. I wasn't far behind, grateful I had worn sneakers. Apparently they're called that for a reason.

"Mr. Brubaker . . . ? Sir, what are you doing here?"

"For crying out loud, this is my house. I live here."

"This is a possible crime scene. No one's allowed in."

"I need to go inside for ten minutes. Ten minutes is all I'm asking."

"Sorry, sir, but I've got strict instructions. No one gets inside until the house is released as a possible crime scene."

Earl ran a hand over his jaw, which once again bristled with whiskers. "How long will that take?"

"Not for me to say. That's up to the sheriff. Never can tell. He might decide to make a second sweep."

"But I need to water my orchids," Earl whined. "If I don't, they'll die."

"Afraid I can't help you, sir." Olsen wasn't swayed by the pleading tone in Earl's voice.

"I'm working on a new hybrid," Earl said as if that tidbit explained everything.

"If you entered, sir, I'd have no choice but to arrest you."

"You're forgetting *I* pay the mortgage, not some dumbass sheriff."

"Like it or not, sir, that's the law. You'd be guilty of obstruction of justice."

Obstruction of justice? That phrase was becoming a bit shopworn. And had a way of popping up at the most inopportune times.

Suddenly, all the starch seemed to go out of Earl. Muttering under his breath, he turned to go back the way he had come. I caught a glimpse of that sad basset hound face and felt my heart squeeze with sympathy. Leaving Officer Olsen standing in the middle of the Brubakers' lawn, I hurried to catch up with Earl.

"Earl, wait," I called.

He paused and turned. "Sure you want to talk to me?" he asked bitterly. "No one else does."

I fumbled for the right words. What could I say to a man suspected of murdering his wife? Should I burst into song? Remind him that the sun will come out tomorrow? That tomorrow is only a day away? "You're developing a new hybrid?" I asked instead, opting for the mundane.

"Yeah, I've been working twenty-four/seven since Rosalie left."

"That's great, Earl. Everyone needs a hobby."

"It's more than a hobby. I plan to turn it into a business. Raise hybrids and sell them on the Internet."

"Wow," I said. "I had no idea."

"Planned to do it up right. Even thinking about getting myself a Web site."

"How did Rosalie feel about all this?"

He dived his fingers through his thinning hair, and stared up at the night sky. "That was what we argued about last time we talked." He blinked back tears. "I wanted to take money out of our savings and invest in a greenhouse. She accused me of throwing good money away. Said I paid more attention to my hybrids than I did to her."

I placed my hand lightly on his arm. "I'm sorry, Earl. Is there anything I can do to help?"

"Nah," he said, shaking his head. "First I lose Rosalie, now my phalaenopsis. If it hadn't been for someone phoning in an anonymous tip about a golf club, we wouldn't even be having this discussion. I thought if I just explained to the officer out front, he'd let me into my own house long enough to water my orchids. He could even stay and watch if he wanted. How's that for being naive?"

"Maybe if you explained to the sheriff —"

Earl cut me off. "The only words Sheriff Wiggins wants to hear from me is a confession." He started to walk away, but then paused and turned back. "Funny thing is, even though we'd grown apart, I still loved my wife." His voice cracked as he struggled to regain his composure.

I watched him walk away, head bent, shoulders slumped in defeat.

I gave Officer Olsen a halfhearted wave as I walked toward home. A cold breeze out of the north chilled me to the bone. One thing was clear — crystal clear. If Earl was innocent — and I believed he was — only the murderer could have planted the weapon in Earl's bag and phoned in the anonymous tip. Find the caller; find the murderer. Simple as that. Piece of cake, right?

"Hi, Kate." Megan greeted me with a smile. "Have a seat. Dr. Baxter is running a little behind."

"No hurry," I said, taking a seat and picking up a copy of *People.* "Will I see you Thursday at bunco?"

"Sure, wouldn't miss it. Where's it at this time? Mom told me, but I forgot."

"At Connie Sue's."

"Cool! Her house is amazing!" Giving me an apologetic look, she turned to answer the phone.

Amazing described Connie Sue's home to a T. With her impeccable taste, if she hadn't worked as a cosmetics rep, she could have had a career as an interior decorator. Unlike Bill's, there was nothing beige or neutral about Connie Sue's home. She loved color and wasn't afraid of using it.

"Mrs. McCall . . ." I looked up from *People* and recognized Caitlin, the girl from my previous visit. "Right this way," she said.

I reluctantly closed the magazine without learning the name of the latest Hollywood celebrity to file for divorce. I'd have to get the details from Polly later. I followed Caitlin down a hallway to the last exam room on the left. Seemed like the uniform of the day was pale blue scrubs imprinted with smiling molars heralding glad tidings of brush, floss, and rinse. Meanwhile my brain was trumpeting a different message entirely: run, retreat, and hide.

Too late. Caitlin motioned me into the dental chair and pinned on a bib. After assuring me Dr. Too-Handsome-for-His-Own-Good would be right with me, she disappeared. Probably to resume her role as modern-day tooth fairy, cheerfully dispensing toothbrushes and mint-flavored floss to the unwary. I sat back to await my fate, determined to be brave.

As a distraction, I let my eyes roam over the room, taking in the decor. Although this was a different exam room than last time, the golf theme still prevailed. This one contained more personal memorabilia. An elaborately carved shelf of photos and golf trophies was mounted on a wall next to the window. One photo in particular caught my attention. It was the same one I'd first seen in the Brubakers' living room. In it, the happy foursome of Brubakers and Baxters, newly proclaimed winners of the His and

Hers Classic, grinned back at me. Even Earl looked happy.

"Kate!" Just-Call-Me-Jeff breezed in, nearly blinding me with his pearly whites. "Sorry to keep you waiting."

"No problem," I answered, mustering a feeble smile. I was never in a hurry when it came to seeing a dentist. Take all the time in the world, I wanted to tell him.

"Let me take another look at your films." He clipped the X-rays onto the light box and proceeded to study them.

I succumbed to the need for nervous chatter. "You were modest about your golf game. I didn't realize you'd won trophies."

"I've been lucky and won a time or two."

"Were you good friends with Rosalie Brubaker?"

He dropped one of the X-rays and stooped to pick it up. "No, uh, why do you ask?"

If I didn't know better, I'd say he was the one who was nervous now. "I couldn't help but notice the picture of you winning the His and Hers Classic."

"We paired up for a tournament once. I believe she and my wife, Gwen, knew each other."

I distinctly remembered thinking how chummy the foursome had looked in the photo. Dr. Good-looking had his arm hooked around Rosalie's waist while she smiled up at him adoringly. Earl and the brunette — Gwen — were hardly more than background scenery. "Hmm, I don't know what gave me the impression you two were friends."

"I'm sure I have no idea. I scarcely knew the woman." He tugged on a pair of latex gloves and reached for the syringe. "Let's get started, shall we?"

The needle stung as it was repeatedly jabbed into my gums. Tears streamed down my cheeks in spite of his assurances it wasn't going to hurt.

"Megan warned me you're dental phobic, so I'm giving you a little extra Novocain so you don't have to worry about pain."

He had barely left the room before numbness began to creep along my lower jaw. In minutes, my tongue felt the size of a kielbasa. Even my nose felt strange. Soon I wouldn't be able to tell if my nose dripped or my mouth drooled. As much as I disliked the thought of pain, I'm not sure if I liked this sensation any better.

Eventually, Dr. Jeff returned with Caitlin in tow. There were no smiles this time; he was all business. "Open wide, Mrs. McCall."

What happened to "Can I call you Kate?"

I wondered as I tried to ignore the whine of the drill. Dr. Isn't-He-Darling must have used up his daily ration of charisma. The procedure seemed to last forever. I was drilled, rinsed, and suctioned. I didn't feel a thing and wondered if I ever would. For all I knew, he could've been drilling for oil or tunneling to China.

At long last, he nodded his approval with the temporary filling. "Have Megan give you an appointment for two weeks. Your crown should be back from the lab by then," he said, peeling off gloves and mask. "Careful what you chew on that side. Stay away from anything sticky." With this, he disappeared down the hall.

Caitlin was left to mop up the drool. "Sure you're all right, Mrs. McCall? Can I get you some water?"

"No thanx," I lisped. "I'm juth peachthy." I wobbled down the hall toward the receptionist's desk, feeling a little woozy after two hours in a dental chair.

"Kate!" Megan's eyes widened at the sight of me. "You're white as a sheet. Let me call Mom to come give you a ride home."

I shook my head. I must look even worse than I thought. I *had* tried to tell her I was allergic to dentists, but no one ever takes me seriously. "An appointment," I managed to say, my words sounding garbled. "Two weeks."

I snatched the appointment card from her hand without so much as a glance and shoved it into my handbag. I didn't care if Jeffrey Baxter, DDS, had a great selection of magazines. I didn't care if he had the whitest teeth in the world. I didn't care that he looked like a movie star. I just wanted out.

"See you at bunco," Megan called as the office door slammed behind me.

Chapter 31

"Y'all help yourselves." Connie Sue, perennially gracious, motioned to the spread she had set out on the granite-topped island in the center of her spacious kitchen.

As if we needed coaxing!

Diane slathered a generous serving of dip on a wheat cracker and almost purred after tasting it. "Mmm, this is so good. I want the recipe."

"Glad you like it, sugar. It's Aunt Melly's spinach and artichoke dip."

None of us seemed to be in a particular hurry to get started. Instead we congregated around the island and snacked on dip and crackers. For the calorie conscious, Connie Sue had thoughtfully provided a colorful array of peppers, carrots, and celery sticks.

"Besides the usual, I made us something special." Connie Sue produced a party-size cocktail shaker. "Who wants an apple martini?"

"I'll give it a whirl." Polly snatched a stemmed martini glass from a nearby tray.

Gloria took a glass also and held it out for Connie Sue to fill. "Where's Thacker tonight?"

"Dave invited the guys over to watch the basketball game," Rita answered for Connie Sue, who was busily pouring martinis. "He's in seventh heaven since we bought that new fifty-inch plasma TV."

"Basketball should be a nice change of pace." Nancy, who has become our semipermanent sub with Claudia still away, dragged a strip of red pepper through the dip. "All anyone wants to talk about is whether Earl's guilty of killing Rosalie. Especially after the sheriff found the murder weapon in his garage."

"The *alleged* murder weapon," I corrected around a mouthful of cracker.

Janine regarded me thoughtfully over the rim of her martini glass. "Do you still think he's innocent, Kate?"

"Hmph!" Monica snorted. "If she does, she's the only one. The man is guilty as sin. What more proof do you need?"

Monica's tone put me on the defensive. "Last time I checked, a man's innocent until proven guilty," I said.

Monica, a teetotaler unless under duress,

helped herself to a diet soda. "Well, I know how I'd vote if I was on the jury."

"Then let's hope you're not on the jury." I couldn't help but think an apple martini or two might smooth Monica's sharp edges.

"I was on jury duty when we lived in Rochester." Janine took a small sip of her drink. "The judge was very specific in his instructions. A juror is supposed to listen to *all* the testimony before rendering a verdict — especially when a man's life is at stake."

"Maybe Earl's being framed," Pam suggested helpfully.

Polly nodded. "Sounds like this movie I watched the other night on Lifetime. Even the man's own wife didn't believe he was innocent. She ended up having an affair with the real killer."

"Yeah," Tara agreed. "I know the one you're talking about. Didn't the husband break out of jail and come after them?"

"Yep, that's the one." Polly shook her head, sending her Clairol curls dancing. "The bad guy nearly killed both the husband and the wife before the cops finally arrived."

Rita leaned back against the counter and crossed her arms over her impressive bosom. "For the sake of argument, Kate, let's say Earl's innocent. Who do you think killed

Rosalie?"

Eleven pairs of eyes fastened on me like moss on a rock.

"What about Bill Lewis?" Megan asked.

Out of the mouths of babes, I thought.

"Yes, what about Bill?" Gloria skewered me with a look. "I've heard Rosalie always arranged for his visit when Earl wasn't there."

"Th-that's ridiculous!" I stammered. My protests earned me more speculative looks.

"Pardon the pun, but Bill fits the bill," Monica pointed out ruthlessly. "Be honest, Kate. It's no secret the two of you are friends, but he meets all the criteria."

"And what criteria is that?" I set my glass down more forcefully than I intended. Some of the martini sloshed over the rim. "Just because a man owns power tools and golf clubs doesn't make him a killer."

Connie Sue grabbed a microfiber cloth and wiped up my spill. "Let's assume Bill and Earl are both innocent. Who do y'all suppose committed this awful crime?"

"Do you think Rosalie was really having an affair?" Polly asked. Her bright blue eyes twinkled behind her trifocals. "I read this quiz in *Cosmo* about how to tell if your spouse is cheating. Rosalie would've had a perfect score."

Gloria rolled her eyes. "Mother, for the life of me, I don't understand why you read that stuff."

Polly shrugged, nonplussed. "It's good to know these things. You never can tell, I might decide to get remarried one of these days."

Nancy helped herself to more dip. "The last few months Rosalie looked better than ever."

"I thought so, too," Diane agreed. "She checked out practically every diet and fitness book we have at the library."

Janine weighed the merits of a celery stick versus a carrot, then chose the carrot. "When I asked her, Rosalie admitted she'd lost fifteen pounds on the Atkins Diet."

"She asked the name of my hairdresser in Augusta." Connie Sue ran her hand over her smooth honey blond locks. "She complained the salon here was too . . . ordinary. Said she wanted something with a little more sass."

Gloria topped off her martini glass, and Connie Sue proceeded to whip up a second batch. "I think Mother's on to something about Rosalie having an affair. She was spending an awful lot of time working out in the fitness room."

"She started coming to aerobics, too,"

Monica said. "I overheard her ask a mutual friend — who shall remain nameless — who did her work."

"Work? What kind of work?" Polly held out her glass for a refill, but lowered it when she caught Gloria's look of disapproval.

"You know." Tara winked at her. "The kind of work celebrities deny having done — the years-younger kind of work."

"Ahh," Polly said as the light dawned. "You mean cosmetic surgery. Why didn't someone just say so?"

"Ladies!" Connie Sue tapped a glass for everyone's attention. "I vote we change the subject. Don't know about y'all, but I'm ready for a little excursion to take my mind off killers and such." She paused, waiting a beat before continuing. "What do you say we drive over to Aiken for a day of shopping?"

"Does that include lunch?" Rita and Gloria asked in unison.

Connie Sue grinned. "Does a cat have whiskers?"

The vote was unanimous. We finally agreed on a date for the following week. No easy feat considering the schedules of twelve busy women. In the end only eight of the Babes would be able to go. Megan, Tara, and Diane all had to work. Nancy begged off, needing the time to pack for a trip to her and her husband's time-share in Aruba.

"Now that that's settled, let's play bunco." Connie Sue shooed us toward the tables set up for play.

Pam hung back. Laying a hand on my arm, she lowered her voice and whispered, "Jack casually mentioned at dinner tonight that Bill once planned to be a doctor. Jack said Bill dropped out of medical school after one year in order to get married."

"What does dropping out of med school have to do with the price of tea in China?" I whispered back.

"I'm just saying someone who went to med school would know how to . . . well . . . you know." She cast a nervous glance in Monica's direction and left the rest unsaid.

I did know. The apple martini in my stomach collided with the artichoke and spinach dip. Wasn't dissection one of the first things doctors learned in medical school?

An hour later, I still felt a tad queasy as I sat across from Megan. We were partnered with Monica and Diane. Fours were the coveted number we were trying to roll.

"Have you recovered from your ordeal with Dr. Baxter?" Megan asked as she slid the dice to Diane. "I thought you were going to pass out right then and there in his office."

I mustered a smile. "You were right about one thing, Megan. I didn't feel a thing." Feeling had been physically impossible, considering the entire side of my face was numb. I had drooled like the village idiot for hours afterward.

"Told you he was good." Megan grinned.

Diane racked up a few points, much to Monica's delight, then passed me the dice. I cupped them in both hands, gave them a good shake, and let them fly. Not bad, three twos — a baby bunco — five whole points.

I continued to roll the dice. "Dr. Baxter's quite the golfer, isn't he? I saw a picture of him and Rosalie after winning some tournament."

Megan picked through the bowl of nuts on the table until she found a cashew. "Rosalie was one of the doctor's biggest fans. She'd come in religiously every three months to have her teeth cleaned. Insisted on having Dr. Baxter rather than Caitlin. Claimed she had some rare condition with a fancy name that required special attention."

I made a mental note to add Dr. Movie-Star-Handsome to my list of possible suspects. My run of luck over, I shoved the dice in Monica's direction.

"C'mon, baby," Monica crooned as she shook and rattled the dice. "Mama needs a tiara." She blew on them for luck and flung them down on the table in a technique reminiscent of one I had seen Rosalie use.

In that instant, I experienced a flashback. If I closed my eyes, I could envision another hand instead of Monica's. A hand with a ring. Rosalie's hand. With everything else going on, I had nearly forgotten about the ring — a striking piece of jewelry Rosalie had once worn while subbing for bunco.

A ring she had been wearing the day she died.

Another memory surfaced. Memory of an almost forgotten conversation. I had complimented Rosalie on the ring's unusual design. She had said the ring was one of a kind, then shrugged off my compliment, saying she seldom wore it. When I asked if Earl had given it to her, she'd laughed. Earl, she had complained, didn't have a romantic bone in his entire body.

"Kate, pay attention! It's your turn." Monica's plaintive voice startled me back to the present.

Preoccupied, I picked up the dice — and promptly rolled a trio of fours. "Bunco!"

I couldn't wait for the evening to end. The

minute I got home, I intended to sketch Rosalie's ring while the memory was still fresh.

Chapter 32

I came away from Connie Sue's the reigning bunco queen. The bunco gods had smiled down on me. Buncos and baby buncos fell from my hands as effortlessly as spring rain. Much to Monica's chagrin — and in spite of my inattention — I'd enjoyed an extraordinary run of luck. And had the tiara to prove it.

I also came away from bunco with a fourth name for my list of possible suspects: Dr. Jeffrey Baxter. Megan's version of his relationship with Rosalie contradicted that of the good doctor. He had led me to believe he barely knew Rosalie. That she and his wife, Gwen, were mere acquaintances, but that didn't seem to be the case. Not if Rosalie was racking up frequent-flier miles sitting in his dental chair every couple months.

And I'd seen the way she gazed up at him in that photo.

I pondered all this as I got ready for bed. Why would Baxter lie unless he had something to hide? It was definitely worth considering. I squeezed toothpaste onto my brush, then stood there thinking of Pam's bombshell.

Bill had gone to med school.

My mind veered away from this disturbing tidbit, and all its nasty implications. I scrubbed my teeth, slathered moisturizer on my face, and climbed into bed. Maybe a good night's sleep would help put things in the proper perspective.

In spite of efforts to the contrary, I was still mulling over the seemingly endless possibilities the next morning. Instead of one person to prove innocent, I now had two. Since instinct told me both Earl and Bill were innocent, I'd zero in on the next name on my suspect list — Brad Murphy.

The golf pro might be flying under the sheriff's radar, but not mine. The good-looking pro reportedly had a hot temper along with a reputation as a ladies' man. He'd mentioned that he and Rosalie often worked together arranging various golfing events. Betty from the putting clinic mentioned he had regripped Rosalie's clubs. That meant time spent in each other's company. A visit to the pro shop was definitely in order.

While I went about housework, I formed, then discarded a laundry list of plausible excuses for my visit. It wasn't until I was changing sheets on the bed that I settled on the perfect ruse. I'd claim I was interested in purchasing a set of hybrid clubs. I'd heard golf pros get a commission on sales, so I'd appeal to Brad's pocketbook. Not especially clever, but it should do the trick.

Since every detective — well, maybe not every, but most — has a sidekick, I elected Pam as mine. Pam's logical, smart, and a veritable fountain of common sense. Besides, she spends nearly as many hours watching *Law & Order* marathons as I do. I'd hate her to miss out on a chance to apply all that know-how. And it had been Pam who raised the possibility that Earl was being framed for Rosalie's murder. It seemed only right she help eliminate suspects. As added enticement, I dangled lunch afterward at the Cove Café. She agreed to meet me at the pro shop at noon.

"What exactly do you want me to do?" Pam asked me as we crossed the parking lot.

"Just follow my lead."

Except for a woman behind the desk, the pro shop looked deserted.

"Is Brad in?" I asked. I'd debated calling first, but instead elected the element of surprise. This approach seemed to work best for the *Law & Order* crew. Even newer cast members favored this route.

"Brad's giving a lesson. Oughta be back any minute." The woman, who had DORIS engraved on her name tag, didn't look up from her romance novel. Instead of giving her a more youthful appearance, her dyed black hair emphasized weariness and wrinkles. Clairol had failed to fortify this woman in her march against time.

Pam and I checked out the merchandise while we waited. We wandered around racks of golf shirts, hats, and visors. I paused to examine golf sandals on clearance at the end of the season.

Pam held up a coral and black argyle sweater vest and matching golf shirt. "What do you think?"

"Cute," I said. "Gonna try 'em on?"

"I'm thinking about it." Pam studied the outfit from arm's length. "I'm trying to decide if I should wait a couple weeks, see if they're marked down one more time."

"Final markdown," Doris said in a raspy smoker's voice, still engrossed in her paperback. "All sales final."

Just then, Brad breezed in a side door.

"Hey, y'all."

Out of the corner of my eye, I saw Doris hurriedly tuck her novel under the counter and pretend to look busy.

"Hey, yourself." *Hey* replaces *hi* as a casual hello here in South Carolina. It's one of the few Southernisms I've adopted since the moving van transported all my worldly possessions across the Mason-Dixon Line.

I casually sauntered over to a display of golf clubs along one wall. I picked up one of the clubs, wrapped my fingers around the grip as I'd been taught, and took an abbreviated practice swing.

Brad moseyed over. "Thinking about new clubs, Miz McCall?"

I pursed my lips. "Actually I might be in the market for a set of these new hybrids everyone is talking about."

Pam joined us. "Me, too. A friend of mine has a set and loves them."

"Great!" He rubbed his hands together, obviously sensing a sale. "Ladies, you came to the right place. Here's a set you might like to take out for a test-drive, so to speak."

Pam picked up one of the hybrids and examined it as if she actually knew what she was doing. Way to go, Pam, I thought, proud she was serious about her role as sidekick.

"Tell you what I'll do." Brad pushed back

his visor and gave us a big old grin. "Since you're such nice ladies, I'll knock off another five percent right here and now. You'll have delivery in seven to ten business days."

"Whoa!" I took an involuntary step backward. I could practically hear a robotic voice boom, "Step away from the clubs." If I didn't watch myself, I'd have these babies signed, sealed, and waiting on my doorstep. "Not so fast. I don't know the first thing about hybrids."

Brad rose to the challenge. Tapping the clubface for emphasis, he expounded. "To begin with, a hybrid is much more forgiving than a fairway wood. You'll hit the ball higher and longer with a hybrid than an iron."

Pam edged closer, hanging on his every word. "Is that true, even for a poor shot?"

"Yes, ma'am. I can see you've done your homework."

Pam preened under the compliment. I gave her a gentle nudge to remind her we were here on business. Our mission was to learn about Brad's relationship with Rosalie. Not to fall for a sales pitch for new golf clubs.

"It all has to do with the club's design," Brad continued. "A hybrid has a wider sole and increased moment of inertia."

Huh?

He must have read the confusion on my face and took pity on me. "All you need to remember, ma'am, is these clubs will shave strokes off your game."

Well, la-di-da! These clubs would also shave dollars off my checking account. If he had promised to shave years off my age, I might've paid closer attention.

"Allow me to demonstrate." He positioned himself behind Pam and slipped his arms around her waist. "Just put your hands over mine."

A closed mouth collects no flies, as my mother used to tell me. So I closed my mouth and watched a fine demonstration of Brad's aw-shucks brand of country charisma. If he gave all the women this kind of instruction, no wonder his dance card was filled. How could Earl possibly compete with this?

"There you go. See how easy."

Before Pam could respond, the door burst open and in walked chaos in the form of Mort Thorndike and Bernie Mason. Mort and Bernie are the same two idiots we encountered on the eighth hole the afternoon we found the Wal-Mart bag containing the arm — Rosalie's arm. The same morons who insisted we play through and thought we found yarn.

Mort held a towel pressed against his forehead. "You did this on purpose."

"Did not," Bernie heatedly denied.

"Did, too."

Brad Murphy released Pam and stepped back, a frown marring his handsome face. Pam and I exchanged looks.

"I asked you to throw the beer *to* me — not *at* me."

"You were supposed to catch it."

"I would've caught it if you knew how to throw."

Brad moved toward the arguing duo. "Gentlemen, please, what seems to be the problem?"

"Look what this fool did." Mort removed the towel to reveal a nasty inch-long gash on his forehead where his hairline used to reside. Without a towel to stanch the flow, blood trickled down Mort's cheek, making him resemble a victim in one of those slasher films young folks seem to enjoy.

Brad paled, his skin the color of wallpaper paste. "I'm feelin' dizzy."

Doris hurried over from behind the counter, but was too late. Brad's legs folded beneath him like a yardstick. There he sat, his eyes glazed, legs splayed, limp as an overgrown Raggedy Andy.

Pam bent to help, but Doris shooed her away. "Don't worry, hon," Doris said, waving a vial of some evil-smelling stuff under Brad's nose. "He'll come around in a minute or two. This happens every time he sees as much as a drop of blood. Poor baby, won't even put on his own Band-Aid."

The door opened again, and I looked over my shoulder to see Bill enter.

"I heard there was an accident of some sort on number nine."

I pointed to Mort and Bernie, who stood glaring at each other near a rack of marked-down golf shirts. Then I motioned to Doris and Brad.

Bill took in the situation at a glance. "Doris, take Brad outside for some fresh air. Kate, if you look behind the counter, you'll find a first aid kit. Would you get it, please, and bring it to me?"

While I went in search of a first aid kit, Pam took one of Brad's arms, Doris the other, and they hoisted him to his feet. Once he was upright, Doris wrapped her arm around his waist and guided him away from the carnage. Bill, meanwhile, used the towel to reapply pressure to the cut on Mort's forehead.

I silently handed Bill a green metal box bearing the familiar Red Cross. "Thanks," he murmured absently, then turned his attention back to Mort. "I'm sure Bernie will be happy to drive you over to the clinic. Looks like this is going to need stitches."

Mort gave his buddy a satisfied smirk. "Told you."

"Don't know why you're making such a fuss over a little scratch," Bernie grumbled.

Bill expertly applied a butterfly dressing to the wound, and the pair bickered their way toward the door.

"You owe me a buck for our bet on the last hole. Don't try to weasel out of it."

"Pure luck. No way you coulda made that shot. You're not that good."

"Wasn't luck. Was skill."

The pro shop seemed unnaturally quiet after the door closed behind the pair. Bill turned to Pam and me. "You ladies OK?"

"We're fine, Bill," I replied, answering for the both of us. "Thanks. You handled that situation like a pro."

He shrugged off the compliment. "As long as it's not a mangled body part, blood usually doesn't bother me."

One positive result from the little drama I had just witnessed: I could cross Brad Murphy's name off my list of suspects. Anyone who'd faint at a small laceration wasn't the type to dismember a body.

Bill, on the other hand, hadn't broken a sweat when confronted with Mort's bloody gash. He remained calm, cool, and collected under pressure. I recalled an earlier conversation in which he told me he had been a hunter all his life. And he also had a year of medical school under his belt. Intuition told me he wasn't capable of murder, but just like in *Law & Order,* life came with unexpected plot twists. I vowed to try harder to keep my investigation objective in spite of my burgeoning feelings for him.

I turned to Pam, who once again was inspecting the set of hybrid clubs. "Ready?"

"Let's wait until Brad comes back," she said. "I'm going to order these babies."

I stared at my friend in disbelief. Who was this woman? Here was someone who hesitated to buy a sweater vest on clearance, yet was primed to buy a pricey set of golf clubs. Would wonders never cease?

I looked from her to Bill. Who knew what really went on inside a person?

CHAPTER 33

I aimlessly wandered the aisles of Wal-Mart. It was time to put my squeamishness to rest and reacquaint myself with deep discount prices. I wondered as I wandered: Had my visit to the pro shop been a waste of time, or not?

On the plus side, I was able to remove Brad Murphy from my list of suspects. That moved Dr. Jeffrey Baxter to the head of the class. He had blatantly lied about how well he knew Rosalie. What other secrets was he keeping? I had to admit, other than the fact he was drop-dead gorgeous and loved golf, I knew little about the man. Unfortunately, I wasn't due to return to his office until next week. I didn't want to wait that long. I wanted answers — and wanted them now.

Shampoo, hand lotion, and a giant bottle of multivitamins later, I ventured into the grocery section. Whether coincidence or subliminal craving, I'll never know, but I happened to find myself in the candy aisle. My taste buds suddenly screamed for chocolate. To silence the internal racket, I reached for the industrial-size bag of peanut M&M's. I'd store these in the pantry, I promised, for a future bunco game. But I knew full well I'd sample them first. I don't believe in serving guests anything that hasn't undergone a thorough taste test. Quality control is my middle name.

Mesmerized by all the selections, I dawdled in the candy aisle. With Halloween right around the corner, the shelves nearly buckled beneath the weight of all those tempting treats. A veritable bonanza of lollipops, candy bars, and bubble gum awaited little trick-or-treaters, causing parents to fret over sugar highs and cavities.

The word *cavities* reminded me of dentists. And dentists reminded me of Dr. Tall-Dark-and-Handsome. Resolutely I wheeled the buggy out of the candy aisle and headed for the produce department. It was here another display caught my attention: a display for caramel apples. Right next to a pyramid of bright red Jonathan and Delicious apples were bags and bags of caramels piled to eye level.

Be careful what you chew on the side with the temporary filling.

The dire warning had barely registered at the time. But it came back to me now . . . loud and clear. If I dislodged the temporary filling, it would mean an unscheduled visit to Dr. Baxter. I reached for the caramels.

Once I returned home from shopping, I made a turkey sandwich and treated myself to some sweets. My brainstorm worked like a champ. Two caramels later, I held the temporary filling in the palm of my hand. I tentatively explored the hole left behind with the tip of my tongue. It felt the size of a moon crater, but thankfully didn't hurt. Dr. Baxter's office had been very accommodating about my unfortunate "accident." Megan said Dr. Wonderful would fit me in at the end of the day.

I just finished getting ready for my four-thirty appointment when the phone rang. It was my daughter, Jennifer.

"You mean to tell me a murderer lives right across the street from you?" Jen shrieked from Brentwood.

I held the phone farther from my ear. Even as a child, my daughter had a voice that carried. As a parent, that often proved embarrassing. More than once, I hustled the child out of McDonald's without a Happy Meal.

"Mother, what kind of a place *are* you living in?

"Now, Jen, no need to blow it all out of proportion." I have to admit this whole conversation was entirely my fault. I should have been prepared for her questions about the missing arm we found on the golf course instead of being caught off guard. "Besides, dear, I don't think a man who grows orchids is capable of murder."

"Orchids!" Jen's voice rose again. "What do orchids have to do with any of this?"

"Growing orchids is tedious work. It requires patience and gentle loving care. Those are hardly the attributes I'd associate with a vicious killer."

"You lost me at *vicious*," Jen said. "I'm getting a headache. I think I need an aspirin."

"No need to get upset, Jen. I'm perfectly fine."

"I wish you'd reconsider and let me book you a flight to LA. You could spend quality time with the girls."

Right. I'd no sooner step foot off the plane than she'd be setting up one of those interventions like I'd seen on TV where family and friends gang up on a poor, unsuspecting substance abuser.

"What about the sheriff or the police?

What are they doing? Are they just sitting by while this . . . this . . . maniac gets away with murder?"

I blew out a breath. "Sheriff Wiggins has to build a stronger case before the judge will issue an arrest warrant."

"Well, I certainly hope he can do it without your assistance."

I winced upon hearing that. I may have overstated my role in helping the sheriff solve this case just a teensy bit. I'd hoped Jen had forgotten that portion of our last conversation. "If the sheriff wasn't competent, dear, he wouldn't keep getting reelected." I had no idea whether competency had anything to do with reelection, but it sounded good when I said it.

"What kind of sheriff needs help from an elderly woman?"

Elderly? This was the second time my daughter had used that term to describe me. I didn't care for it any more now than I did the first time. It had the same effect as chalk screeching on a blackboard. It set my teeth on edge. I struggled for forbearance. "Sheriff Wiggins needs more hard evidence before he can make an arrest."

"I thought you said they found the murder weapon in the man's garage."

"We won't know for sure if it's really the

weapon or not until the forensics report comes back from Columbia."

Jen heaved a sigh. "Mother, you worry me. Why can't you stay home and bake cookies like other grandmothers? You're much too old for this sort of thing."

Now it was my turn to sigh. "More's the pity, dear. If I was younger, I'd seriously consider a career as a criminalist. Maybe it's not too late to go back to school, take a few courses."

"Mother!" Jen fairly exploded.

Ignoring her outburst, I continued in the same vein. "But math and science aren't really my strong suits. I'd probably make a better detective than a criminalist."

"Now I'm more than worried, I'm scared. You're losing touch with reality."

"Settle down, Jen," I said with a laugh. "I was only kidding." But what I didn't tell her was that I was only half-kidding. The other half of me was dead serious.

"Well, I don't think it's funny," Jen huffed, then changed the subject. "By the way, have you heard from Steven lately?"

"No, not since before his trip to . . . ?" The name of the place escaped me. Those darned senior moments always pick the most inopportune times. Here I was, trying to impress my daughter with my mental acuity, and I couldn't remember which country my son had jetted off to in his eternal quest for gadgets.

"Sri Lanka," Jen supplied for me. "I got an e-mail from him yesterday. Said he'd be home next week at the latest." She hesitated a second. "Steven wondered if you had received the information he forwarded."

"Oh, yes," I replied, my tone subzero, "I received it all right." I had not only received information on assisted-living centers but promptly placed it in a cylindrical file commonly called a trash can. What a waste of good paper, not to mention the cost of postage. Steven and I needed to have a talk about going green and the benefits of eliminating junk mail.

"Have you had a chance to look it over?"

I glanced at my watch and felt a wave of relief when I saw the time. "Hate to cut this short, honey, but I've got to run. Don't want to be late for the dentist."

Megan sat at the receptionist's desk, her face a portrait of sympathy and commiseration. "I felt so bad when you called. I know how much you hate coming here."

I gave her my best martyred look and shrugged. "Just one of those things."

"What happened?"

"Car—" I started to say *caramel,* but caught myself in the nick of time. "Karma," I amended. "Bad karma."

"I hate to tell you this, but Dr. Baxter's running behind schedule."

He had probably allotted too little time for patients to admire his glow-in-the-dark smile. "No problem."

It seemed like I had barely settled into a chair in the waiting room when Caitlin called my name and asked me to follow her. "I don't know what could've gone wrong," she said, apologizing profusely for my misfortune. "This almost never happens with Dr. Baxter's patients. His temporaries are the best."

"These things happen."

The minute Caitlin left the exam room, I hopped out of the chair and started poking around. I inspected the various plaques, studied the photos. A glossy of Phil Mickelson, sporting the coveted green jacket from his win at the Masters, smiled down at me. His pearly whites were impressive, but couldn't compete with those in the photo of Tiger Woods in the adjoining room.

The walls were lined with more of the handsomely crafted shelves I had admired on my previous visit. Like the others, these held trophies interspersed with plastic models of dentures and a high-tech vibrating toothbrush. My respect for Dr. J.'s golfing prowess climbed a notch or two when I realized he often placed in the top ten in tournaments for such notable causes as Habitat for Humanity, United Way, and Juvenile Diabetes. One photo in particular caught my attention. I stepped closer for a better look. There, in the gallery of fans clustered around the winner's circle, I thought I spotted a familiar figure.

"Afternoon, Kate." Dr. I'm-a-Hunk came into the room. He stopped in midstride when he found me out of the chair and perusing his memorabilia. "Didn't realize you were all that interested in the game."

"This golf course." I tapped my finger against the picture frame. "Is it around here somewhere?"

He gave it a cursory glance and motioned me back in the chair. "No, that was taken last spring when I played in a pro-am tournament in Myrtle Beach."

"Do many people from Serenity Cove come out to watch you play?" I asked as I obediently returned to the dental chair.

"No." He reached for a pair of gloves and tugged them on. "Why do you ask?"

I might have only imagined it, but it seemed his smile dimmed a kilowatt or two.

"No special reason. It's just that the woman in the background — the one wearing the red shirt — looks a lot like Rosalie."

"Rosalie?" He picked up the temporary I had "accidentally" dislodged and started scraping off remnants of the bonding agent.

"Rosalie Brubaker," I said. "I believe you two were partnered in the His and Hers Classic once upon a time."

"No offense, Kate, but you strike me as a curious woman with too much time on her hands. Megan mentioned you were recently widowed. Don't take this the wrong way, but maybe you should find yourself a hobby."

Was he really telling me to mind my own business? Were my questions making him uncomfortable? And if so, why?

He continued to clean residue from the temporary filling. His brows drew together as he encountered traces of a sticky substance buried in one of the crevices. "Hmm," he muttered, then leaned so close I could see the pores in his face. "Now, why don't you tell me exactly how this came off?"

Uh-oh. I drew as far away as the headrest would permit. Once again the scene from *Marathon Man* flashed through my mind. In it, I could hear a wary Dustin Hoffman whisper, *"Is it safe?"*

It was déjà vu all over again, to quote my favorite philosopher, Yogi Berra. Only this time I was prepared. The shrill bloodcurdling shriek came just as I was about to drift off to sleep. Even with the Sandman filling the bedroom with the sound of rippling waves, the cry penetrated every corner of the room. Leaping out of bed, I grabbed the flashlight off the bedside stand, raced across the room, and flung open the French doors. I swept the beam around the deck and stifled a scream when I practically stepped on a blob of gray fur.

What was it? Or rather, what had it been? A squirrel? A rabbit perhaps? Maybe a mouse? And how did it get there?

Whatever it was, I didn't need the crime lab in Columbia to tell me it wasn't human. Flashlight clutched in one hand, the other pressed against my chest to contain my bounding heart, I ventured farther out onto the deck. Just a few ceramic pots of purple pansies, but nothing out of the ordinary. Next, I swept the beam across the lawn toward the woods beyond.

And there I spotted it.

An animal, orange in color with translucent green eyes, stared back at me. At first I thought it might be a fox, but reconsidered as I continued to watch. It was too small for a fox, more the size of a house cat. Then it dawned on me. It was a cat all right — a feral cat. I'd heard of them — helpless animals that had been abandoned along the roadside to roam wild — but I'd never actually seen one before. This little creature was a sorry sight. Scrawny and battered, it looked as though it had gone ten bouts with the world's welterweight champion and lost. But judging from the "gift" on my doorstep, it had a generous and giving nature. It also explained, to my mind at least, how the bone happened to come into my possession. Like the blob of fur at my feet, it was another present, another bid for attention.

The wild thing looked half-starved. I thought of the canned tuna sitting on a pantry shelf, and got down on my haunches. "Here, kitty, kitty," I crooned.

Turning tail, the cat turned and disappeared into the woods.

Chapter 34

The day for our outing finally arrived. Aiken, beware: The Bunco Babes are armed and dangerous and primed to shop.

After much debate, we ended up taking two cars. It would be a disaster of epic proportions if we didn't have ample room to store our spoils for the trip home. I opted to drive with Pam, as did Polly and Gloria. I had offered to play chauffeur, but Pam insisted it was her turn. As much as I love her, I hate driving with her. To be brutally honest, she's better at navigating a golf cart than she is her PT Cruiser. Her poor car has the dings and dents to prove it.

Aiken, South Carolina, one of my favorite towns, is situated a little more than a half hour's drive northeast of Augusta, Georgia. I make it a point to visit at least a couple times a year. Known for its mild winters and early springs, Aiken once attracted movers and shakers of the Gilded Age.

Notables such as Vanderbilt, Whitney, and Astor built cozy sixty-nine-room cottages here. Today, while the main drag, Whiskey Road, offers a plethora of chain restaurants, a mall, and megastores, it's the downtown area that draws me. Specialty shops, restaurants, and galleries line a section of Laurens Street. After finding parking stalls — not always an easy task — the Babes and I agreed to go our separate ways and compare notes over lunch.

We scattered. Some went north; some went south. Shopping, however, wasn't at the top of my to-do list. I'd bigger fish to fry. I'd drawn a sketch of the ring I recalled Rosalie wearing at bunco — the one that had been on her hand when she was killed.

While the rest of the Babes shopped, I planned to make some discreet inquiries from store owners and jewelers. Since the ring's design was unique, I hoped someone would recognize it. Since Pam was on a self-imposed austerity program since splurging on golf clubs, she readily agreed to accompany me.

Pam and I concentrated on the boutiques that sold unique jewelry. There, I'd ask to see the owner or manager and whip out my sketch. I'd then go into my spiel about wanting to duplicate the ring in memory of a dear friend who had recently passed away. Everyone listened sympathetically, but alas, the ring remained a mystery. Along the way, Pam forgot about her austerity plan and bought a sterling-silver charm bracelet.

"I guess this wasn't such a good idea after all," I admitted as we headed toward the restaurant to meet the rest of the Babes for lunch.

"Even if we did find the jeweler who made the ring, it doesn't necessarily follow that it'll lead us to Rosalie's murderer," Pam pointed out.

"I know." I couldn't help but feel discouraged. If this didn't work, my stint as a detective was over. Sheriff Wiggins, I sensed, was getting ready to arrest Earl. I was convinced the person Rosalie was having an affair with was the person who gave her the ring. Find him, find a viable murder suspect.

I glanced up and saw Janine and Monica heading toward us. We met them at the door of the restaurant about the same time Connie Sue and Rita joined us from the opposite direction. Gloria and Polly had arrived early and had already been shown to a table. Everyone except me talked a mile a minute, exchanging information about where they shopped, what they bought, and what they almost bought.

Finally, Connie Sue held up her hand for silence. "One at a time, y'all. I don't want to miss a teeny-tiny detail."

Conversation swirled around me. Janine and Monica took turns raving about their wonderful time exploring Hitchcock Woods, a two-thousand-acre tract preserved for the exclusive use of people on foot or on horseback. Connie Sue went on and on about the perfect gift she found for Thacker's birthday. Gloria was pleased as punch with some new cookware to add to her already impressive collection. Rita had discovered the garden shop and had already made a trip to the car with the squirrel-proof bird feeder she'd purchased. Last, but by no means least, Polly showed off chandelier-type earrings suitable for the Academy Awards.

Janine turned to me, puzzled. "What about you, Kate? You're awfully quiet."

"We mostly window-shopped," Pam said, answering for me. "Let me show you the bracelet I bought Megan. It's going to be a Christmas gift."

"Who wants to split a dessert?" I asked. There was no better distraction for the Bunco Babes than a dessert menu. The ploy worked like a charm — as always.

After lunch, we decided on a final shopping blitz before heading home. Once again we separated. Janine and Rita went off in search of a bookstore. Connie Sue and Polly wanted to check out a boutique the waitress had mentioned. Gloria thought she might like a bird feeder like the one Rita had bought. The kitchen specialty shop beckoned to Monica.

"Game for one more try?" I asked Pam.

"How about the place where Polly found those fabulous earrings?" she suggested. "I think she said it was called Art on the Park."

I nodded agreement. "Lead the way."

Art on the Park was my kind of place. Open, airy, it practically begged us to browse. Polished hardwood floors and overhead track lighting provided a stunning showcase for the work of local artisans. Jewel-colored art glass, unique pottery, and some interesting sculptures were strategically arranged around the gallery. Pam and I paused to admire handcrafted one-of-a-kind jewelry in a display case.

"Don't you dare let me buy a single thing," Pam instructed, lowering her voice. "If you see me take out my credit card, you have my permission to smack my hand."

"Isn't that a beauty?" I pointed to a handsome carved wood bowl of burled cherry on a nearby pedestal. "It would look great in your dining room."

Pam ran her hand over the bowl's smooth finish. "Kate McCall, I swear you're a bad influence on me. I promised myself I'd cook dinner every night for a month instead of eating out to make up for the fortune I spent on those new clubs."

"I don't know why you're always so worried. If Jack were here, he'd tell you that if you like something, then buy it."

"I know," Pam said on a sigh. "It's just that I still remember how I struggled after my divorce and before I met Jack."

"But you did meet Jack."

"Yes, and he's the best thing that ever happened to me."

I felt a lump in my throat. I envied Jack and Pam their closeness. Pam had been a single mom with two young children when she met Jack, a confirmed bachelor. It had been love at first sight. At age forty she discovered she was pregnant with Megan. She claims she didn't know who was happier, her or Jack.

A gray-haired clerk approached wearing a polite smile. "Can I help you, ladies?"

I jerked my attention back to the task at hand. Pulling out the sketch of Rosalie's ring, I went into my monologue.

"Hmm." The clerk's brows knit in concentration.

"My friend had this specially made. Now that she . . . passed . . ." I let my voice trail off for dramatic effect. "Passed" is my euphemism of choice for dying. As an alternative, I could have used "entered into eternal rest," as do some of the newspapers. Euphemisms, I wholeheartedly believe, make death so much more palatable than the bald truth. I haven't tested my theory, understand, but I assumed people might react differently if I told them my friend's death had been hastened by a blow to her head with a sand wedge.

"It's quite striking." The clerk continued to examine the sketch, which I took as a good sign. "I can't be certain, of course, but this looks like the work of Whit Kincaid. Whit owns and operates a small boutique jewelry shop nearby."

"Could you tell us how to find him?" A little spark of hope fanned into a raging forest fire.

"He calls his shop Whit's End. Here, let me draw you a map." She used the back of a brochure to draw a quick diagram and wished us luck.

Thanking her profusely, Pam and I left the gallery. As we stood at the corner waiting for the traffic light to change, I noticed an oddity. The crossing buttons were on two levels: one set for pedestrians, a second, higher set for those on horseback or carriage. I recalled reading once that in Aiken horses have the right-of-way. I hadn't thought much of it at the time, but it gave credence to Aiken's love for everything equestrian.

Someday, I promised myself, I was going to organize an excursion to Aiken that didn't involve shopping. The Babes and I would dress up in our Sunday finery, wide-brimmed straw hats and all, and attend one of the polo matches that were held here. We'd have ourselves a tailgate party to end all tailgate parties. We'd sip mimosas and nibble crackers and pâté. Since Monica was resident teetotaler, I'd appoint her designated driver.

Today, however, I had more important things on my mind than horses and polo. The light changed, and I glanced at my watch as we crossed the street. I quickened my step. "We better hurry if we're going to meet up with everyone for the ride home."

"Don't get your hopes up," Pam cautioned. "This could be another blind alley."

"I can feel it, Pam." I looked at the map in my hand, then up at a neat redbrick building with white trim, black shutters, and a dark green awning with WHIT'S END scrawled across it. I shoved open the door. "Here goes."

The only person in the shop was a tall, well-groomed woman in her forties who was busily attacking the shelves with a feather duster. She put down her duster when she saw us and gave us a friendly smile. "May I help you?"

I decided to skip the appetizer and go straight for the entrée. "Is Mr. Kincaid available? If so, we'd like to speak with him for just a moment."

"I'm sorry." The woman's smile shifted from friendly to apologetic. "Mr. and Mrs. Kincaid are in Charleston for the weekend. It's their anniversary."

Disappointment shot through me faster than a speeding bullet. Couldn't the Kincaids have stayed home on their anniversary and just gone out for a nice dinner? I'd tried not to pin all my hopes on Mr. Whit Kincaid, but I'd been so optimistic we were finally on the right track. I'm old enough to know better than to put all my eggs in one basket, but guess I'm a slow learner.

"It's their fortieth," the clerk confided.

Pam nudged me in the ribs. "Go ahead,

show her."

Halfheartedly, I pulled out the sketch, which by now was looking a bit grungy, and handed it to the woman. I went into my song and dance about how I wanted a similar ring made in a friend's memory.

Vertical frown lines appeared between the woman's brows as she studied my crude drawing. "It looks like Mr. Kincaid's work, but I can't say for sure," she said, returning it. "I only work here part-time. My youngest started college — USC in Columbia — and I was suffering from empty-nest syndrome."

"Yes, that can be a difficult time," I commiserated, tucking the sketch back into my purse. "After my daughter, Jennifer, left for college, I volunteered as a teacher's aide at the local grade school."

I always marvel how easily a casual conversation with a perfect stranger can take a personal turn. Another of those eccentricities here in the South. It hadn't taken me long to fall into the pattern.

"If you like," the woman continued, "I could make a copy of your sketch and show it to Mr. Kincaid when he returns on Monday."

"That would be wonderful!" I said, brightening at the prospect. Maybe all wasn't lost.

Maybe small talk did pay off. I didn't question my good fortune. Digging out the drawing, I scribbled my name and phone number at the bottom. "Here, give this to Mr. Kincaid and ask him to call if he remembers the ring."

I was unusually quiet on the drive home, but Gloria and Polly picked up the slack. I had to content myself knowing I had done my best to solve a homicide. I wondered if Nancy Drew ever felt discouraged.

Chapter 35

The morning was gloomy, just like my mood. Sullen gray clouds blanketed the usually cornflower blue Carolina skies. The threat of rain hung in the air, the result of a tropical depression that hovered over the coast. I hoped Tai Chi would lift my spirits. I needed to tap into *calm and relaxed.* Needed to rid myself of the restless, edgy feeling that had nagged me all weekend. It was Monday. If I didn't hear from Whit Kincaid by nighttime, I'd hoist the white flag of surrender.

Pam had gotten to the rec center ahead of me and was already running through a series of warm-up exercises. I set my purse down, took off my jacket, and tried to slip into the place next to her as unobtrusively as possible.

"Kate!" Marian cried, spotting me. "Nice of you to come. We missed you Friday."

The rest of the class turned toward me as

if to say "We were here. Where were you?" So much for being unobtrusive. I could feel my face growing warm. A mini hot flash or embarrassment, it was hard to say.

"We went shopping." It was Pam, dear sweet Pam, coming forward to supply the alibi.

"In Aiken," I added.

"Well, we're glad you decided to join us this morning."

Sometimes I think Marian dislikes me. She has a habit of singling me out for minor infractions. Granted, I'm not the most graceful person in the class, but I'm faithful. That should count for something.

Marian pressed a button on the boom box, and the sounds of a babbling brook filled the room. Along with the rest of the class, I repulsed the monkey, parted the wild horse's mane, and grasped the bird's tail. It wasn't until I waved hands like clouds that I felt that first tingle of well-being. My arms swayed rhythmically as I stared up at the ceiling envisioning fluffy clouds drifting across the acoustic tiles.

That sense of peacefulness lasted throughout breakfast at the Cove Café, where Pam and I met up with Connie Sue and Monica. Unfortunately my good humor dissipated about midafternoon while I was wondering if the phone would ring.

In spite of attempts to distract myself, my mind kept revisiting the jeweler's shop in Aiken. Would the clerk remember to give my sketch to her employer? And if she did, would Whit Kincaid recognize the ring as Rosalie's? It was a conundrum — one about to drive me nuts.

Thinking my long-postponed pot of chili might be just the thing on a gray, dreary day. I chopped a green pepper, diced an onion. The phone rang as I waited for them to brown. I rushed to answer it, praying whoever was on the other end of the line wouldn't hang up before I got there.

"Hello," I said, a bit out of breath after my mad dash.

"Kate, it's Bill."

Any other time I'd have been overjoyed to hear his voice, but not today. Today I was disappointed. It was nearly five o'clock, and I had hoped the caller would be the jeweler.

"Bill . . . hi. How are you?"

"Hope I'm not interrupting anything important."

Judging from the uncertainty in his voice, my lack of enthusiasm must have carried across the wires. "No, nothing important. Just making chili."

"It's been a while since we've seen each

other or talked. I, ah, just wondered how you were doing."

"I'm fine, Bill. And you?"

"Fine, fine. I'm just fine."

How lame was that? Here we were, two adults in the prime of life, acting like a couple of middle schoolers.

"I, uh, thought maybe you'd like to go see a movie with me."

I blinked at hearing him name a particular film. "Are you sure that's the one you want to see? It's a chick flick."

"Don't know much about movies anymore. I read about it in the paper, and thought it sounded good. Maybe we can go out for a bite to eat afterward?"

I lowered myself into a chair. Dinner? A movie? This sounded suspiciously like a date. The notion was unsettling. And scared me half to death. I hadn't gone out on a first date since Jim asked me to a football game when I was barely twenty. I could feel my heart race. If this was any indication what a genuine date did to my cardiovascular system, I'd have to add one of those portable defibrillators to my Christmas list.

"I, uh, maybe this wasn't such a great plan after all. I realize it hasn't been all that long since your husband died. Chalk this up to a bad idea. See you around." And Bill disconnected.

I continued to sit where I was until the whiff of burning onions roused me from my stupor. "Damn, damn, damn," I muttered, bolting to turn off the stove.

Between Bill's call and the burnt offerings, I no longer had a taste for chili. Bill was such a nice man. I wouldn't hurt his feelings for the world. I was scraping crispy bits of onion stuck to my no-stick pan when the phone rang again. I snatched it up on the first ring, prepared to fix whatever was broken. "Bill, I'm sorry —"

"Hey, Kate. It's me, Pam."

I pretended I wasn't disappointed at the sound of my best friend's voice. Cradling the phone between my ear and shoulder, I ran soapy water into the sink and dropped the pan in to soak. "Hey, yourself. What's up?"

"Have you heard the news?"

"News? What news?" I stood at the kitchen counter and idly flipped open a catalog that had arrived that afternoon.

"Everyone's talking about it. I was sure you must've heard by now."

I stopped scanning pictures of high-tech camping gear and mountain bikes. "Are you going to tell me, or do I have to beat it out of you?"

"No need for threats," Pam chuckled. "I sent Jack to the Piggly Wiggly for ice cream to go along with an apple pie I made for dessert. He said the town's buzzing with news that the forensics report on the golf club found at Earl's came back from the crime lab in Columbia."

"And . . ."

"Seems like Earl's sand wedge is the murder weapon."

"Are they positive?"

"Jack heard it from Bootsy, who heard it from Shirley Buckner. Apparently, Shirley's manicurist is the niece of a woman who cleans Judge Blanchard's office. She overheard the judge talking to the sheriff. She heard the words *hair, blood,* and *DNA* all used in the same sentence as *golf club.*"

"Everyone knows clubs are routinely left on golf carts while people are in having lunch or a drink at the Watering Hole. Anyone could have slipped that sand wedge into Earl's bag when no one was watching."

I heard Pam sigh. "Yes, but . . ."

"A lot of clubs look alike." I knew I was being obstinate, but didn't care. "Remember the time Connie Sue accidentally picked up my nine iron and put it in her bag. It took her a week to notice she had an extra club and return it."

"C'mon, Kate. Admit it isn't looking good for Earl."

I picked up a ballpoint and doodled on a page of *Outdoor Adventures.* Even as my mind rejected the notion, I knew Pam had a point, yet I couldn't let it rest. "Just because they found the murder weapon doesn't necessarily mean Earl killed Rosalie. Were there fingerprints?"

"That's the amazing part," Pam said. "According to Bootsy, the club had been wiped clean. Odd, isn't it, that whoever wiped away fingerprints missed a bunch of telltale evidence?"

I stopped doodling as a scenario sprang to mind. "Unless the murder weapon was planted . . ."

"Kate, what are you getting at?"

"Don't you see? If someone else murdered Rosalie, that would explain why Earl's prints weren't found. The killer wiped the club clean, but deliberately left hair and blood, then framed Earl by putting the club in his bag." I could feel enthusiasm begin to bubble as my theory took shape. "What if it isn't even Earl's club? Don't many sand wedges look so much alike as to be interchangeable? Has Earl been arrested?"

"Not yet, but it's only a matter of time."

We talked a bit more about Earl and the

case before the conversation veered onto other topics.

"Hey," Pam said. "Before we hang up, tell me why you thought I was Bill when you answered the phone."

I stared down at the curlicues I'd drawn. They bore an uncanny resemblance to Rosalie's ring. Guess there is something to be said for the subconscious at work. "Bill called and invited me for dinner and a movie."

"A date . . . ?" I could hear excitement creep into Pam's voice. "What did you tell him?"

"While I was fending off an anxiety attack, he took my hesitation for a no and hung up. I'll probably never hear from him again."

Pam sighed, loud and clear. "Maybe it's for the best, Kate. Until we know for sure who killed Rosalie it might be wise to err on the side of caution. Remember, even though you might not want to admit it, Bill *is* a possible suspect."

"Well," I replied, continuing to draw an elaborate series of loops and swirls, "knowing the sand wedge is the real murder weapon eliminates Bill's Louisville Slugger as the culprit."

Pam hung up to feed her hungry husband

beef stew and apple pie. I opened cupboard doors and stared at refrigerator shelves, trying to decide what to fix for dinner now that chili was no longer an option. A peanut butter sandwich vied with grilled cheese. I used to be a beef-stew and apple-pie wife, too, but it's no fun cooking for one. Bill Lewis struck me a man who would enjoy home cooking. But, as far as Bill was concerned, I had probably burned my bridges right along with the onions.

The phone rang again — for the third time — and snapped me out of the pity party where I was guest of honor.

"Mrs. McCall?" asked an unfamiliar male voice.

"Yes, this is she." A glance at the clock told me it was well after six. Dinnertime. The hands-down favorite hour for telemarketers. My house didn't need aluminum siding, my magazine rack was filled to overflowing, and my carpets were clean enough, thank you very much. I intended to hang up the instant the caller launched into his sales pitch.

"This is Whit Kincaid of Whit's End in Aiken," the voice continued smoothly. "Emily mentioned you'd been in last week, and showed me your sketch."

"Yes, thank you for getting back to me."

Was I finally going to piece together the puzzle? I pressed a hand against my chest as if that could quiet my racing heart. I don't know how much defibrillators cost, but maybe the kids could chip in for the gift.

"Sorry to be calling this late. I tried a couple times earlier, but your line was busy. Thought I'd try once more before locking up for the night."

"No problem." I made a mental note to call the phone company tomorrow and sign up for call-waiting. I took a deep breath and popped the question. "Did you, by any chance, recognize the ring from my drawing?"

"It's my work all right. No doubt about it."

I ordered myself to remain calm. Too bad I needed one hand to hold on to the phone, or I'd raise both arms and wave hands like clouds. Where was Tai Chi when I needed it? I cleared my throat and asked, "Do you remember, by any chance, who you sold it to?"

"Let me assure you, Mrs. McCall, there's nothing wrong with my memory. I was once a contestant on *Jeopardy!*"

Well, whoop-de-do! While the rest of us mere mortals are lamenting senior moments, this man is boasting a memory bank worthy of Alex Trebek. "I'm impressed," I cooed, all saccharine sweet. "Mr. Kincaid, do you recall the person who purchased the ring?"

A lengthy pause followed, then finally, "I, um, don't know how ethical it would be for me to divulge such information. But I can tell you, it was one of a kind. The purchaser designed the ring himself."

Himself? Hmm, just as I suspected. Rosalie hadn't bought the ring for herself; a man had purchased it for her.

"Did . . . Emily . . . happen to mention that my friend recently passed away? I'd dearly love to have one like hers as a memento of sorts."

"I'm sorry to hear about your friend's passing, but I'm still not sure I can disclose the customer's name." His tone was polite, but firm.

I wanted to scream — to let out an ear-piercing shriek of frustration worthy of the feral cat I had seen. Then an idea popped into my head. Memory Man seemed to enjoy games, so I dredged up one from childhood called Twenty Questions. "Since you can't tell me his name, let's see if I can guess. Was the purchaser of the ring under the age of sixty?"

"Why, yes, he was."

Score a point for my side. That ruled out both Bill and Earl. "Was this person tall?"

"Yes, the person in question was quite tall."

Another point for my side. Apparently Whit Kincaid was up for my little game of wits — pardon another bad pun. Since no one in his right mind would ever describe Bill or Earl as tall, much less "quite" tall, both were home free once again. Only Brad Murphy and Dr. Too Good-looking were left to eliminate. I took a wild guess. "Does this person have unusually white teeth?"

"Amazing, Mrs. McCall," Whit Kincaid praised. "Yes, indeed, he does."

"Is the purchaser Dr. Jeffrey Baxter, a dentist from Brookdale?"

"Right again!" He congratulated me with far more enthusiasm than Alex Trebek ever shows contestants after "Final Jeopardy!" "How did you guess it was Dr. Baxter?"

"Just a stab in the dark." I flinched. Not exactly a stab. More like a blow to the head.

"Dr. Baxter — Jeff — and I were partners in a member-guest tournament a while back. We got talking, and when he found out I was a jeweler, he asked if I could make a ring he designed for his wife. He even supplied the gold." He hesitated, then asked,

"Is Mrs. Baxter the deceased friend you referred to?"

I heard worry seep into his tone and hastened to reassure him. "No, you can rest easy; it wasn't Mrs. Baxter who died. You've been a great help, Mr. Kincaid." I thanked him again and hung up before he could ask any more questions.

I had found out everything I needed to know and then some. Only problem was — what did I do with the information?

Chapter 36

I paced. I prowled. If there was one thing of which I was certain, it was that I was losing my mind. If I knew a good shrink, I'd get my head examined. Why couldn't I stop obsessing over Rosalie and Dr. Dreamboat? Why couldn't I let the matter rest?

Maybe time had come for a reality check. My friends and daughter were probably right. I had gotten too caught up in all this. I'd been lured by the mystery, the excitement, and a misplaced sense of duty. Standing there in the middle of my kitchen, I had an epiphany. A scene from my beloved *Gone with the Wind* flashed before my eyes: Scarlett, bowed but not broken, raised her fist to the sky and proclaimed, "As God is my witness . . ."

I'd take a lesson from Scarlett. As God is my witness, I'll reform. Painful though it might be, I'll cut back on my favorite TV shows. No more *Law & Order* marathons for me, no sirree. I'll limit *CSI* to one episode per week. *The Complete Idiot's Guide to Forensics* will be relegated to the top shelf of my bookcase. And most painful of all, I'll turn Tools of the Trade into a sewing box.

But my mind wouldn't let the matter rest. I picked up the newspaper, then tossed it aside, wandering from room to room. Rosalie was a good bit older than Jeff-the-Dentist, but weren't older women–younger men all the rage these days? Polly was forever regaling the Babes with stories from the tabloids. After seeing Rosalie and Dr. Hunk in the photos, anyone could tell the pair were more than mere friends. Why would the good doctor insist they hardly knew each other? Unless, of course, he wanted to keep their relationship secret.

What did I know about the man other than the fact he was blessed with drop-dead good looks? I continued to pace. Continued to prowl. I also knew he was an avid golfer. Would frequent outings on the links make it easy for him to substitute one sand wedge for another? Was he the person who made the anonymous phone tip that led Sheriff Wiggins to search Earl's golf clubs for the murder weapon?

I paused in my relentless pursuit for answers to peer through the kitchen blinds.

The Brubaker house across the way remained dark and deserted. Time was running out for Earl. Brick by brick, the sheriff was constructing an airtight case. It wouldn't be the first time circumstantial evidence was deemed enough for an arrest.

I gnawed my lower lip. In spite of well-meaning intentions, Earl's arrest would be partly my fault. I'd been the one who told the sheriff that he and Rosalie had argued. Now I strongly suspected Rosalie had been having an affair with her dentist. I didn't have to guess what conclusion the sheriff would draw once he knew this. Rosalie'd become a cheating wife killed by a jealous husband. A sad but tragic cliché. Garth Brooks, country music icon and philosopher at large, even wrote a song about that some time back. Something about Mama being in a graveyard while Papa's in the pen.

Heartsick, I plunked myself down on the sofa in the great room. Hoping for a distraction, I picked up an ankle-deep stack of catalogs that had been accumulating, and started sorting through them. It was already late October, and a steady stream of them arrived as a daily reminder the holidays were fast approaching. One pile I designated "recycle"; the other I set aside to page through at my leisure.

I methodically went through the pile, stopping when *Country Cuties* caught my attention. Every year, the Bunco Babes and I do Secret Santa. This way, instead of gifting each and every one on birthdays and Christmas, we buy only for the person whose name we've drawn. A single gift instead of eleven. Simple and economical. Perfect for those on pensions.

This year it had been my good fortune to draw Diane's name. Unlike Monica or Connie Sue, Diane's easy. She dotes on anything and everything country. Paper-towel holders, bird feeders, bookends shaped like owls, you name it, Diane loves it. I was halfway through *Country Cuties* when all thoughts of Christmas shopping fled. I paused, staring at a page featuring handcrafted wooden shelves.

The shelves reminded me of those I had seen in the dentist's office, but with a striking exception. In comparison, the shelves on the glossy page of the catalog were plain and functional. They lacked the artistic carving and scrollwork of Dr. Charisma's. Those in his office had put me more in mind of Bill Lewis's prettily carved cradle.

I closed my eyes and tried to visualize the shelves. I remembered satiny smooth oak and gracefully curved brackets on either end with carvings of a palmetto, South Carolina's state tree. They weren't the run-of-the-mill kind found in a mail-order catalog. More the type crafted by a man skilled at woodworking. A man such as Bill.

A man such as Baxter?

Bill had an extensive woodworking shop at home. One with all sorts of tools. All types of saws. Did Baxter have a woodworking shop? And access to saws?

I sat up straighter, my pulse racing. Suddenly the memory of what I had discovered in a Wal-Mart bag flashed in front of me. A man with Baxter's background would possess ample knowledge of anatomy to perform the unspeakable. If Baxter did have a woodworking shop, I'd risk another anonymous phone call to Sheriff Wiggins. But before I made that phone call, I needed to know for sure. No way I was going to send the sheriff's deputies on another wild-goose chase. Better a slow learner than a no-learner, as the nuns at St. Agnes Elementary used to say.

I quickly formulated a plan to lure the good doctor away from home while I performed my reconnaissance. I didn't want any nasty surprises lying in wait. Proud of my creativity, I checked my supply of caramels before dialing Pam's number. Caramels had worked like a charm once; hopefully they would again. I was relieved when Megan answered the phone.

"Hi, Megan. It's Kate."

"Hey, Kate. Mom's not here. Dad took her out to a movie."

"It was you I wanted to talk with anyway, not your mom. I, um, I'm worried about that temporary filling coming loose again. I don't suppose Dr. Baxter ever sees patients after hours at his office?"

"Sure. He's always available for emergencies, but he's out of town."

"Out of town?" I repeated. I could scarcely believe my good fortune.

"Dr. Baxter and his wife are in Hilton Head," Megan said. "He's playing in a pro-am tournament this week. I can give you the name of the dentist in Augusta who's covering for him."

"No, no, that won't be necessary. I'm just being a worrywart. I'm sure the temporary is just fine."

I disconnected and grabbed the telephone directory, where I found a home address listed for Baxter, Jeffrey, DDS. The road he lived on was a short drive from Serenity Cove Estates — ten minutes max. Just one quick look, I promised myself. In and out like a flash. Grabbing car keys and purse, I headed for the door. Putting my earlier resolution on hold, I grabbed Tools of the Trade for one last outing before its conversion into a sewing box.

The area surrounding the Baxter home reminded me much of Vera's with houses set on large tracts of land. But unlike those on Jenkins Road, homes here were bigger, much bigger, and looked considerably more expensive. I double-checked the address to be sure, but the two-story white brick home with dark shutters belonged to Dr. and Mrs. Jeffrey Baxter. Except for a single porch light, the house was dark. All the better for my little foray.

I pulled into a gravel turnaround partially hidden by a copse of sweet gum just beyond their drive. I sat for a moment, marshaling my courage. It was now or never. If I turned tail and ran, I'd forever be plagued by what-ifs. I repeated my promise like a mantra: One quick look, then leave, one quick look, then leave.

Drawing a deep breath to settle my nerves, I opened the car door and stepped out into the night. The air was cool and crisp, the sky lit by a smattering of stars and a crescent moon. I stood statue still and listened. Cicadas and tree frogs greeted me with an off-key chorus. Taking the flashlight out of my jacket pocket, I aimed the beam along the ground. A low split-rail fence separated the Baxters' from their neighbor's. Switching off the light, I followed the fence line toward the back of the property, all the while keeping one eye on the house for any sign of activity. Like I mentioned, I wasn't in the mood for any nasty surprises.

I skirted the house. It was then I noticed the pole barn at the far edge of the property. The building appeared well maintained and fairly new. Could it be a storage shed for a riding mower and various lawn equipment?

Or a woodworking shop?

My palms grew slick with sweat. I crept closer, careful to stay in the shadows. The front of the building boasted a single, double-hung window and an overhead door. I cautiously rounded the side and found an offset entry door — locked, of course — and yet another window. Rising on tiptoe, I pressed my nose against the glass, thumbed on the flashlight, and peered inside.

The beam of light illuminated a trademark yellow and green John Deere lawn tractor hunkered near the overhead door. I angled my flashlight a little to the left. And sucked in my breath.

The remainder of the pole barn was

devoted to a woodworking shop that would make even Bill drool with envy. I was able to make out several workbenches, a desk in one corner, and utility shelves neatly stacked with lumber. Occupying center stage, however, was a table saw. Even to my untrained eye, it appeared top grade, state-of-the-art. Its metal teeth gave off an evil reflection in the flashlight's glare. The thought of those jagged fangs ripping through flesh and bone sent a shiver down my spine. Should I leave now and call the sheriff? I wondered. Common sense said yes. Curiosity said no.

Curiosity won.

Just because a man owns a wicked-looking table saw doesn't justify a search warrant. I might not know much about the law, but I had learned at least that much in my stint as wannabe detective. Motive, weapon, and opportunity. Those are the three buzzwords I hear bandied about on TV when it comes to solving a murder. As for opportunity, I'd leave that to the experts. But if Dr. Handsome and Rosalie were having an affair, and one of them wanted to break it off, it could supply motive. That left only weapon. According to the rumor mill, Earl's sand wedge had been positively identified as the murder weapon.

But Rosalie's arm didn't just fall off.

Still I needed a good excuse for dialing 911.

Lowering my heels to the ground, I looked around for something to stand on. Since the front and side of the pole barn were clear of debris, I went around back. The rear of the building wasn't nearly as neat. Clay pots, a half-empty bag of potting soil, and a wheelbarrow with a rusted-out bottom caught my eye before my attention fell on a discarded window box. The paint was chipped and peeling, and it no longer held flowers, but it looked sturdy enough to support my weight. I dragged it around the side and tested it gingerly. Perfect. All I needed was one quick glance. Afterward I'd call the sheriff and give up sleuthing once and for all.

Always be prepared. I pulled a couple latex gloves from my pocket and slipped them on. Once a Girl Scout, always a Girl Scout, I guess. I didn't know much about the legality of what I was about to do, but didn't want to leave any incriminating evidence behind. I wasn't going to enter the building, just poke my head inside. Technically, I don't think this could be construed as breaking and entering. Plus, I had no intention of taking anything that didn't belong to me. I just wanted a look. To the best of my knowledge, looking wasn't a crime. As to the matter of trespassing, my mind refused to go there. I'd plead temporary insanity.

Once perched on the window box, I employed a technique I practiced when washing windows, and popped off the screen. I gave the window a push, and much to my surprise, it slid upward. An owl shrieked just then, causing my blood pressure to rocket into the stratosphere. I nearly dropped the flashlight that I still held in one hand, but recovered it before it slipped to the ground.

I stuck my head through the partially opened window. Instantly, my nostrils were assailed with the smell of paint and the lingering odor of chlorine. Fresh paint? Bleach? I swept the light around the interior. The metal walls appeared newly scrubbed, so clean they fairly sparkled. The floors were pristine under a coat of battleship gray paint. Bill was meticulous, yet not even his woodworking shop was this spotless. No self-respecting shop was *ever* this spotless. My eyes automatically zeroed in on the table saw.

I itched for a closer look, to get down on my hands and knees and search for telltale signs that a crime had been perpetrated here. If I were a CSI tech, I'd spritz my magic chemical on a Q-tip and swab for traces of blood. But, alas, I wasn't a CSI tech, or any other kind of tech. It was time to go. I shut off my flashlight and started to pull my head back.

"Stop right where you are," an all-too-familiar voice commanded.

Startled, I cracked my skull against the window frame with enough force to send fireflies dancing in front of me. Busted! Dr. Too-Handsome-for-His-Own-Good had caught me red-handed.

That was my last coherent thought before I lost consciousness.

Chapter 37

When I came to, I found myself lying on a cold cement floor. Instantly I knew where I was — Baxter's woodworking shop. I blinked against the harsh glare of a fluorescent light, then blinked again. But no amount of blinking in the world could dispel the sight of the gun Baxter held in his right hand.

"I'm tempted to shoot you right here and now," he said, his tone conversational.

He stepped closer, in no apparent hurry, the pistol aimed at my chest. "I'd claim I'd shot a prowler out to rob me blind. Man has a right to defend his property."

My head throbbed. I didn't know whether it was from whacking my skull against the window frame or if the not-so-nice doctor had added to my misery. Wincing, I turned my head slightly and found myself staring at the underside of the table saw occupying the center of the shop. Dark splotches marred the shiny steel undercarriage. Blood? I wondered. Rosalie's blood?

I eased up on one elbow. "Aren't you supposed to be in Hilton Head?" I asked, stalling for time.

His mouth curled in a humorless smile. "Checking up on me, were you?"

"For what little good it did." I fingered the lump on my head. It felt the size of a lemon, but in reality was probably more the size of a walnut. In any case, definitely larger than a peanut.

"You're pretty sassy for a nosy old broad who's about to die."

My blood ran cold. I've heard that expression numerous times, but never, until this very moment, had I actually experienced it.

"Just couldn't leave well enough alone, could you, Kate?"

I slowly pushed to my feet. The pole barn seemed to do a full rotation before resuming its original position.

Baxter didn't seem to notice my unsteadiness. Or didn't care. "I told Gwen you were dangerous. That with you asking so many questions someone was bound to figure out what happened to Rosalie."

"Gwen?" My voice came out barely more than a squeak.

He flashed his pearly whites in a parody

of friendliness. "That's right, Gwen. My wife, Gwendolyn 'Moneybags' Baxter. I don't believe you two have met, but I have a sneaky feeling that'll be remedied before the evening's over."

I swallowed. No easy feat with a mouth as dry as burned toast. "Why bring your wife into this?"

"Because, my dear Kate, I think it's only fair you know the whole truth before you die."

Was it fair, I wanted to scream, that my children would blame themselves for not shipping me off to a home for slightly demented and foolish elderly women? Was it fair I learned the truth, but no one else would? I tried to form a plan of action, or any plan at all, but my brain stubbornly refused to cooperate. Like the time I tried to crank the engine of the Buick with a dead battery. Zip, zilch, nada.

Dr. Murder-on-His-Mind made a casual gesture with his gun hand. "Shooting would be the easiest way to dispose of a busybody, but messy. My wife and I just finished cleaning up an even bigger mess. It was a lot of hard work. A task we're not anxious to repeat. No," he said, "I have something else in mind."

I ran my tongue over my lips to moisten

them. "You said you were going to tell me everything. About how you killed Rosalie."

"Therein lies the real kicker." He chuckled. "I didn't kill Rosalie. Gwen did."

I shook my head to clear it. I wasn't sure I'd heard right.

He smiled at my confusion, but his eyes were cold, lifeless. The smile of a sociopath. The type I imagined Charles Manson and Jeffrey Dahmer gave their victims right before killing them.

"I — I don't understand," I stammered.

"My wife has an awesome temper. Rosalie and I planned to take a weeklong cruise to the Bahamas. She told that stupid oaf of a husband she was going to Poughkeepsie to visit their daughter. I, in turn, told Gwen I was headed for a dental convention in Cleveland. Since it was Gwen's bridge-club night, just like tonight, we arranged to rendezvous here. Somehow Gwen got wind of our plans. As luck would have it, I had an emergency and was running late. Gwen was waiting here when Rosalie arrived. They argued — things got . . . heated. According to Gwen, Rosalie, after flaunting the ring I'd given her, turned her back to leave. Gwen lost it. She picked up a golf club I'd just finished regripping and struck her with it. Rosalie, poor dear, died instantly."

I took a baby step toward the door. If I could distract him, I'd make a run for it. Anything was better than just standing here, an easy target. "But I still don't understand. If Gwen killed her, where do you fit in? From what you just told me, you weren't even here."

As if on cue, Gwen Baxter stepped through the doorway and into the workshop. The photos I'd seen of her didn't do her justice. Tall and slender, she was strikingly attractive in tailored black pants and a cherry red jacket that flattered her brunet beauty. Her face was narrow, her features sharp and foxlike. Her eyes were a brown so dark they appeared almost black.

"What's going on?" she demanded, taking in tableau-in-a-woodshop.

"Hello, darling. Bridge finish early?"

"What's *she* doing here? Isn't she a little old for you?"

If I weren't in dire straits, I'd object to being called old.

"You're timing's impeccable as always, my love," Baxter replied, never taking his eyes — or the gun — off me. "I found the biddy snooping around. I was about to explain how we work as a team."

"Yes, we're quite a pair." Gwen joined her husband's side. "I have the money. You have the charisma."

"Following her little . . . altercation . . . with Rosalie, Gwen made me an offer I couldn't refuse: She transfers a cool million to my personal account, and I help dispose of the body. I have to hand it to her. Gwen's a great gal. And clever, too, not to mention gutsy. She was the one who came up with the idea of replacing Brubaker's sand wedge with the murder weapon. She made the switch herself when no one was looking."

"And you, sweetheart," Gwen sneered, "were supposed to dispose of the body — or rather what was left of it. Fine job you did, too. Do I have to do everything myself if I want it done right?"

I didn't want to be the audience for a family feud, so I asked, "Doesn't it bother you that an innocent man is about to spend the rest of his life behind bars for something you did?" Silly question to ask a pair of psychopaths, but any port in a storm, as my daddy used to say.

Gwen laughed, she actually laughed, her wide mouth a scarlet slash against her pale skin. Ignoring me, she addressed her husband. "In case you've forgotten, we've a long drive ahead of us tomorrow. Let's get on with this, shall we? How do you plan to dispose of our uninvited guest?"

"I was hoping you'd ask. My idea's brilliant — and involves no messy cleanup."

"Do tell. I'm all ears."

"Kate, here, has an irrational fear of dentists. A fear she broadcasts to anyone who'll listen. A pity, but the unfortunate soul is going to suffer a fatal overdose from the barbiturates she took to calm her nerves when that nasty filling came loose a second time."

Chances for escape were dim before, but now with two people blocking the only exit, they were downright grim. Belatedly I remembered I still wore the latex gloves I had donned what seemed like a lifetime ago. I wouldn't leave as much as a single fingerprint behind to show I was once here. I had outsmarted myself.

"How do you intend to explain my dying in your woodshop?" I asked, so terrified I could barely speak.

"That won't be a problem. According to my script, the next scene takes place in my office. Gwen is going to drive us there. I happen to keep a supply of sedatives locked away and have the means of . . . how shall I say? . . . persuading? . . . you to take them. She'll witness how I valiantly rose to the occasion and tried to revive you." He smiled a mirthless smile. "But, alas, my heroic efforts failed. Your death will be viewed as a tragic accident. Now" — he waved the gun at me — "move!"

My ankles felt shackled by ten-pound weights as I stumbled to obey. I tensed at the hard press of a gun barrel between my shoulder blades and sluggishly moved toward the door. I paused for a second on the threshold, drawing in a lungful of cool night air. I caught a slight movement out of my peripheral vision but, before I could locate the source, felt another jab of the gun urging me forward.

"Hurry up," Baxter ordered. "If you're waiting for the cavalry, it ain't coming."

No sooner were the words spoken than a flurry of motion exploded just to my right. I heard a sickening crack followed by a bloodcurdling howl. I half turned to find Bill Lewis wielding his Louisville Slugger over Baxter, who was down on his knees cradling his broken wrist against his chest.

Springing into action, I scrambled to retrieve the gun that had flown from his grasp upon impact with the bat. Gwen, though stunned at first by the unexpected turn of events, dived for it, too. Luckily I was quicker. I'd like to think my reflexes were faster than the younger woman's, but credit an adrenaline rush for the lucky save.

I aimed the gun in her general direction, using both hands like I'd watched Mariska Hargitay do on *Law & Order: Special Victims Unit.* I was shaking so much I couldn't have hit the broadside of a barn at ten paces. But in spite of my attack of palsy, Gwen froze, apparently not wanting to chance my marksmanship — or lack thereof.

"You OK?" Bill asked.

I gave him a shaky smile meant to reassure. "Call Sheriff Wiggins."

Nodding, he pulled out his cell phone and dialed 911. When the brief conversation ended, he came over and put his arm around my shoulders. "Sure you're all right?"

In the aftermath of the adrenaline overload, my teeth started to chatter and my knees wobble. If Bill weren't there for support, I'd be on the ground alongside the blubbering doctor. "J-j-just peachy," I managed.

"That's my girl."

Seeing Bill's baby blues light with approval, a slow, steady warmth began to seep through my body. Warmth from the inside out.

A nice feeling.

CHAPTER 38

It was all over but the shouting.

Maybe the cavalry hadn't arrived, as Baxter had been so kind to point out, but my white knight had arrived in the nick of time armed with his trusty Louisville Slugger. Bill kept me company while I explained to Sheriff Wiggins what happened. And believe me, I had some 'splainin' to do, as Desi used to say in the old *I Love Lucys*. Afterward Bill and I watched from the backseat of a patrol car while Deputy Preston hustled Dr. Death, whimpering and threatening assault charges, to the emergency room. Their final stop would be Brookdale County Jail. Gwen Baxter, looking more petulant than fearful, glared at me as she was led away in handcuffs.

The sheriff barked orders to his men. The pole barn was draped in the now-familiar yellow crime-scene tape. SLED would arrive first thing in the morning to examine every square inch of Baxter's woodworking shop for trace evidence. I had no doubt they'd find what they searched for. All in all, it had been an eventful night. I couldn't wait to see the looks on the faces of the Bunco Babes when I described my exploits. As for my children, I decided mum's the word.

I turned to Bill and asked, "How did you ever happen to find me?"

"If I tell you, you've gotta promise you won't think I'm some kind of stalker."

"Promise."

"You're not the only curious person, Kate," he said with a rueful smile. "I saw you head out of town and decided to see where you were going. I was worried, you out late at night and Rosalie's murderer still not found."

"If you hadn't come along when you did . . ." I shuddered, remembering Baxter's cold smile and even colder eyes.

"But I did." He reached over and took my hand, which was no longer sheathed in a latex glove. "I saw your car parked alongside the road and decided to wait it out. When you didn't return, I thought you might've gotten yourself in trouble. So I went to check on you. I wanted to make sure you were all right."

"Thank goodness you did. Baxter and his wife would have killed me without batting an eye."

He gave my hand a squeeze. "Not with me around."

I squeezed back. Who would have thought a guardian angel would have baby blue eyes and a tool belt?

The next day, Tammy Lynn phoned to say the sheriff wanted to see me. When I arrived at his office, she gave me a big smile and instructed me to go right in.

"Miz McCall. Please, have a seat," Sheriff Wiggins greeted me.

I sat, perched on the edge of the chair, poised for flight. I wasn't sure what this meeting was all about, but hoped I wasn't being charged with trespassing.

Somehow I didn't think the sheriff would accept an excuse of temporary insanity. Temporary meddling, perhaps, but not temporary insanity. I plunked down the little gift I'd brought before he had a chance to launch into the business at hand.

As with my previous offerings, he eyed the square plastic case with suspicion.

"Don't worry, it won't bite — and won't leak."

Frowning, he picked it up. "What am I

supposed to do with this?"

"It's a download of a *Law & Order* episode. Just pop it in your DVD player some night when there's nothing on TV but reruns. Watch it once, and you'll be hooked."

He set it down on his desk, but I could see a teensy smile play at the corners of his mouth. "Miz McCall," he drawled in that deep, velvety baritone of his, "I feel it's my duty as Brookdale County sheriff to warn you about the dangers of civilians interferin' with police work. You mighta gone and got yourself killed last night."

I held up my hands in mock surrender. "Sheriff, I've learned my lesson. From now on, I'm going to mind my own business. Besides, I think it highly unlikely Serenity Cove Estates is going to experience a crime wave any time soon."

He leaned back in his chair, appearing more relaxed than I'd ever seen him. "Just between the two of us, I wasn't entirely convinced Mr. Brubaker killed his wife. Some things just didn't add up."

"Did SLED find anything out at Baxter's shop?"

"They found blood trace all over that table saw just like you said. I asked 'em to put a rush on the DNA, but I'm positive it'll match Miz Brubaker's." He grinned at me then, a flash of perfect white teeth that could put Tiger Woods's smile to shame. "Brookdale's going to be needin' a new dentist right quick. Once the DA offered Doc Baxter a deal, he was only too happy to confess his role in the murder and place all the blame on his wife. Both are goin' to be guests of the state for a mighty long time."

I was just about to pick up my purse when the doorbell rang. I glanced at my watch as I hurried to answer it. Tonight was bunco night, and I didn't want to be late. Gloria and Polly were hostessing, and I knew we'd spend time rehashing the events of the past couple days.

Much to my amazement, I found Earl Brubaker on my front step. A new and vastly improved version. Hair neatly trimmed. Clothes crisp and clean. And not a single nose hair in sight.

"Earl! What brings you here?"

"I'm taking off for Poughkeepsie first thing in the morning. I wanted to thank you before I left. Here," he said, shoving a clay pot into my hands.

I stared down at a beautiful peach-colored orchid. "Earl, it's lovely. Thank you, but you really shouldn't have." I didn't have the heart to tell the man about my deplorable absence of a green thumb.

"It's the least I can do for someone who saved my life." His brown, basset hound eyes looked suspiciously bright. "You're the only one who believed in me. Everyone else thought I killed Rosalie."

I felt my own eyes well up. "Are you going to return to Serenity Cove?"

"I'm not sure." He shrugged. "I only know I want to spend some time with my daughter and get to know my grandkids."

"But what about your orchids while you're away?" I asked, mentally crossing my fingers and hoping he wouldn't entrust me with their care.

"Your friend Rita's a master gardener. She said she'd be happy to look after them for me." With a final wave, he turned and walked down the steps.

Later, just as I predicted, the first forty-five minutes of bunco were spent reviewing everything that happened since four of us Babes made a startling discovery while golfing. At last, Gloria picked up the brass bell from the head table and rang it.

"Ladies! Let's play bunco."

And so we did. Monica went home that night wearing the tiara, but I felt as though I was the real winner. After all, Bill was coming over tomorrow night for a home-cooked meal. What man can resist pot roast?

The employees of Thorndike Press hope you have enjoyed this Large Print book. All our Thorndike, Wheeler, and Kennebec Large Print titles are designed for easy reading, and all our books are made to last. Other Thorndike Press Large Print books are available at your library, through selected bookstores, or directly from us.

For information about titles, please call:

(800) 223-1244

or visit our Web site at:

http://gale.cengage.com/thorndike

To share your comments, please write:

Publisher
Thorndike Press
295 Kennedy Memorial Drive
Waterville, ME 04901